Hilary Koprowski

Yelena Dubrovina

IN SEARCH OF VAN DYCK

To my friends
The Lisols
in remembrance
of the good time
we had together
Hilary
5/20/97

Portrait of Charles I by Anthony Van Dyck

Hilary Koprowski

Yelena Dubrovina

In Search of Van Dyck

Effect Publishing, Inc.
New York, 1993

Hilary Koprowski, Yelena Dubrovina
IN SEARCH OF VAN DYCK

Cover designed by Andrei Efremoff

ISBN: 0-911971-81-5
Library of Congress: 92-55139

Published & Distributed by
Effect Publishing Inc.
501 Fifth Ave. Suite 1612
New York, NY 10017

Acknowledgements

The authors first would like to express their gratitude to Ms. Christa Binder for her help in typing the manuscript of the book and Katherine Regan for her invaluable editorial assistance. They also would like to thank Ms. Valentina Sinkevich and Professor Alexander Riasanovsky for translating poetry from Russian into English, and Mr. Alan Morrison of the Art Library of the University of Pennsylvania for his computer search of references. We would also like to thank Mrs. Nicole Hubert, Curator of the Museum of Malmaison, for her valuable information concerning the collections of Josephine and her children, and Ulrike Zeiger for providing photographs of Seeon Castle.

Contents

List of Illustrations

Introduction

This work was inspired by a painting that is in my collection. In 1987, I bought a portrait of Charles I, painted by the seventeenth century Flemish artist, Anthony Van Dyck, at a gallery in Germany. The sales catalogue stated that the painting once belonged to the Grand Duchess Maria of Russia, and then Nicholas and Serge Leuchtenberg. Being a curious person, I decided to trace the painting's history. I spoke to a Russian colleague about my intention and we began our search. The more we learned, the more excited we became, and we decided to write this book.

In Search of Van Dyck is a work of fiction. Names, characters, places and events are either the product of our imagination, or are used fictitiously. Certain elements within the book — the story of Van Dyck and of the Leuchtenberg family and the history of art collecting in Russia — are factually based and supplied with references.

I find I can often enjoy
a half-hour with the glories of Goya.
At the end of that time
I acknowledge that I'm
averse from the glories of Goya.
— Max Beerbohm

Chapter 1

I Am What I Am

> Hoc opus, hic labor est.
> (This is the tough part.)
> — Virgil, The Aeneid

I was just reaching my office in Scotland Yard when my boss's secretary caught me at the door.

"Hurry up! Sir Alex has been waiting for more than twenty minutes," she whispered. "You're late as usual, and he's in a foul mood."

Sir Alex's office was at the end of a long corridor. The walk to his office reminded me of the procession to an execution.

I tried to put my thoughts in order.

The boss was sitting in his favorite armchair and smoking a cigar when I entered his office. He was frowning and his face had a strained look. He had a letter in his hands, and it was obvious that he had been impatiently awaiting my arrival. But he greeted me warmly and asked me to sit in the chair across from him. Since he didn't explode, I knew he must truly need my help. I breathed an inner sigh of relief. Immediately he began to discuss business.

Sir Alex told me that the Government of Bermuda had asked Scotland Yard's help in identifying a painting found on an abandoned yacht near the mysterious Bermuda Triangle. The forty-eight foot motor-sailor had been found unattended at sea. It was a luxuriously equipped yacht with only one *objet d'art* — a portrait by the hand of a master.

"According to information from Bermuda," Sir Alex said, "the boat is in perfect condition. There is no evidence of damage or looting, except for the removal of all documents identifying the boat and its owner. Even the name of the vessel has been obliterated."

I nodded my head and remembered those stories about the Bermuda Triangle. "A phantom boat," I said with a smirk.

But Sir Alex was serious. "Not exactly a phantom. The owner was identified as a Mr. Berg and his boat was registered in Panama. We know next to nothing about Mr. Berg, except that he is not listed in the Interpol Rogue Gallery of Art Thieves."

"What does the Government of Bermuda want from us?" I asked, looking intensely at Sir Alexander.

He got up from his chair, lit the stub of his cigar, and continued.

"They are all interested in the portrait, the only valuable object found on the yacht. It could be the key to solving the mystery of 'Mr. Berg'. Ultimately, the Government intends to sell the painting. It is necessary to identify the origin of the painting — both the artist and subject — and its value in the present art market."

Sir Alex turned towards me, furrowing his brow. "First, I want you to indentify Mr. Berg," he continued with meditative seriousness, "and then trace the history of the painting and find out its market value."

My head was pounding. Somehow the prospect of going to the Bermuda Triangle, with its fantastic history of disappearing people, turned my stomach. Sir Alex's shaved head and slanted eyes loomed large in front of me. Why hadn't I become an art professor or an art critic? I cursed my life.

"But, Sir Alexander," I replied, as respectfully as I could, "investigations of crime on the high seas are not within my expertise as an art theft investigator."

"Who told you there was a crime on the high seas?" asked my chief.

"Well," I said, "Berg is in all probability the scion of his family, and now he's been kidnapped or killed outright."

Sir Alexander rolled his eyes to the ceiling and laughed.

"You are a romantic, my dear Jerry," he said. "A true romantic posing as a policeman. They simply want you to inspect the yacht in order to ascertain the identity of the painting and its owner. The Government of Bermuda graciously sent you a first-class ticket."

"Are you sure someone else wouldn't be better suited?" I asked hopefully.

"Find out the painting's value, Gramtrub. We need to know if it has something to do with Berg's disappearance. Your plane takes off at 5:00."

"Yes, sir."

"And, Jerry," Sir Alexander leaned toward me, "don't let me hear any reports of your affairs with the ladies while you're in Bermuda."

I left Scotland Yard in a daze. I had no intention of getting involved in a 'yacht affair.'

"We can't all, and some of us don't," said Eeyore in *Winnie the Pooh.* I remembered this phrase as I walked to my home to pack my bags. The city was covered by a dense, cold fog, not unusual for London this time of the year. I still had a tremendous headache from the whiskey I drank with my friend Tom the night before. To keep alert during the walk, I repeated two lines from an almost forgotten poem written by Walter Scott:

> The way was long, the wind was cold,
> The minstrel was infirm and old.

13

It was windy, and the way was long. But I was neither infirm nor old — even if my head was pounding. As another diversion from the weather and my health, I thought back through my meeting with the chief. Then I reminded myself how I had chosed this sedate, intellectual career.

Due to my parents' interests and influence, I almost became an art historian instead of a detective. I had been granted a fellowship to study art history at Oxford. With retrospect, I wonder if I would have been happier studying paintings — determining their value and age, detecting which ones were forgeries and which were real — instead of drudging up the filth and crime of London's sewers. Yet, I had always been interested in police work and always wanted to work for Scotland Yard. And to my father's great despair, I applied for a position there and thus set my career.

My father did not want the family name Gromotrubov to be "sullied" as he put it, with police work. My father, may his soul rest in peace, apparently forgot that his great-grandfather was a General in charge of police in St. Petersburg, and was model for the "important personality" in Gogol's tale, *The Greatcoat.* I know this remarkable family tale thanks to my mother, who slipped me the story with pride after I was given the position as a Scotland Yard detective. My father, however, refused to speak to me because of the shame I had brought to the family.

After years of haggling and bickering with my father, I finally got him to consent to my new career and to my name change. I had been christened Jerichon Afanasievich Gromotrubov by my Russian parents who had immigrated to England shortly before my birth. As I grew older, I refused to be addressed as Gromotrubov, a name too long and too often a mangled utterance by Englishmen. My shortened name, I proudly thought, could be easily pronounced — Jerry Gramtrub. Yet I've lately thought that perhaps my father had been right about my choice. Gramtrub is horrible-sounding, compared to the lilt of my former Russian name.

My parents insisted I learn their native tongue, which I now speak fluently. They also added to my regular school work by demanding that I learn Russian history and literature. My parents loved music and art almost as much as literature. However, they could not accept that anything worthwhile had taken place in Russia since the end of the nineteenth century. Russia died for my parents in 1918. When I tried to convince them that the poets Alexander Blok, Anna Akhmatova, Marina Tsvetaeva and Osip Mandelshtam were as great as Alexander Pushkin and Mikhail Lermontov, they shook their heads in sorrow. Their tastes were definite, but I am grateful that they instilled me with Russian culture.

At work in Scotland Yard, my background and proficiency in art put me in charge of their art-theft squad, a department at first consisting of only me. Under my supervision, this department has come to hold over a half-dozen detectives and assistants.

My chief, Sir Alexander Mongol, was a Baronet, descendant of a noble line, originating from one of Charles II's whores. The woman's child was born with slanted eyes and therefore, of course, would not be the son of the Monarch. The name of Mongol was bestowed on him and his progeny.

Sir Alex liked me, probably because I was better educated than my colleagues, and I had a reputation of being successful with women. My chief was also a bit of a ladies' man, and I think he found in me the young man he used to be. He had a round face and a clean- shaved head that women were probably fond of caressing. Gossip was always circulating the office concerning his somewhat illicit adventures — but nobody was ever sure of anything.

His presence was powerful. When staff members were called in to talk with him, they were known to make irrelevant statements and move nervously in the chair beside Sir Alex's desk, a combination that stirred Sir Alex's anger.

15

His slanted eyes had a piercing look, and as he talked, they penetrated whomever he addressed deeply. But Sir Alexander always spoke in a soft voice, and his manners were charming. He intimidated us, but we still respected and admired him.

My thoughts shifted from my past, the chief, and my meeting with him, and as I approached my flat I hurried my walk. I quickly prepared for the trip — yes, Bermuda, I thought to myself — an unexpected addition to my schedule. I did sense this morning a dreadful premonition that it would be "one of those days".

I was alone with my thoughts in the airplane bound for Bermuda. Fortunately my flight neighbor slept through the entire trip, and I could utilize the time to ponder the fragments I knew in this case. This "abandoned ship" story in the Bermuda Triangle seemed bizzare, despite how often I had heard of other disappearances there. Should I take this one seriously, and would I be able to solve this mystery? I questioned my involvement as I imagined myself confronting a murderer still on board this yacht — while I went aboard to investigate a painting. Yet, the painting did lure me there. I was curious why a theif or owner would leave this painting and abandon ship. The art historian awakened in my soul. If it was painted by a master I could call upon my expertise, but if it was merely a poor copy then I was wasting my time traveling to Bermuda. Gradually my head became heavy with thoughts. I fell asleep and woke up only when a hostess announced our arrival in Bermuda.

I was greeted at the Bermuda airport by a tall, heavyset man in Saville Row tweeds who looked like John Bull himself. He was the Chief of Criminal Investigations in Bermuda, and he immediately started to reminisce about the "good old days in London" when he had also worked under Sir Alexander. He became quite nostalgic and kept cleaning his monocle on his tie with a thoughtful look, or frantically puffing on his pipe as if he were quitting the habit tomorrow.

After taking me to his club, where he drank twice as much whiskey as I did, John told me that we should meet tomorrow at the yacht. He said the boat was easily accessible since it was moored at the island's main harbor. I asked him as a favor to let me search the yacht on my own. I do work better alone, but I also couldn't picture myself listening to any more of the chief's stories.

I started my inspection of the yacht early the next morning. The morning air was cool. The temperature was fifty degrees Fahrenheit, the landscape obscured by a water fog. When I entered the boat I was surprised to see that the staterooms exuded an aura of luxury. The panels were made of maple and mahogany, and the bunks were wide and covered with satin and velvet cushions. The bathrooms were tiled in the finest marble and contained highly polished brass fixtures in which one could see a reflection of the entire room. But what impressed me most, what I kept returning to again and again, was the painting I had been sent to inspect.

The work was a life-sized, half-length portrait of King Charles I. The English King was posed in warrior's armor, looking straight ahead, his left hand resting on a tarnished helmet. Next to the helmet on the same table was a crown, its jewels set off by the dark and mottled reds of the velvet cloth that covered the table. The silver armor and the jeweled crown were painted to catch the light and shine. But the most striking feature of the portrait was the King's eyes — soft eyes in a long pale face — expressing both sadness and dignity.

The portrait was obviously Flemish, painted during the seventeenth century. The pigments, style, and brush strokes led me to conclude that it must be the work of Anthony Van Dyck, and if not him, then a fellow worker from his studio.

The rest of my inspection, however, was proving fruitless. I searched the closets, the drawers and table tops, but I found nothing. As I was leaving the boat, I discovered a small room adjacent to the master stateroom. Inside, there was a small chest of drawers made of lacquered rosewood, and in one of its drawers I found a folder. This folder contained a copy of an old drawing of a handsome couple. In the background of this picture I immediately recognized the Russian Imperial family's crest. I remembered seeing it as a child, in books my father read or papers he always carried with him.

Why, I wondered, would Berg be interested in the Russian Imperial family? How was the couple related to the portrait in the other room? I asked my questions aloud, but the only one who could hear me was the portrait of Charles I. His sad, brown eyes followed me everywhere.

When I finished, the heavy fog had already been dispersed. John Bull was waiting for me at the pier. I asked him about the photograph of the Russian couple, but it meant nothing to my companion. He looked blankly at me through a clouded monocle, and quickly asked what steps Scotland Yard would take next.

"I will have to take the painting to London," I replied. "It should be examined by experts."

"That can be arranged," said John Bull confidently, ready to assist me however he could.

The next morning I departed for London with the painting of Charles I on the same flight, paid for by the Government of Bermuda. The Government of Bermuda had also insured the painting for 100,000 pounds, even though I told them that it might be worth only a fraction of that sum, depending on whether or not Van Dyck was the actual painter. By now I was determined to know who had painted the portrait. It had captured me, just as it must have Berg — wherever Berg was.

When I arrived in London, I immediately called Sir Anthony Blunt. Blunt had been my teacher and mentor when

I was at Oxford. He was a foremost art expert and I trusted his opinion implicitly. I described the painting to him and he advised me to compare the features of Charles I in the Berg portrait with those of Charles I in the triple portrait, now in the possession of Her Majesty, the Queen. Blunt was in charge of the Queen's Gallery of Art, and he obtained permission for me to visit the Gallery. To my astonishment, the face of the King in the triple portrait's full-face view was absolutely identical with the face in the Berg portrait.

I learned from Blunt that the portrait in Her Majesty's Gallery was ordered by Queen Henrietta Maria, the consort of Charles I. Queen Henrietta Maria, an ardent Catholic, wanted Charles I to convert. In an intricate plot with Pope Urban VIII, Queen Henrietta Maria sent the portrait to Rome, where the famous sculptor, Giovanni Bernini, used the portrait as a model from which he sculpted a bust of the King. The Queen and the Pope both hoped to endear themselves to the King by presenting him with the bust, and influence him through these maneuvers to convert to Catholicism — the faith of his grandmother, Mary, Queen of Scots. The King did not convert, even though his adherence to the Protestant religion was lukewarm, a fact he was reminded of when Oliver Cromwell later ordered his execution.

Since Blunt had been so helpful, I thought he should see the Berg portrait himself. I knew he would want to see it, so I invited him to my office at Scotland Yard.

"Jerry, my friend," Blunt said, "I'm sorry to say this. But I can not meet you at Scotland Yard. Perhaps you could bring the painting to me?"

"But that would be impossible. The portrait belongs to the Government of Bermuda. I am not authorized to take it out of the office." I replied.

"But it is really most inconvenient for me to go all the way to Scotland Yard," Blunt claimed.

"Why?" I asked, growing puzzled.

19

"I can't tell you now, but the trip would be very dangerous."

"Don't you want to see the portrait?" I asked.

Finally Blunt agreed to come if we met after business hours. His nervousness confused me at the time, until later I discovered he was suspected of being a Russian spy and he was concerned about any move he made.

When Blunt first saw the portrait, he was very enthusiastic about its artistic value. "Jerry," he said, "it is an extremely difficult task to identify beyond a doubt whether or not this portrait was painted by Van Dyck or by one of his assistants. He used studio help, as did his teacher, Peter Paul Rubens."

"Rubens?"

"Yes. Both were essentially commercial artists. They earned their money painting portraits. The more they painted, the more money they made. They employed a number of assistants who, being good craftsmen, were able to execute their master's commissions — except for the original design and the final touches. Here the Master's intervention was necessary."

At the end of his speech my Oxford mentor advised me to research Van Dyck's sojourn in England for clues. If the Berg portrait was painted in Van Dyck's studio, it had to be painted while, or very soon after, he was here in England. Blunt suggested I might find some reference regarding the artist's terms for the commission, and gave me some books and notes concerning Van Dyck's activities as Charles' court painter.

I was glad to be alone after my teacher left. I gathered together Blunt's notes and studied the painting that hung before me. I wanted to ask the portrait so many questions. I soon noticed that my right hand was clenched in the same position as Charles'. If I was wearing armor and had a crown positioned on the table at my side, the man in the portrait and I would have made a perfect mirror-image. I could have been posing as Charles for Van Dyck himself.

Chapter 2

A Painter and a Courtier

Man's lovely, peculiar power
to choose life and die.
— Robert Lowell

I closed my eyes for a moment and suddenly felt the presence of the painter near me, here in twentieth century London. I was so frightened by the apparition that I could hardly move. Anthony Van Dyck looked exactly as I would have expected, of low stature but well-proportioned, with piercing dark eyes and a short beard. His handsome face and delicate features would attract any woman's attention. An aura of benevolence characterized his whole appearance.

He seemed so close I could almost feel his heartbeat. I wanted to ask him questions. I wanted to know what his life was like, and what type of relationship he had with Charles I — and if he had painted the portrait hanging before me.

"Do you mind if I sit here?" he asked, moving a chair toward the desk. "It's been a bit of a journey."

"What? Who said that?" I quickly asked.

"I did." The painter coughed and scratched his short beard thoughtfully. He was wearing white tights and a blue doublet, and his skin looked terribly pale.

"Not at all," I said though I could hardly move my dry lips. "Please do."

"Thank you," he replied, sitting down.

"My pleasure," I said. Feeling foolish, I hoped no one would walk in on this discussion. It's bad form to talk to a painter who's been dead for almost three-hundred years.

"You know," Van Dyck said, "I did not die from excessive love affairs or drinking. That's just a myth they put in text books to incite people to read about me."

"Really?" I was quite bewildered.

"Yes. It's a shame, you know. Poor Margaret. I loved her the best. Not Margaret Lemon, that viper, but Margaret Ruthven, my wife."

By now I was sufficiently recovered from my shock to ask him a question of more intimate nature.

"But I'd heard you had an illegitimate daughter," I said, despite myself. I had not intended to be rude.

"Listen," he said. "I'll tell you things about my life that may or may not be helpful for your work. Please sit with me for a while and let me do the talking."

I nodded my head in agreement, and the three hundred year old painter smiled.

"That's better," he said. "You know, I was thought to be quite a talker in my day."

His dark eyes shone.

"I was born in Antwerp, Belgium in 1599. The first time I came to London was in 1621. Thomas Howard, the Earl of Arundel, invited me after we met in Paul Rubens's studio. Paul, the old scoundrel, taught me everything I know about painting and about women. You name it... he was a good teacher. I was proud to be his apprentice — not like the assistants you find these days."

"Anyway, the Earl had me paint him more than seven times. He made a name for himself as being the first great

22

British collector of painting. And it was through him that I got to meet King James I, the reigning King of England! I worked for James at 100 pounds a year, but I could only stay a few months. I had wanted to meet Prince Charles, the future King of England, but that was to come later."

"When I returned to Antwerp, Rubens received me with open arms. I painted a portrait of Rubens' wife, Isabella Brant, and a portrait of Rubens and myself. Rubens, the scoundrel, almost stopped talking to me — all because I had painted him without a hat. I had exposed his old, round, bald head. He was so vain. He hated the fact he was bald and always painted himself wearing a big hat in order to hide the reality. But he got over it. The painting was splendid, one of my best early portraits. In return for the two paintings, Rubens gave me the best grey horse from his stable. He told me I should go to Italy and learn from the artists there. I set out to Florence, Venice and Rome atop that beautiful grey horse."

"Italy was fantastic, but you don't want to hear about that, do you? You want to know what I did in England. But I must say, that while I was in Italy, I learned how to really paint well. My admiration goes to those great Masters in Italy during the Renaissance!"

"Anyway, I visited London again in the spring of 1627, on my way back from Italy to Antwerp. By this time, Charles I had ascended the throne. He had become King in 1625, and I hoped to meet him. Unfortunately, Lord Arundel, my patron who had introduced me to James, was not in favor with the new King. He was replaced by the Duke of Buckingham. I had no way in which to meet His Majesty. I was disgusted and returned home. At least my fellow Flamands received me with pride!"

The great painter seemed rather upset, and I took it upon myself to ask him a question. I didn't want him to vanish and there were so many things to know.

"Why did you want to meet Charles I?" I asked, hoping this question would encourage Van Dyck to talk again.

"Excuse me." He coughed and looked rather pale.

But I couldn't stop myself from asking the question again.

"Why did you want to meet Charles I?"

"Charles had excellent taste and an intuition for evaluating artists and their work," the master answered.

I nodded and allowed him to continue.

"He himself drew and painted, and he had started an admirable collection immediately after his accession to the throne. His art collection consisted of 1,387 paintings and included Titian's *Twelve Caesars,* Raphael's *Holy Family* and works by Andrea del Sarto, Caravaggio, Tintoretto, Correggio, Holbein, Rubens and others. You should have seen the walls of his palace. The King's principal residence was the Tudor Palace at Whitehall, a building of 2,000 or more rooms. Charles kept more than 400 paintings there![1]

"There was a terrific scandal concerning a collection he received from Mantua. Perhaps you know of it? The King's agents, Daniel Nys and Nicholas Lanier, purchased the paintings from the Duke of Mantua. The sale of the Duke's paintings caused an uproar among the Mantuan citizens. Rubens said that the Duke should have died rather than part with his treasures. But perhaps the transaction was for the best. Just after the collection arrived in England, enemy troops captured the land and ransacked the Duke's palace, but fortunately the collection was safe. It could only be compared with the collection of Maximilian I, Elector of Bavaria.

"In 1629, two years after my return from Italy, I was asked by another of Charles' agents, Endymion Porter, to paint a picture for the Royal Collection. I painted *Rinaldo*

---

[1]The art collection of Charles I was sold by Oliver Cromwell after the King's execution in 1649, but many paintings were saved by George Geldorp, the faithful agent of the murdered King.

and Armida[2]. This painting, and my portrait of Nicholas Lanier, greatly impressed Charles. The King finally decided to invite me to England.

"I was very anxious this should happen, quite frankly. Confidentially speaking, the competition in Antwerp between myself and Rubens was growing very fierce. We were barely on speaking terms, something I now regret tremendously. I was also ready for some new adventures and Charles, as an art collector, intrigued me. I arrived in England a renowned artist and confident of my talents. I was ready to take on London!

"Sir Kenelm Digby introduced me to Charles In 1632. I knew Sir Kenelm's wife, Venetia, and had painted her numerous times. We even had a bit of a romance, but enough about that. When she died quite suddenly, I was grief-stricken. Sir Kenelm asked me to paint his Venetia on her death bed. She was beautiful! I painted her as if she were sleeping and at peace. Only the dying rose she held gave any indication of death."

Van Dyck lifted a lace handkerchief from his pocket and proceeded to wipe his eyes. I was impressed that after so many years, he could still be moved by this woman's death.

"And Charles I?" I asked, hoping to elicit the information I needed.

"Yes, yes, I'm getting to him. Don't be so impatient. The King took to me immediately. Within the first three months of my arrival, Charles made me his principal court painter and conferred upon me the honor of knighthood. He even presented me with a gold and diamond chain. The

---

[2]Following the death of Charles I in 1649, the painting *Rinaldo and Armida* was sold from the Royal Collection. From the mid-eighteenth century until 1913 it was owned by the Duke of Newcatle. In 1927 the painting, considered to be Van Dyck's "finest allegorical work", was purchased by Jacob Epstein of Baltimore and in 1951 placed in the permanent collection of the Baltimore Museum of Art.

King was quite generous. He also granted me an annuity of 200 pounds a year for life.

"I deserved it, too. I worked extremely hard and didn't even employ any assistants. Later, after my reputation and popularity were established, I could afford assistants. During the height of my commissions I sometimes spent less than an hour on each portrait.

"First I would draw the sitter's figure and features, using brown paper and black and white chalk. Then I would decide on the sitter's pose, and my assistants would finish the picture. Of course, before the painting was turned over to the patron, I would add my finishing touches. I would never release a painting in its raw state.

"In those days, it was considered common practice to use assistants in this way. Rubens, being a bon-vivant and a ladies' man, in addition to holding the office of Ambassador, would never have had time to execute all the paintings attributed to him without using assistants. Holbein, active at the court of Henry VIII, also employed a number of assistants to help with his work.

"My own atelier contained many known names such as Jean de Reyn, whom I brought with me from Antwerp; Jan Van Bockhorst, who imitated me quite successfully; Remigius Van Leemput; Thomas Willeborts, called Bosschaert; Theodor Boeyermans; Peter Thys; and the well-known David Beck (Beeck). You would have a hard time distinguishing their strokes from my own. Most likely there were many others who worked on my portraits, but I've forgotten their names."

"But what about King Charles? Didn't you paint him?"

"Patience, my dear Jerry," the artist said. "Try to relax. You're not talking to a twentieth century man. Try to be civil!"

"I'm so sorry, Sir Anthony," I said, paling.

"That's quite alright. Now where was I? Oh yes. In those days, I lived and worked in a house at Blackfriars designed by Inigo Jones, the most wonderful architect of his time. My house faced the Thames, and had a garden and a landing. When the King visited, he would come by royal barge directly to my workshop. Imagine the scene: the short, bow-legged monarch ascending to my studio to sit for a portrait, chattering all the while about art and haggling about the price of the next portrait. Charles loved to talk. We enjoyed many a conversation. If I do say so myself, I believe he was as much taken by my courtly qualities and conversation as by my talents as a painter.

"Charles loved to be painted and he commissioned more than thirty-five portraits. He didn't always sit for all his portraits. Sometimes I reconstructed the King's features from drawings and other times from memory. I painted Charles In a variety of poses: as a horseman, a hunter, a warrior, and in full coronation regalia.

"I think the triple portrait I painted of Charles was my best, though. Queen Henrietta Maria chose that one to send to Giovanni Bernini. She wanted him to sculpt a bust that would please the King so much he would convert to Catholicism! Bernini said he had never seen a face 'which showed so much greatness, and withal, such marks of sadness and misfortune'. I was quite proud he should say that. I've never forgotten it."

"I saw that portrait today," I said, "in the Royal Collection. It's exquisite."

"Thank you, Jerry," Van Dyck said smiling, "but that triple portrait may have brought the King bad luck. The King's bust, modeled from my portrait, was brought to England shortly after it was sculpted by Bernini. However, when Charles and his courtiers arrived at his residence, a hawk flew over the procession with a wounded bird in his claws. A few drops of blood fell on the sculpture's neck where it remained without being wiped off. This event was an ill omen for Charles. The sculpture perished in a fire in Whitehall at the end of the seventeenth century. King Charles I was beheaded in 1649."

"Surely you don't feel responsible," I said.

"No, not completely. Still, I wonder if King Charles would have suffered such an unfortunate demise if Queen Henrietta Maria had not sent the triple portrait down to Bernini...if he had not made the bust and sent it up here...but let us change the subject."

"Of course."

"My most frequent sitter, aside from the King, was Queen Henrietta Maria herself. I painted more than twenty-six portraits of her.

"When I met Queen Henrietta Maria for the first time, I was surprised to find that the Queen was a little woman with long lean arms and crooked shoulders. When she laughed she showed teeth protruding from her mouth like guns from a fort. In spite of this, I did my best to present her as an elegant lady, particularly in the portrait of her with a dwarf. She looks much more beautiful in this portrait than she really was[3]."

Van Dyck grinned, waved his hands and continued his monologue, "The King and Queen set a fashionable trend by me. Soon all the nobility were competing with one another, vying for my attention and time. I was very much in vogue.

"There are still many portraits of both noblemen and women at my workshop in London. In painting the court ladies, however, I must say I tended to cheat a bit. I used the same background, and even the same dress and jewelry on different subjects. In Lady Herbert's portrait, she wears the same dress and jewels as the Queen. I incurred the royal wrath for that sacrilege!"

"You must have made a lot of money," I found myself saying, before I could keep from asking the very rude question. But Van Dyck just laughed.

"I became very rich in England, but I didn't have the knack for saving. I spent money lavishly, sometimes on

---

[3]The portrait is now in the National Gallery of Art in Washington, D.C.

28

friends, sometimes on women and wine. Charles himself once asked me what I did with all my money. I told him, 'When one keeps an open table for his friends and an open purse for his mistresses, he soon reaches the bottom of his money chest.' Oh, but those were the days."

Suddenly the painter's mood changed. His face flushed and he seemed to have trouble breathing. I asked him if he wanted some water, but he shook his head: No.

"I died in London on December 9, 1641 — three months before my forty-second birthday and on the day of my baby daughter's baptismal ceremony. No one really knew what caused my death. I think it was the tuberculosis I suffered from for four dreadful years.

"Rumors circulated that my health suffered because of excessive love affairs and drinking. My goodness, have you ever heard of anything so ridiculous? Sir Lionel Cust, a renowned art historian, claimed that 'Women were the fatal attraction of Van Dyck's life and on them he wasted his health and his money.' What a fool. He'll never find my love letters!

"I didn't have time for many love affairs anyway. I only remember two, aside from the legitimate affair I had with my wife. One was with a woman I met in Italy. She gave birth to my daughter, Maria-Theresa. I made a provision for the dear thing in my will. That's probably why I have the reputation I do. But would you ignore an innocent daughter, even if she was not born in wedlock?

"My other lover was Margaret Lemon, who lived with me in London for some years. Oh, but she was a feisty, hot-tempered woman. Why I almost lost a finger because of her. Margaret bit me when a particularly beautiful noblewoman appeared at my house without a chaperon — Margaret was furious! That unsightly incident signalled our love's end.

"She was beautiful. I painted several of Margaret's portraits. She inspired me in a way no court sitter ever could. I painted Margaret in the style of the courtesan pictures of the Italian Renaissance, such as Bellini's *Young Woman Looking in a Glass* and Raphael's *Fornarina.* In one portrait of Margaret, I painted her in a fur stole — her right breast exposed. The painting is similar to Titian's *Girl in a Fur.* But my portrait caused an uproar. It immediately became famous throughout Europe as well as in England.

"I wouldn't marry her though. I was not about to marry a woman who bit my finger," Van Dyck said, laughing.

"One day at a court reception I noticed a lovely girl standing alone in the corner of the room. When I looked more closely at her I saw tears in her eyes. I realized that she was uncomfortable being alone among the dressed up courtiers. I asked the King to be introduced to her and found that her name was Margaret, daughter of Sir Patrick Ruthven. He was a distant relative of the Stuart family. The girl was quite shy in my presence, but slowly opened herself and told me about her unhappy upbringing in a household of a strict military discipline. I found her graceful and charming. I slowly fell in love with her and finally proposed marriage. Sir Patrick agreed so eagerly to my proposal that I suspected the King had his hand in fostering my romance with Margaret. Sometime after our wedding the King admitted that it was his wish for me to be married to a nice English girl, and Margaret fulfilled this role admirably. After our wedding we left England. It was 1640. I wanted to go home.

"Upon our arrival in Antwerp, I learned that Rubens had died. He was a great painter — one of the best. I will always remember him fondly and with gratitude, despite the competition between us.

"His death prevented him from completing a commission from the Cardinal Infante Don Fernando. The commission, ordered by the Cardinal's brother, Philip IV of Spain, was for four large-scale paintings. When I arrived in Antwerp, the Cardinal-Infante asked me to complete Rubens' work. But I could not agree to this. I would execute a new painting of the same subject, but I refused to work on Rubens' unfinished canvas. Eventually it was arranged that Caspar de Grayer would complete Rubens' work — the sod!

"That's when Margaret and I went back to England, and from there, soon after to France. Everywhere was the cry, 'Painters needed, commission to decorate the Louvre available for takers.' However, once we got to Paris, I was quite disappointed. After trying to negotiate for several months with Louis XIII, I was denied the commission to paint the ceiling at the Louvre. Poussin got that job.

"I was so disillusioned. Rubens, the only one who could help me, was dead. I wasn't getting any work, so I sent Margaret back to England and followed her a few weeks later. Exhausted and sick, I arrived in London for the last time in November, 1641. I knew I was dying. King Charles promised his personal physician 300 pounds if he could save me, but the efforts were in vain. My only legitimate daughter was born on December 1, 1641 — and I died five days later on December 6."

I could not believe that this handsome individual, who now seemed so close to me, actually perished in the prime of his life.

"I'm so sorry, Sir," was all I could muster.

"That's quite all right," Van Dyck replied. "It all happened a long time ago."

"And the paintings? What happened to them?"

"In 1645, Patrick Ruthven, my father-in-law, requested that the English Parliament pass a law prohibiting the pilferage of my paintings from the studio at Blackfriars. Apparently, someone by the name of Richard Andrew was instrumental in smuggling the stolen canvases out of England. Patrick Ruthven filed a new petition with the same complaints two years later, exasperated by Parliament's inaction. There are no records showing that Parliament acted on his request. The majority of my collection was already taken out of England by the time Margaret's father made his second request."

"How awful!" I repeated over and over. "How truly awful!"

Van Dyck's vision slowly dissolved and I looked at the painting from which the Master had appeared only moments ago. The notes I had been studying were scattered everywhere.

I still had so many unanswered questions. Who painted the portrait of Charles I found on Berg's yacht? Was it Van Dyck or one of his talented pupils? Or, was the painting a copy skillfully executed by an unknown hand? I felt shocked, sad and deceived. I still saw his image before my eyes but he was not there any more... Had he really been there?

Chapter 3

Experts, Experts

> Experience is the name everyone
> gives to their mistakes.
> — Oscar Wilde

In my capacity as head of the Art Department at Scotland Yard, I used to shy away from the so-called experts who claimed they could determine, without question, the origin of any painting. But in spite of my negative opinion about such experts, I needed assistance in tracing the origin of the portrait found on Berg's yacht. I finally decided to consult Dr. Leo van Puyvelde, an art expert and the Director of the Museum of Fine Arts in Brussels, whom I had met when I was investigating an art robbery at the Castle of DeWaart.

I liked old Leo. He was a soft-spoken Belgian of short stature, with pleasant manners and kind, clever eyes. He apparently liked me as well, since he often invited me to join him for the excellent Belgian beer at the Grand Place. As the beer loosened our tongues, we would find ourselves engrossed in some rather philosophical discussions. At that time, I thought that rapid advances in technology would adversely affect creativity. But Puyvelde held a different viewpoint.

"The time will come," he said, "when robots and the most sophisticated machines will free us from our daily chores. This will permit us a feeling of security. Mankind will be able to maintain its position in the universe without any further struggle. Only then will we dedicate ourselves to 'labor for pleasure.' And art will flourish as it never did before."

Draining the contents of my glass, I wiped my mouth thoughtfully before expressing my point of view.

"Robots and the most intricately built computers will reach their limitations," I said. "They could not be a substitute for man's intelligence in spite of what we have been told. And the energy deriving from intelligence could be channeled into good deeds and into bad deeds. Creativity as expressed in art, for instance, belongs to the good deeds."

We could talk in this manner for hours and rarely agree, but we always enjoyed the controversy.

Reminded of our conversations, I decided to call him in Brussels. Faced with the difficult search for the origin of the Charles I portrait, I remembered that Dr. Leo van Puyvelde was not only a brilliant art theorist, but that he was also one of the world's experts on Van Dyck and had written several books about the painter. Hearing my situation, Leo said he would be very glad to inspect the painting now that he had retired as the Director of the museum.

Dr. van Puyvelde greeted me cordially at his house. We reminisced over the DeWaart case and talked of our recent interests. I showed him the photographs of the painting found on the mysterious yacht and he became quite enthusiastic.

"I know this portrait!" he said, barely able to contain himself. "A few months ago, a stranger brought this same painting to me for identification."

34

Suddenly, I saw the old Leo I had known at DeWaart, passionate and keen.

"I am sure the portrait is a Van Dyck," Puyvelde said. He looked at me and smiled. "I'll show you a copy of the letter I gave to the stranger."

While Leo went to get the letter, I wondered who this stranger was and realized Dr. Puyvelde would be even more help than I had originally anticipated. Apparently this stranger had visited Leo a few months before the Bermuda Triangle incident.

Leo immediately handed me the letter when he returned. The letter read:

> I have examined the painting, size 104.5cm × 85cm, presented to me in Brussels on November 13, 1964. It is a remarkable work by the Antwerp painter, Van Dyck, executed in his own hand. I recognize in this painting Van Dyck's spirit and the characteristic techniques typical of his work in the years 1635–1636. This painting has different dimensions from, but is executed in the same style as, a painting known to me in the Duke of Norfolk's collection in England.

"I am positive the painting is a Van Dyck!" Leo repeated.

I nodded. I was almost certain of that, too. But now, I had another question. Who was the stranger who brought the painting?

Dr. van Puyvelde thought for awhile and then explained that the owner of the painting did not identify himself — but after paying for Puyvelde's expertise, the stranger ventured to inform him that the portrait had originally belonged to the Grand Duchess Maria of Russia, and then to Serge and Nicholas Leuchtenberg.

This was all that Puyvelde learned from the uniden-tified stranger, for obviously, as an art historian, he was more interested in the painting than in its owner. Nev-ertheless, Leo did mention that he was impressed by his visitor's strikingly handsome appearance.

"He was tall," Puyvelde said, "and slender with big, penetrating eyes and a protruding forehead. He had a rich complexion and a dark mustache. He spoke French with a slight accent, and although he had perfect manners, he seemed to be nervous and reserved during his visit. Only after my final judgement of the painting did he seem to relax."

Over this surprising information I mused, then asked, "The painting has a Russian history?"

"It's quite possible, Jerry. Russian nobility were known for their love of art."

In the back of my mind, I could hear my father talk-ing, instructing me on Russian history, Russian aesthetics. Would he have known of the Leuchtenberg family?

Dr. Van Puyvelde looked tired and I realized that my visit was taking longer than expected. I thanked Dr. Puy-velde for his hospitality and expressed my hope to see him again.

Leo died shortly after my visit. So many of the questions I had intended to pose to him would remain unanswered. In my despondency, I was unsure of what to do next. I decided to approach two other art experts. I sent one of them a color transparency of the painting and he pronounced his verdict:

> Unfortunately, I do not see Van Dyck's hand in this painting. This portrait is most likely a copy of a well-known portrait of which many copies are known. The best version is the portrait at Arundel Castle, owned by the Duke of Norfolk.

So, the painting found on the Berg yacht was a copy of a Van Dyck original? Similar but inferior to the 'copy' owned by the Duke of Norfolk? This letter not only contradicted Dr. van Puyvelde's assertions, but it also did not make any sense. The Duke of Norfolk was a descendant of the Earl of Howard — a man who knew Van Dyck quite well, commissioned numerous paintings from him, and was responsible for bringing Van Dyck to England. It did not make sense that the Duke would own a copy of Van Dyck, and not an original.

The second expert was even less helpful. He only wanted me to buy the books he had written on Van Dyck, and for quite a large sum of money. Sir Alexander did not authorize this expense.

I decided to do my own research. Anyone associated with the arts is familiar with the Witt's Library at Grosvenor Square. I spent several days searching through volumes of Van Dyck archives at the library and discovered a few interesting facts. As I already knew, there were more than thirty-five known portraits of Charles I supposedly painted by Van Dyck, and most of these paintings were owned by the various nobility in England. These paintings were listed by their owners or by the auction date of the portrait. Only in some instances did the Witt's archives refer to a Van Dyck "copy".

Several of the Van Dyck portraits looked similar to the one found on Berg's yacht. The painting owned by the Duke of Norfolk was, indeed, strikingly similar. In addition to a slight discrepancy in size, the Norfolk painting contained a scepter between Charles I's helmet and crown — whereas in the painting found on Berg's yacht, the scepter was not seen.

Another similar portrait was listed as being in the Glasgow Art Gallery. But after writing the Director of this gallery, I received the following letter:

37

With reference to your letter on January 12, 1964, I am writing to inform you that there appears to be a mistake in the catalogue for the exhibition "Flemish Art 1300–1700" at the Royal Academy, 1953–1954. We do not own a copy of the Van Dyck portrait in question.

The letter puzzled me but I did not want to be the sleuth for yet another mystery, on yet another Van Dyck portrait. I still had a lot to do in searching the background of my mysterious painting. I only had to decide what to do next.

Chapter 4

Berlin Interlude

And you had to tear yourself
from the embrace which you
had conquered.
— Karel Čapek,
Don Juan's Confession

I was on my way to Berlin. The reason for my trip was to investigate a massive sale of *objets d'art* ordered by the Soviet government during the 1920's. The art was sold abroad as a means to earn hard currency for the newly formed Communist state. At that time several galleries, such as the Hammer Gallery in New York, had specialized in disposing of Russian art. Another of these major galleries was in Berlin. I had an idea that if I could find this gallery's sales records from the late 1920's, I could obtain a list of paintings that had passed from the Soviet government's hands to capitalist collectors — one that included the portrait found on Berg's yacht. But the likelihood of finding these records was slim and was only an excuse for my trip to Berlin. My real interest was to retrace the places I had liked as a child with my parents, before the Brown Shirts took over Berlin and Germany.

Sinaya Ptitsa, also known as *The Bluebird* — how well I remember the name of this cabaret theater. It was internationally famous in the years 1922–23, when well-known Russian poets and writers wrote for its stage. My father, who disliked modern Russian poetry, loved sentimental Russian songs. *The Bluebird* in Berlin in the early twenties was the place where my parents enjoyed the art of Alexander Vertinsky, a lyricist, composer and an interpreter of songs of post World War I decadence. We owned many of his recordings and my father knew the songs by heart. I could still hear my father's voice, twenty years after his death, chanting Vertinsky's *Tango Magnolia* or *Pani Irena.*

A good number of emigré Russian artists were known to have performed at *The Bluebird* cabaret. My father even claimed that he heard the legendary Russian Basso, Feodor Chaliapin, sing *Si Vous Avez Compri* and *Ochi Chornye* there, but I doubt that Chaliapin ever sang at *The Bluebird.* I think that father must have confused him with somebody else.

In England, my father became acquainted with Sergei Zharov, the leader of the *Don Cossack Chorus.* Zharov was a tiny, agile man with lively features and an incredible love for music. He arranged simple Russian folk songs for a male chorus in such a way that individual voices sounded like instruments in an orchestra. My father attended almost all their performances in London.

When I was fourteen or fifteen years old, Zharov's chorus was invited for lunch with Queen Mary, and the invitation was graciously extended to my father. He took me with him. I found myself among a group of well-dressed, well-fed Russians, who chatted gaily with Her Majesty. She was quite taken by them and invited Zharov to tell her the chorus' history and why it was called *Don Cossack Chorus,* since obviously none of the members were Cossacks anymore.

I don't remember the explanation given to Queen Mary, but I vividly remember another scene, when the waiter

40

placed a bowl of water with a slice of lemon in it before each chorus member. The Cossacks looked rather bewildered at the lemon water in front of them and then, at a signal, they all rose, lifted the bowl in their hands, shouted *Zdravia Zhelaem Vashe Velichestvo,* (Long Live Your Majesty), and drank the contents with one gulp. The Queen didn't bat an eyelash as the chorus drank from their finger bowls, and she continued to chat amiably with the leader and members of the Chorus.

My parents often talked about their Berlin experiences.

"Do you remember, Mashenka, our first night, in the *Esplanade Hotel?*" asked my father.

My mother would blush and not answer him. I learned later that my father was referring to their wedding night, and that my mother did not consider the event an appropriate topic of conversation in the presence of their adolescent son.

The *Esplanade Hotel!* Before we moved to Berlin my parents took me there several times. The hotel was located in *Bellevue Straße,* very near *Potsdamer Platz.* The porter in his golden livery knew my parents well and took a great liking to me.

"How is the young Russian Master?" he asked whenever we came for a visit.

He always had candies in the pockets of his heavy over- coat and whenever he saw me, to my mother's dismay, he would sneak me a few as a treat. My mother was always afraid that my teeth would become full of cavities (it never happened) as the result of these treats.

In my childhood memories, the *Esplanade Hotel* was luxurious, furnished with thick carpets, a magnificent can- delabrum, grand, comfortable rooms, and impeccable ser- vice. The tub in the bathroom was so large that my moth- er never left me when I was bathing, for fear that I might drown.

We used to take walks to the *Tiergarten,* where I learned German history from my father while we stopped

41

at the statues of German Kaisers. The *Friedrichstraße* and *Leipzigerstraße* were not far from the hotel, and as a child I liked to window-shop at the stores that carried what I thought were luxurious goods. I particularly remembered our visits to the *Wertheim Department Store,* probably one of the first department stores in Europe. After the Second World War, Wertheim had been an on-and-off lover of Coco Chanel and part-owner of her enterprise. During the war, Chanel, through her German connections, tried to expropriate Wertheim from his share in her business. She was not very successful in her endeavors. Today Wertheim's son is the owner of Chanel — so turn the wheels of fortune.

My father spoke German fluently. His wealthy Russian parents employed German Frauleins to take care of him as a child. In school he perfected his knowledge of German and became very interested in German literature. Even in London, his library contained the complete works of Goethe, Heine, Schiller and many other German writers and poets whom he could quote by heart. My knowledge of German has become rusty, but I still remember the poems by Heine and Rilke that my father liked to recite. He enjoyed not only Rilke's poetry, but he considered Rilke's novel, *Aufzeichnungen des Malte Laurids Brigge,* a masterpiece.

If a guest were dining in our home and happened to spill wine on the tablecloth, father would interrupt the guest's apologies to my mother and recall an episode from Rilke's *Malte.* Malte's grandmother, the old Countess Brahe, would make horrid remarks to any guest, who, at her huge and elegant dinner table, happened to spill a few drops of wine on the snow white table cloth. Count Brahe, who was usually subdued by his wife, rebelled at one such party. While his wife engaged in her sarcastic remarks, he asked the butler to fill his glass with red wine. When the glass was full, Count Brahe ordered the butler to continue pouring the wine until it was flowing on the tablecloth. The guests were petrified by the thought of the Countess Brahe's reaction. But the Count took one look at his wife and started to laugh loudly. Slowly the guests joined him in his laughter, and finally, the Countess was unable to resist and soon started laughing with everyone else.

My father not only knew the major German writers, but also the minor poets. Once he showed me a poem by Christian Morgenstern entitled *Fisches Nachtgesang,* translated as *Fish Nightsong.* It consists of several lines without words and only signs.

Occasionally, I have also selected a German writer from the shelves of my library — indulging in an evening of reading in a language that has become more and more difficult for me.

We left Berlin when I was nine years old. Brown Shirts were already marching up and down the main streets of the city. My father took me to *Charlottenburg* with the excuse of wanting to visit the *Zoological Garden.* But once we were there he pointed out to me, with feelings of nostalgia, the locale of *Kurfurstendamm* where *The Bluebird* was located years before.

From the reports that reached my family during and after Wold War II, we knew that Berlin had been heavily bombed. I didn't know whether the *Esplanade Hotel* still existed, or if *Bellevue Straße* was in the Russian or Western power zone. I landed at the *Tempelhoff* airfield with a strange feeling. Here was the city where my parents spent several happy years, and which I vaguely remembered from childhood memories. But I did not know if my memories were based on real places and events, or if they were figments of my imagination. As the taxi sped through the city I did not recognize my surroundings. Then suddenly, I exclaimed so loudly that the taxi stopped.

"What is the name of that church in ruins before us?" I asked the cab driver.

"That was the *Kaiser Wilhelm Kirche,*" he replied.

"We must be near *Kurfurstendamm,*" I remarked.

"We are on *Kurfurstendamm,*" he said.

I recognized the street. It was greatly changed and yet I could still recognize it. We were in the *Charlottenburg* district, now the center of life in West Berlin.

I registered at the *Hotel Kempinski,* and the next day I paid my visit to the Scotland Yard agent at the headquarters of the British Occupation Forces. I took a taxi to the British Sector and entered an imposing building which probably served during the War as headquarters of an important segment of the Nazi hierarchy.

The Scotland Yard agent was a tall, almost gaunt, individual with jerky movements when he walked. He also spoke stoccato with a marked Welsh accent. He fancied a sandy-colored mustache and a beard *á la mode de* Van Dyck (it beats me why his name always crops up).

"I have known about you, Gramtrub. You have the reputation of the world's expert on stolen art."

"Far from it — I am just a policeman who, instead of having an assigned beat to patrol the streets, is assigned to art libraries, galleries, and history books in order to discover the identities of stolen art treasure," I replied.

I then proceeded to tell him all I knew about the Bermuda yacht, the painting and my frustration in tracing the original owner or his predecessors.

"Leuchtenberg...wait a second," interrupted my colleague. "I have something in our archives connected with this name. Let me see."

He unlocked his file cabinet and pulled out a file.

"This is a dossier of a young woman who arrived in Berlin about one year ago, purportedly to study, but contacted the German police for help in finding a relative of hers with the name Leuchtenberg. Since she introduced herself as a Russian, the German police classified her as *verdachting* and tipped us off. I presented the case at our weekly meeting, venturing my opinion that it was a loss of time to investigate anybody who claimed to have a Russian relative. I was, however, overruled by the Chief who held the opinion that, following the example of Mata Hari, the Government should rely more on women as good spies because they are more sensitive and more intelligent than men. Therefore, I was then ordered that she be followed closely. We discovered absolutely nothing surprising about her activities. She went daily to the *Stadtbibliothek*, where she spent many hours, and then went for solitary walks in the park. She was never seen with anyone Russian or otherwise who has been on our *verdachtig* list, and after two weeks I called off the posse."

I became curious and asked, "Because of her relation to Leuchtenberg, I may want to talk to her. Where does she live?"

"I do not know. She moved from her old apartment and prohibited the concierge from informing anyone of her new address. Apparently she suspected that she was being followed. But as I read here she may be found four or even five times a week at night in a cafe on *Kurfurstendamm* called *Stolze Kraniche*."

Standing up, I thanked my colleague who refused my invitation to a meal, and went to visit a few places from my childhood memories. At night *Kurfurstendamm* was very much alive with many young people filling the streets, holding hands, embracing and kissing. I heard music everywhere. At one point a familiar tune reached my ears. It was from *The Threepenny Opera* by Kurt Weill — an example of the decadent music my father had loved. The sound came from an entrance to a cafe. The name over the entrance door was *Stolze Kraniche*. I decided to explore this place, frequented by the mysterious girl with the Leuchtenberg connection. I found a dimly lit room with a bar, ten tables and a stage. The stage was empty except for a large electronic assembly and speakers that played the music of Weill.

I sat down at the only unoccupied table and, feeling good, ordered a Graf von Metternich Sekt — the only German Sekt besides Deinhart Lila I find drinkable. I do not know how long I sat alone at that table, but suddenly I heard the rustle of feminine clothing and a very handsome young girl occupied the next table.

I got up, approached her and asked, "Is this seat free?"

"By all means," she replied.

The woman was elegantly dressed, tall and slim. She had large blue eyes and a chin showing determination — or even stubbornness. She ordered a Negroni and, while sipping her drink, she eyed me carefully, deciding whether or not to initiate a conversation.

I must have met her approval because she asked in her melodious, heavily accented German, "Are you familiar with Berlin?"

"Yes and no," was my elusive answer.

"What do you mean?" asked my table companion.

"The last time I was here was more than thirty years ago," I said.

"What were you doing then?" asked my interlocutor.

"I was a child with my parents staying at the *Hotel Esplanade.*"

She was too young to know anything about the *Hotel Esplanade,* but for the next half-hour, she queried me about my birth, childhood, studies and profession. It took me some time to realize that she had learned a lot about me, and I knew virtually nothing about her. When I tried to turn the tables on her, I received evasive answers or no answers at all. She would only admit that German was not her native tongue, which I had noticed anyhow, and she confessed to a native French. Since my French is much better than my German I changed the conversation to French, but was immediately interrupted.

"What a strange accent you have," she said.

"I don't listen to myself speaking French often enough to hear my accent," I replied.

"What is your native tongue?"

"Russian."

"Not true," she exclaimed. "You do not have a Russian accent when you speak French."

"Then English?" I suggested.

"No, you do not have an English accent."

I became impatient with the constant interrogations, and risked asking what I had been wanting to ask for some time.

"Shall we go?"

"Yes, it's time,' she said smiling.

When we walked out, I realized she was almost my height and beautifully built, with long, slim legs and enough curves to look slightly voluptuous. We started to walk along *Kurfurstendamm* without talking to each other.

Then suddenly she turned to me and said, "You may take me home."

"With pleasure," I nodded.

"I don't know whether this is a matter of pleasure or of chivalrous behavior," she rebuked.

We lapsed into silence again, and turned on *Joachim-stalerstrasse*. After walking a few blocks we crossed onto a quiet street, the name of which I missed, and stopped in front of an apartment building.

"You can take me to my apartment," my companion said.

I opened the elevator door for her and we rode to the fourth floor, again in silence. We got out of the elevator and she opened the door with a key and entered the apartment. I hesitated over what to do, but she left the door open. I decided to follow her. I found myself in a beautifully furnished, cozy room with a small bar in the corner. The walls were covered with patterned silk and were bare of pictures. On the credenza and several scattered tables, I observed silver, gold and porcelain boxes of different sizes.

"I collect them," she explained. "Some are quite old, others are new. Some are of exquisite workmanship, and some are ordinary. This is the only thing I collect."

"What about men?" I almost asked, before biting my tongue. It would have been a stupid question. I knew next to nothing about her.

47

"A drink?" she asked.

"Yes, sekt, if available."

"I have no sekt, but perhaps vodka instead?"

She poured generous amounts into two glasses and motioned for me to sit next to her on the couch. When I got near her, I had a strong sensation of her warmth. Her body emanated heat.

She looked straight into my eyes, without any trace of emotion. Then parting her lips, she began to smile. I put my vodka aside, lifted the glass from her hands and started to kiss her palms. She bent toward me and I gathered her in my arms. Her skin was soft and fragrant and I started to kiss her neck, slowly, opening her blouse and touching her breasts. She moaned and I lifted her gently from the couch.

She led me to the next room where her bed stood in the middle of an elegant room. On the bureau was a bronze candelabra containing four white candles. She started to light them as I began to remove her skirt, her shoes and her stockings. She was laughing, trying to light the last candle as I undressed her. But she wouldn't let me take off the rest of her clothes.

"Wait here," she said, and then disappeared.

I took off my jacket and shoes and loosened my tie. After a few minutes she entered the room in a transparent negligee.

"Are you still dressed?" she asked.

I was suddenly self-conscious. I got up from the bed and started to undress myself with as much self-possession as possible, but for some reason, I was ashamed to appear naked in front of her. There she was, radiant and calm, and there I was, unable to take off my shorts.

"You look so funny," she said laughing, inspecting me from top to bottom, "Like a Russian on vacation, who sits on the beach but does not bathe."

"This is too fantastic," I said.

"Nonsense!" she said smiling, and I started to laugh with her, losing my self-consciousness. "Blow out the candles so you won't be ashamed to take off your shorts."

Her laughter freed me and I approached her again, the heat of her body was making me frantic. I started to explore her body, removing her peignoir, removing my shorts. I lifted her into bed and we melted into each other's bodies. Not a word was spoken.

In our sleep (were we sleeping?) we found each other again, her lips tender and yielding. My desire was strong again. Afterwards she curled against me silently and I was peaceful. For just a moment I hesitated, not knowing if I should remain there or if I should go.

"Stay," she said, as if reading my mind.

I kissed her as gently as I possibly could as she fell asleep. I still didn't know her name.

Oh, dreams! I can still remember the dream that haunted me that night. I was walking on the deck of a large boat, when suddenly I was pushed from behind. I turned around to see two corpses pursuing me. I ran as fast as I could, but the corpses were on my heels. Glancing up at the mast, I saw a pirate's flag, skull and cross bones on a black background. Crazy from fear, I decided on a desperate step and jumped into the water — but there was no water. I was falling into an abyss and landed in a room with a painting on the wall. The painting was of a sculpture of Pauline Bonaparte by Canova and I could not understand, even in my sleep, why anybody would paint a sculpture.

I woke up in a terrible mood, but one look at my companion made me smile with pleasure. She looked as fresh and as beautiful in full daylight as when I first saw her in the dim light of the evening before.

"You're bright-eyed and bushy-tailed this morning," I lightly teased.

"What does that mean?" she asked me.

"Have you read *Winnie the Pooh* by A.A. Milne?"

"Only in Latin."

I thought she was joking. Only later did I find out that a Hungarian physician, living in the Brazilian jungle, had translated *Winnie the Pooh* into Latin. *Winnie ille Pu* was the title. If she had been able to read this book, she must have had considerable knowledge of Latin.

We made breakfast together in her rather spacious kitchen. While drinking my tea and watching her drink coffee, I ventured to ask her name.

"Anastasia, and yours?" she asked.

"Jerry."

"You don't look or even sound like a Jerry."

I decided to let it pass.

"What brings you to Berlin?" she asked.

"I am looking for the records of a painting exported from Russia shortly after the revolution and sold to the West."

"What is the painting?"

"Van Dyck's portrait of Charles I."

"Why this particular painting?"

"It's a long story, but if you will get me another cup of tea, I will tell you all about it."

I still don't know why, but I was tempted to tell somebody about my work, and this woman knew how to listen. I proceeded to tell her about the Bermuda Triangle, the abandoned yacht, and my study of Van Dyck's life in England. I also told her about my visit to Dr. Leo van Puyvelde and about the mysterious man who brought the painting to him. Then I mentioned that the painting was supposed to have belonged to the Grand Duchess Maria and Serge and Nicholas Leuchtenberg. On hearing this, Anastasia's hand, now lifting her third cup of coffee, froze in mid-air. Her eyes stared at me with utter astonishment.

"I am a Leuchtenberg!" she exclaimed.

It was my turn to be surprised. "Are you Duchess von Leuchtenberg?"

"Oh, no," she said, "That isn't my title. My natural father, the Leuchtenberg, never married my mother. They met in Canada. My mother fell in love with him, and with the glamour of his origin and his name. It wasn't difficult for my father to convince her to sleep with him. I was conceived and born in Quebec. The Leuchtenberg never intended to marry my mother, and she was too proud to plead for a wedding ring. He expressed only a casual interest in me when I was small, and did not protest when my mother told him that she was leaving Canada."

"What name do you use then?" I asked.

"That isn't any of your business. I didn't ask for your name. We shall know each other as Jerry and Anastasia. That is sufficient," was her ultimate verdict.

"Anastasia," I begged, "I need to know the story of your family. In fact, I am dying to know it."

"No Jerry, please. I have already told you too much about myself. I like you and trust you — it does not happen often — and I've already said too much. But I'd like to go with you while you search for your records."

She was a strange and remarkable woman. I felt attracted to her and was driven by an incredible curiosity to find out more about her. I had the desire to penetrate, not only her body, but her mind. Yet I didn't have the slightest idea how to approach her. I was happy she suggested that we spend the day together in search of my painting.

We left Anastasia's flat and started our search, but there was no trace of the gallery that had sold the Soviet art treasures abroad. After careful inquiries at the Berlin Archives, I learned that the records of this gallery were taken over by another gallery, which in turn was bombed in a night raid during the war. Although I found this disappointing news, I discovered a person in the Berlin archives who was knowledgeable and helpful. He told me to visit the State Museum of Prussian Culture in Dahlem.

"If there is any trace of the records you are looking for, the archives at Dahlem are the place to look," he informed me.

The Dahlem Gallery has one of the best collections of Medieval, Renaissance and Baroque paintings, and the Dutch and Flemish schools were very well represented. At the time it contained two or three rooms of Rembrandts, including the *Man in the Golden Helmet,* now considered to be painted by someone else, and the famous Dutch painting by Peter Bruegel with 118 proverbs woven into a picture of a village with its inhabitants performing daily tasks. The Van Dyck collection was also fabulous, containing six paintings and one drawing. Four portraits, one of Marchioness Geromina Spinola, were of remarkable beauty. Two paintings of unnamed apostles were so unusual for Van Dyck that I stood dumbfounded in front of them and will remember them forever.

While looking at this enormously rich collection, I wondered who had counseled the Prussian Kings and German Kaisers on their purchases. I knew that Leo Cassirer had advised Wilhelm II to buy Cézanne and other impressionists. But apparently the Kaiser refused to buy a particular Cézanne and the painting was snatched up by the painter, Max Liebermann, a noted collector. I had no idea, however, how the paintings by the great masters of the past found their way to the Prussian court. I asked Anastasia, but she did not know much about the history and origin of these paintings, although I found she was quite knowledgeable and intelligent.

Finally, after spending several hours looking at the marvels of the Dahlem collection, I went to the museum's archive collection. The archivist, a dour-faced spinster of uncertain age was, at the beginning of our conversation, uncommunicative and uncooperative. Anastasia, however, started to tell her about the painting whose provenance we were tracing, mentioning the mysteries surrounding the yacht found in the Bermuda Triangle and the Leuchtenbergs. The archivist's attitude changed completely. She showed us several catalogues and the sales records from 1922 to 1933. But she had no knowledge of the gallery that was supposed to have been used by the Soviet Government as a channel to dispose of paintings in Russia to the West. I searched through the records in the Dahlem archives for any mention of Van Dyck's Charles I in vain.

In the taxi returning from Dahlem, Anastasia noticed my disappointment and suggested a spontaneous visit to the Pergamon Altar.

"But that is in East Berlin," I exclaimed.

"So what," she said. "We can cross to East Berlin. You're English and I'm a Swiss citizen. Nobody will stop us."

Even though I was not very comfortable with her suggestion, I wanted to revisit the places I hadn't seen since I was a child. I acquiesced, and we directed the taxi to take us to Checkpoint Charlie. After passing the perfunctory examination given by the West German officials, we entered another world. We weren't spoken to, but barked at and ordered about in a most crude and impolite way. One East German guard looked like an ex-SS man, and his female counterpart, the last guard to examine us, looked like the infamous Ilse Koch. I wanted to forget the whole idea and return to West Berlin, which now seemed like heaven, but Anastasia refused. When we were finally ready to leave the barracks and enter East Berlin, we heard a piercing whistle. We looked back and saw the Ilse Koch woman motioning for us to come back.

"You forgot to change your currency into our marks," she said.

"But we're only visiting Berlin for a few hours — to see the Pergamon Altar," I stated.

"That doesn't matter," she said. "You must change your money now. And remember, you cannot take it out of East Germany."

We changed the money and started to walk along the street that was apparently *Leipzigerstraße;* I did not recognize at it all. Gone were all the wonderful shops and boutiques, replaced by drab, ugly-looking structures. The street was empty — no cars, no people. I felt, however, a thousand eyes looking at the back of my neck. The feeling was so intense that I put up the collar of my coat. I had the same sensation walking through the streets of communist Prague. Anastasia seemed oblivious to all this. She was marching happily at my side, whistling some tune of a French chanson. We turned from *Leipzigerstraße* onto *Unter den Linden,* a beautiful villas-alle I remembered from my childhood. Nothing remained that would have even remotely reminded me of the street that I once knew. I almost cried aloud.

There were crowds in the building housing the Pergamon Altar. I recognized the altar from reproductions, but I never expected it to be so impressive. Anastasia knew very little about its origin, and I told her, briefly, the history of the King of Pergamon, Eumenes II, who reigned over the vast territory of Asia Minor — including Phrygia, Ionia and Casia. Eumenes II was a brave warrior who won the battle over the Gauls. To commemorate his victory, he built this fabulous altar to Zeus in 180 B.C. The altar sculptures represent the finest one can expect to find in Greek art.

Next to the Pergamon Altar building was the National Gallery of Arts. As we started to check our coats, the cloak attendant told us that there was nothing to see here because all of it had been robbed by West Berlin! We turned from the Gallery and started to make our way back to West Berlin.

I still wanted to see the *Friedrichstraße* — which, again, bore memories of my childhood. We went in that direction, knowing that there was a crossing from East to West Berlin by U-Bahn from the *Friedrichstraße* stop. Walking along *Friedrichstraße* was as disappointing as going through *Leipzigerstraße* and *Unter den Linden.* When we tried to board the underground, we were stopped by another guard of the East German police.

"You can't go back through here," he barked at us.

"Why not? Isn't this an official crossing point?" we asked.

"You have to go back the way you came through at Checkpoint Charlie," he retorted.

We realized there was no sense in arguing. Our day's worth of activities finally ended with a sigh of relief when we found ourselves back in West Berlin.

Eating our evening meal in one of the taverns on *Kurfurstendamm,* Anastasia started to talk about herself after several glasses of sekt, first quoting a German proverb.

"Für das Gewesene gibt der Deutche nichts," she said. "A German cares nothing about his past."

Anastasia told me that when she was three years old, her mother married a Swiss who after one year, moved the family from their home in Canada to Switzerland. They settled in his native village, *Le Peutapache,* in Jura, where Anastasia went to school. Her mother maintained a correspondence with the Leuchtenberg in Canada, informing him about Anastasia and herself.

"When I was ten years old and alone at home," Anastasia said, "the door to our house opened suddenly, and a handsome and distinguished-looking man came to the house. He was wearing a dark grey overcoat, spats, a beautiful, black Homburg hat, and was carrying a cane with a golden handle. I was somewhat intimidated by this stranger's appearance, but he had such a benevolent expression on his face, even when he put on a monocle, that I approached him and extended my hand.

He took my hand in both of his and said, 'You must be Anastasia.'

'Yes, I am,' I shyly answered.

'I am your father!'

I was quite surprised and pleased at the same time that this good-looking man was my father.

"Mother returned to the house shortly after father's arrival and was overjoyed to see him. She even kissed him on his mouth. He embraced her and they behaved as if they would stay together forever.

"My step-father was away for several days on business, and mother invited the Leuchtenberg to stay at our house. She served what I later learned was a typical Russian meal with several brands of vodka, and when I went to bed they sat chatting at the fireplace. I woke up later that night and, while walking in the corridor, I saw my mother and the Leuchtenberg entering her bedroom with their arms wrapped tightly around each other's waists. Nothing seems surprising to a ten-year-old and I found it quite natural that the Leuchtenberg, in his pajamas, and my mother, in a rather transparent negligee, emerged from the bedroom in the morning and sat with me at the breakfast table.

"When we finished eating, my father dressed and took me for a walk in the park. After we had seated ourselves on a bench he said,

'Do you know why you were named Anastasia?'

'No, father,' I said, shaking my head.

'Let me tell you, then, the story of another Anastasia."

At this point of the story, the Anastasia to whom I was talking finished her sekt.

"May I get you another drink?" I said.

"Please," she answered. "Have I been talking too long?"

"Not at all. I want you to go on," I quickly replied so she would continue telling me about her childhood.

Anastasia laughed and took my arm.

"Well, alright, my father and I were seated on the park bench and he was telling me the story about my name."

" 'Our late Tsar,' he said, 'and his entire family were supposed to have been shot by the Bolsheviks in 1918. Almost ten years later there appeared in Germany a woman in her late twenties who claimed to be Anastasia, the youngest daughter of the late Nicholas II. She said that she had been miraculously saved from the Bolshevik slaughter by her father's devoted soldier, and, after recovering from her wounds, hid from the Bolsheviks for years and then emerged in Germany. When trying to commit suicide, Anastasia was taken to a Berlin asylum where she was recognized by a Russian nurse,' my father continued.

'The news spread immediately. You can imagine the uproar created by the appearance of this lady! Most of the Imperial family, now living in exile, considered her an impostor — especially the Grand Duchess Olga Alexandrovna, Nicholas II's sister, who was residing in Canada, and her youngest sister, Xenia, who was living in France. They probably feared the loss of the Romanov's heirlooms, which were supposedly hidden in a Swiss bank. But the Leuchtenbergs thought otherwise. My cousins invited Anastasia to their Castle in Seeon, Bavaria, and they also invited several other people who knew Anastasia as a child – such as the son of the late court physician to the Tsar's family, Gleb Botkin, whose father was so devoted that he refused to leave the Tsar's family on the day of their execution, and was shot with them.'

'In spite of the doubts expressed by many members of the Royal household, Botkin and my cousins recognized Anastasia as the real daughter of the Tsar. She stayed in Seeon until she was invited to the United States by other members of the Russian royalty, but she did not endear herself to her American relatives. She was impossible to live with because of her strange — almost paranoid — behavior. In the end, she was placed in an asylum under the assumption that she was mentally deranged.'

'Was she the real Anastasia?' I asked my father.

'I don't know. If she wasn't, she was an excellent actress. Many women claimed to be Anastasia. The Grand Duchess Olga used to tell us about one such impostor from Japan! There were also many men who claimed to be Tsarevich Aleksei and, of course, not one was real — the poor boy was brutally killed. As for our Anastasia, she met with Maria Feodorovna, the widowed mother of the last Tsar, who lived in Denmark to a ripe old age. Some say the Tsarina thought Anastasia was an impostor and some say that she recognized her as being the real product of the Romanovs.'

Anastasia turned to me, sipping her fresh glass of sekt.

"I liked this story," she said, "it was romantic. But I was, as any child would be, even more interested in the mysterious Castle at Seeon — where my relatives had once lived. When I asked my father if his cousins were still there, he replied,

'Oh, no. They are both dead. And the castle itself, and all its contents, were sold in 1947.' "

Anastasia finished her story and smiled. I was thoughtful and kept silent.

"Do you realize," I finally said, "that this may be the best clue to finding the origin of my painting? You must tell me more about your father's family."

"It's a long story, Jerry," she answered, sighing. "Within a year of his return to Canada, Father literally disappeared. Mother's and my letters were returned to us with a Canadian stamp: 'Address Unknown.' We tried to call him but the telephone was disconnected. Mother contacted several of their mutual friends and they were as puzzled as we were about his disappearance. I am still trying to find him. He might not even be alive! I've even researched his history, but without much success... For now, let us go back to my apartment."

As we sat drinking more sekt in Anastasia's apartment, we looked at each other with the same thought in mind. I took Anastasia's hand and slowly led her into the bedroom. Without words, we helped each other undress — caressing each other's bodies, sliding into bed. Just the smell of her hair shook my body with anticipation and yearning. Looking into her eyes, I knew that my body spoke for what was in my heart.

Afterwards, I was too excited to fall asleep and I started to kiss her again — this time more tenderly than passionately. She resisted my advances.

"Maybe it's time to tell you about the Leuchtenbergs," she said, laughing and tired. I nodded, smiling, and still holding her in my arms, she began the story of the Leuchtenbergs from beginning to end. I tried to memorize every word she said so that later I could write it down and think about it. We both fell asleep just before daybreak and woke up late in the morning.

When I opened my eyes and looked through the window, I saw that it was raining and the sky was grey. Anastasia was up and fully dressed. She sat near me, pointed outside, and in her low, melodious voice recited a poem:

> It was invented by an artist —
> this grey daybreak.
> Again — hunting game for a time.
> Two burning arms.
> Morning still keeping warm our harms,
> the blueness of your Russian blood,
> fir tree silvery sweat,
> two lines — uneven, unwritten by me,
> as yet,
> the alarm of a guilty grin.
> Nothing stays with us - within.
> Everything is just a game.
> Mist spreading thin.
> Unforgiveness.
> Forgiveness.
> Departure.

"Is it yours?" I asked. "Is it about us?"

"No," Anastasia answered. She seemed to be annoyed with me.

While we were eating a late lunch, Anastasia started telling me about her present interests. I noticed that when she talked about herself, she looked straight at me, with her sparkling, light blue eyes, and she gestured freely, showing her animation. When she evaded my queries she did not

59

meet my eyes — looking rather downcast, with her stubborn jaw thrust forward. But now she was talking excitedly.

"I am currently studying the heroines of great men — ladies whose identities were only recently discovered or surmised, hundreds of years after their death."

"Who are some examples?" I asked.

"Well, at present I am researching Beethoven's Ferne Geliebte, his immortal beloved, and Antonie von Brentano. Beethoven probably had a short but passionate love affair with Antonie, sometime before he wrote his famous letter to Ferne Geliebte in July, 1812. The other mysterious lady I am interested in, Emilia Lanier, has only recently been identified. She was the Dark Lady of Shakespeare's Sonnets. She is a much more difficult subject to research since there is hardly any material about her."

I was constantly surprised and amazed by Anastasia's interests — I knew nothing about these women. While I was searching in my mind for facts that would match what Anastasia knew about the mysterious ladies, she started telling me more about herself.

"I am like Niels Klim in his *Unterirdische Reise.* I have fallen in a hole in this world, looking for a paradise."

I professed complete ignorance of Niels Klim.

"He is a character in a book by Ludwig Holberg, the Danish Moliére," Anastasia explained.

"I only know Grieg's Holberg Suite. I play it on the piano," I informed her.

"Grieg is probably referring to the same Holberg. I don't know the suite, but I know Holberg's plays — and also this wonderful book, Niels Klim's *Unterirdische Reise,* in which the hero falls into a hole in the ground near Bergen, Norway. He finds himself in a country that he calls Potu, governed by an enlightened Monarch, and then visits other underground states."

We decided to go for a walk, and Anastasia suggested that we visit a park near Wannsee, where Kleist killed his beloved, who was suffering from an incurable cancer, and then killed himself. Was the idea of making this morbid pilgrimage mere caprice on Anastasia's part? Or was she truly interested in the life of Henriette Vogel, Kleist's beloved, and wanted to relive the last moments of her life? I never discovered Anastasia's motive since we never reached Wannsee. A torrential rain made us run for shelter in the nearest building, which happened to be my hotel. We sat at the bar and ordered sekt.

After a few glasses, Anastasia told me that the subject of her thesis was the *Protocols of the Elders of Zion.* But when I asked her the name of the university where she studied, she evaded my question.

"I know quite a lot about the *Protocols,*" I told her.

"How so?" she asked, quite interested.

"I proved the fraudulent nature of the *Protocols* when I served as a witness during a trial in London. The Crown was accused by a publisher — who was prohibited by the Lord Chancellor to publish the *Protocols* in English. I know that the *Protocols* were fabricated by Okhrana, the Tsar's secret police, in 1895 and that they represented a combined composition of the novel, *Biarritz,* written by Herman Goodsche forty years before, and a French publication, *Dialogues aux Enfers Entre Machiavell et Montesquieu,* by Maurice Jolly," I explained to her.

We drank more sekt, ate some hors d'oeuvres, and at one point Anastasia got up to leave. Accustomed to her changes in mood, I kissed her good night without offering to take her home. While disappearing through the revolving door of the hotel, she looked at me with what I thought might have been tears in her eyes, and then she was gone.

I slept late the next morning and when I was ready to leave the hotel to go to Anastasia's flat, I noticed a piece of paper in my key slot at the porter's desk. When I retrieved it, I found a handwritten poem addressed to me:

> Shrouding my tenderness in a white silence.
> Painting over with Van Gogh's slant strokes.

61

Of God and myself asking forgiveness —
your generosity taking my breath.

This ascent or descent - flight into skylessness.
Rays not gleaming and the stars out of reach.
Repenting before God, if not plunging into the abyss.
In your memory I, just a shadow, will I remain?

I knew this was a farewell but still hoping for a miracle, I ran to Anastasia's apartment. I rang the bell and knocked at the door. There was no answer. I searched for the superintendent and finally found him in the cellar of the house.

"Do you know the young lady who lives in the apartment on the fourth floor?" I asked the superintendent. He looked unkempt and judging by his accent, was Russian.

He must have realized that I spoke Russian, too, because he answered in my mother tongue.

"There is no young lady in this apartment," he said. "Once, many years ago, a very famous Russian writer, Count Alexei Tolstoy, lived in the apartment. Since then it has changed hands many times. At present, a certain Bogamarov owns the apartment, an elderly gentleman with no family."

"But what about the young lady who uses it now?" I asked desperately.

"There is no such lady who occupied even for an hour this apartment!" replied the old man.

I realized that Anastasia must have bribed the man to keep her existence secret. For a moment I thought of bribing the man with an even larger offer. But after a few moments of reflection, I felt that if she wanted to disappear from my life and become my Ferne Geliebte, I should let her go her own way — leaving me with only memories of these wonderful two days and nights.

I was saddened that the girl I fell in love disappeared without a trace for me to follow her. My colleague in the

British Sector had told me that after she moved to an unknown address she still frequented the cafe *Stolze Kraniche.* I went to the cafe every night, becoming almost a *Stammgast,* but Anastasia never appeared there. Berlin was big, and being divided into four occupational sectors, it would be difficult, if not impossible, to find a person who meant to elude you.

"Damn it," I told myself. Here was someone to whom I had grown attached, at last, and she had become a phantom overnight. I remembered the name of the small Swiss town where her real father found her, and in despair, I hired a car and drove recklessly to *Le Pentapache.* When I arrived there, I realized that I did not know her real name as I attempted to describe to the local police both the girl and her Leuchtenberg father. The Swiss immediately grew suspicious in spite of, or because of, my credentials as an agent of Scotland Yard.

"Can you describe to us the parents of this young woman?" they inquired.

"I have never seen them in my life."

"Well we cannot help you then. Even though all our citizens are registered in our archives they are not open to anybody except when they are involved in a crime. We bid you adieu."

I swore to myself never to deal with Swiss police. I spent my time walking through the few streets of the town and found no trace of Anastasia. Finally I gave up, drove to Zurich and took a plane to London.

The sky was still grey and the fog rather dense when I boarded the plane to London. I felt desolate and sad. "No Van Dyck, no Charles I and what is worse, no Anastasia," I kept repeating to myself, rather depressed — not over my love for Anastasia, but over the realization that I would never see her again. And my attachment to this mysterious woman, to this shadow that passed through my life, was as strong as that of Peter Schlemiel to his own shadow.

Seeon Castle

Chapter 5

Scotland Yard in Munich

> Woe to the specialist who
> is not a pretty fair generalist,
> and woe to the generalist who
> is not also a bit of specialist.
> — Samuel Butler

After returning from Berlin, I sat in my study every night for a week, obsessed by my memories of Anastasia. I didn't have a clue as to where I could find her. I would drink enough whiskey to put me to sleep, but I spent fretful nights tossing in bed from side to side, dreaming about Berlin, the Leuchtenbergs, the painting... and then I would wake up with a terrible hangover. Even Sir Alexander noticed the change in my disposition. I began drinking cup after cup of Turkish coffee, needing caffeine to wake me up in the morning — needing alcohol to put me to sleep at night. After an entire week of this, I knew that I had to find Anastasia soon.

I kept thinking about the discussion Anastasia had with her father on the park bench in *Le Peutapache,* Switzerland, the first and only time she met him, years ago. Her father had mentioned that the Leuchtenbergs, after being exiled from Russia, had resided at the Seeon Castle in Chiemsee, just outside of Munich. Perhaps the castle would hold some clues concerning Anastasia's whereabouts.

I decided to speak with Sir Alexander, realizing that in order to convince him to send me to Munich on a Scotland Yard mission, I would have to tell him about Anastasia. I was prepared for some subtle form of ridicule, but Sir Alex's reaction to my tale was unexpected. Instead of playing the role of a cool intellectual, or of a high official of the British government, he became quite supportive of my plan.

"Go on, my boy," he said in a kindly voice. "Try to use all your knowledge as a detective to find your beloved. I'll make your mission to Munich and the Seeon Castle official."

"You won't be sorry, Sir."

"Just make sure to research the origin of the Charles I painting in the Leuchtenberg archives while you're there," he added. Sir Alex wasn't a fool. Visiting the Seeon Castle was just as necessary for the case as it was for finding Anastasia. I was on a plane to Munich that very same night.

I had never been to Munich before and I had to rely on a travel guide in order to choose my hotel. The two with the highest ratings were *Vier Jahreszeiten* and *Bayerischer Hof.* I called the latter from the airport and was told that a single room was available. The room was cramped and poorly ventilated, but I was so tired that I went to bed immediately. I slept uneventfully, without the intrusion of a dream, until the late hours of the morning. After breakfast I asked the concierge directions to Chiemsee and the Seeon Castle.

"It's quite a long way from here," he told me. "The best way to get there is to travel by car — which you can rent here if you'd like."

Within half an hour I was on my way, travelling at top speed through rolling hills covered with tall trees. There was a long view of the quays and irregular hills. To my left I could see Seeon Lake, the Castle rising above it on a small islet to its right.

An ancient custodian greeted me at the Castle gates. He was a tall thin man, and his skin folded about his neck, layer upon layer. He told me that, except for a young man who had come yesterday, nobody had bothered to visit the Castle for more than a year. Then, without pausing for breath, this frail and half-deaf custodian insisted on telling me the history of the Castle. He was obviously quite pleased at having any type of audience for the information he was paid to impart.

"The Castle of Seeon," my friend began in a quavering voice, "was built as a cloister by the Bavarian palatine, Aribo I, in 994. The monks became famous for their illuminated manuscripts and the founder of the cloister was memorialized in 1395 by Hans Halber, who sculpted a tombstone showing the palatine in full armor, with a sword and flag in his hands and his feet holding down a lion. It is supposed to be one of the best representations of late Gothic art in Bavaria! Perhaps it may interest you also that Mozart visited Seeon as a young man and played on the organ in one of the chapels!"

"Well that is interesting," I admitted. The custodian nodded, relieved by my appreciation.

"And when the Leuchtenbergs moved from Russia to Seeon, a Russian Orthodox Church was built on the grounds of the Castle. They are buried in the cemetery that they helped establish."

The custodian went on to explain that the last Leuchtenberg, Dimitrii Georgievich, sold the Castle to the Stein Brewery in 1947. The Castle was purchased from the brewery by a certain Hirshfeld who leased it to the local police. After Hirshfeld's death, his widow sold the Castle for 2,500,000 German marks to the Catholic church, which was interested in preserving the Castle as a tourist attraction. My friend here was in their employment. I inquired about the Leuchtenberg archives and if they contained their memoirs or lists of their possessions. The custodian mentioned that those documents could be found in Münich, at the *Staat Bibliotek*.

"And where is this cemetery you mentioned?" I asked.

"Behind the chapel," the old man answered. "I'll show you if you'd like."

Even though the custodian was quite helpful, I wanted to avoid any type of discourse about each and every Leuchtenberg buried in the cemetery. Knowing that the old man could prove to be of more assistance in the future, however, I didn't want to insult him.

"I would very much like to see the place, but I really do not want to take up more of your time. May I see it without your assistance?" I asked most politely.

He pointed the way and after a few more exchanges concerning the Leuchtenbergs, I soon found myself wandering amongst their tombs. In the afternoon, a wind rose, muffling sounds from below but the landscape was very still and beautiful. My thoughts turned to Anastasia. I wondered if she had ever visited the site where her ancestors were buried and I imagined walking here with her, her arm looped in mine, while we tried to read the inscriptions written on the various gravestones. Suddenly it seemed as if the day darkened. I glanced around quickly and discovered that while I was indulging in my romantic fantasies, I was also being watched.

In the far corner of the cemetery, a man was half-hidden behind a tree, standing absolutely still, observing my every move. He was tall and lean with shoulder-length black hair, probably no older than twenty-three — but he was too far away for me to distinguish his features. I lit a cigarette and continued to walk as if I hadn't seen him, but when I took a few steps in his direction, he quickly ducked behind the tree and started down the hill toward the lake. I wondered if he were the same man the custodian had mentioned — the one who had visited Seeon the day before. I ran to the other side of the cemetery, hoping to spot him before he entered the woods, but the young man had vanished from sight.

Who, besides Sir Alex, knew that I was in Munich? Did Anastasia have something to do with my being followed? The last idea proved too unnerving for me to pursue and I quickly dismissed the notion.

It was late afternoon when I returned to Munich and I wanted to forget the rather unsettling feeling of being followed. I decided to try my luck and see if I could obtain a ticket to the opera. The performance at the main opera house was sold out but the box office offered me a ticket to the *Volksopera* at the *Gartner Platz.* I was afraid that I would be obliged to listen to *The Merry Widow* or some other similar form of entertainment, but to my great surprise they were performing *The Nose* by Shostakovich.

After the opera I treated myself to a typical Bavarian dinner consisting of pig knuckles, potatoes and cabbage. I had terrible difficulty falling asleep because of indigestion, but the next morning I awoke refreshed and went immediately to the *Staat Bibliotek.* After asking for the head librarian, I explained the purpose of my research to her.

"We have drawers and drawers of Leuchtenberg archives," the librarian said. "Some boxes contain documents only written in Russian. You would have to spend days searching through all the papers."

"They were never catalogued?" I asked. For some reason her discouragement aroused my suspicion.

"In a certain fashion," she answered, elusively.

"And may I see the catalogue?"

"Yes, but you must sign for it with your name, where you are currently staying and the institution you represent."

The librarian brought me a fat ledger and after giving her the requisite information, I made a perfunctory search through several files. At first, my duties were parochial and dull. Most of the documents dated back to the late

69

eighteenth and early nineteenth centuries and referred to Eugéne de Beauharnais who was the first Leuchtenberg and also the son of Joséphine de la Pagerie, Napoleon's first wife. I found a list of paintings apparently owned by Beauharnais, and even though he had collected some very great artists such as Domenicino, Garofalo, Guercino, Ruysdael and Van Ostade, there was no mention of Van Dyck or of the portrait of Charles I. Yet in spite of the boredom there were some interesting documents. I was so involved in my research that when the librarian informed me that they were closing the library early, I became very upset. She noticed the changed of my mood and kindly recommended me to spend the rest of the day in the country and take a train to Ansbach. After a late lunch in the old cloister and a glass of their dark beer, I returned to my hotel for an early night's sleep. I left in the morning under dark sky to present myself once more to the librarian at the *Staat Bibliotek.* She greeted me with some surprising news.

"Excuse me, Mr. Gramtrub," she said, "but no one has asked for the Leuchtenberg archives for ages, and now, within two days, two people have searched the same files — you and a young man."

I looked at the librarian inquisitively. Why was she mentioning this now, instead of yesterday?

"When I just casually mentioned that another person had searched the same archives,' she continued, "the other man asked me for your name and I told him. Was this wrong?"

I couldn't believe the woman's audacity.

"Of course you were wrong in giving my name to a stranger!" I nearly shouted. "And besides, how could this man have gotten such information when I've been here at closing yesterday, and at opening today?"

"Oh, Mr. Gramtrub. We did close early yesterday, but the young man came just after you left. And he was so insistent. He seemed desperate. I hope I haven't done something too terribly wrong."

I was quite angry, particularly because I knew I should have hidden my affiliation with Scotland Yard in the first place. I wondered how much this mysterious young man had bribed her to reveal my identity. Maybe he'd arranged for her to close the library early, before I had even arrived.

"Now you can do me a good turn for a change," I said gruffly. "First tell me what this man looked like and what you know about him."

Immediately the librarian jumped to attention. She described the man as being between twenty and twenty-five, tall with long black hair to his shoulders, wearing black jeans and a leather jacket.

"But he was quite well-spoken," she added, "even if he did seem to be a bit of a derelict."

"And his name?" I asked, leaning toward her.

By this time the woman was nearly in tears.

"He never told me his name, Mr. Gramtrub."

She was a stupid woman and I told her so. But I also believed that she was relatively harmless. I needed to worry more about this young man.

Knowing that I couldn't get any more information from the librarian, I decided to spend the rest of the day continuing my research. However, the only other files that contained nineteenth- and twentieth-century documents merely held information concerning the construction of streets, bridges and certain industries. Obviously these files had nothing to do with Anastasia or her father or with the Charles I portrait. I interrogated the librarian, asking if any information was missing from the files. By this time she was completely undone, and I realized that she was probably telling the truth, her only misdemeanor being the one to which she had already confessed.

After giving a somewhat more courteous nod to the librarian, I returned to the hotel. There, another surprise was awaiting me — a note slipped under my hotel room door.

The envelope contained a single sheet of paper with a message composed of clumsily cut-out letters from newspapers. The text was as follows: "If you treasure your life, stop investigating the Leuchtenbergs and go home. Staying in Munich may become dangerous for you." I almost laughed aloud, thinking about the absurdity of my situation.

Here I was, an art investigator, not exactly the type to chase down criminals. And yet I was not only being followed — but my very life was being threatened! Why? What could I possibly discover that would endanger someone to the point where he'd threaten me? I am not a coward but my training as a detective had not taught me to deal with such encounters. I decided, therefore, to return to London and make a detailed report of these strange occurrences to Sir Alexander.

Back in London, immediately after discussing my findings with Sir Alex, a messenger brought me an envelope. It contained a copy of a recent letter from the Government of Bermuda inquiring about the progress being made in identifying the provenance of the Charles I portrait. I was not amused by Sir Alexander's not-so-subtle reprimand and fell back into my ghoulish mood. I felt like a medieval knight wounded by an arrow. And while trying to pull the arrow out from my wound, I was tearing up even more of my own body. Some time later, Sir Alex entered my office and strongly suggested I channel my grief into my work.

I started to search the London libraries for information on the Leuchtenbergs. I needed to find out if Serge and Nicholas Leuchtenberg had indeed owned the Van Dyck painting, as the mysterious stranger had mentioned to Puyvelde. And I needed to determine his personal relationship to the Grand Duchess Maria, Nicholas and Serge Leuchtenberg.

And, perhaps most importantly, I was still trying to find some clue as to Anastasia's whereabouts.

Chapter 6

Saga of the Leuchtenbergs

> The body of writing takes a
> thousand forms and there is
> no right way to measure.
> — Lu Chi Wen Fu

The desk in my study was covered with texts from the London libraries, out-of-print memoirs, and scrambled notes I had pertaining to the Leuchtenberg family. It was two in the morning and nearly one and a half weeks since I had returned from Munich. My nerves were fraught with overwork and Sir Alex wasn't making my life any easier. If I didn't come up with some definitive information concerning the provenance of the Charles I portrait by the end of this week, I would be put off the case. And then, as Sir Alex undoubtedly knew, I would have no recourse for investigating Anastasia's whereabouts. I wasn't about to let Anastasia slide through my hands again. There had to be a reference to the painting somewhere.

Outside, the streets were dark and silent. Everyone in London was probably already asleep, curled up warm and happy in their beds. I decided to play my favorite recording of an opera composed by Michael Ivanovich Glinka, entitled *Ruslan and Ludmila,* and pour a little brandy into my coffee. Perhaps if I could relax a bit, the work would be accomplished more easily. As I listened to the overture, the melodious notes slowly began to soothe my nerves.

"You're playing the opera inspired by my wedding," a young woman said to me, her voice as clear and melodious as Glinka's music.

"Hmmm?" I answered, now very relaxed, my eyes closed.

"That music," she said. "Glinka was sitting on the balcony of the Winter Palace observing my wedding banquet. He wrote in his memoirs that it was the clinking of forks and spoons that inspired the overture to *Ruslan and Ludmila.*"

"Anastasia?" I mumbled, my eyes still closed. I couldn't quite hear what this woman was telling me. "Anastasia, is that you?"

"Anastasia? Are people still wondering about her?" the voice asked, somewhat askance. "Can't people remember past their own century?"

"Not the Tsar's daughter," I said, trying to clarify.

"Excuse me, but I am the Tsar's daughter. Nicholas I's daughter! The Grand Duchess Maria."

My eyes flew open. Before me stood a woman of striking beauty, tall and slim with magnificent blue eyes. She wore a heavily embroidered silk robe, covered with diamonds, and her hair was piled on top of her pale face in soft, intricate waves.

"Your Grace," I said, falling to my knees. "Please pardon my horrible rudeness."

"My dear man," the Grand Duchess answered graciously, "please get up. How were you to know who I am? I've been dead for over a century."

I quickly got up and pulled out a chair for her.

"Thank you, Jerry. And thank you for making me feel wonderfully alive. The music has pulled me back as I was on my wedding day, that beautiful sunny, summer day — July 2, 1839. I was nineteen."

"Your Grace, you look exquisite."

We both sat down and looked about us with some discomfort. The Grand Duchess Maria tapped her foot nervously, in time with Glinka's music, while I drummed my fingers on the arm of my chair, waiting for the Grand Duchess to speak, which finally she did.

"Shouldn't you tell me why I'm here?" she said.

"Your Grace," I said paling, "I have no idea. I thought you could tell me."

"But you must have wanted something from me, or I would never have been able to come. It's your will that brought me here. Perhaps you need to know something?" she suggested.

"Oh Your Grace, I think I'm just overworked," I said. "You see, I've been researching for days, looking for clues as to the origin of the Charles I portrait, looking for clues that will help me to find Anastasia, the woman I mistook you for — the Leuchtenberg history is extremely confusing."

"Now Jerry," the Grand Duchess Maria said, interrupting my somewhat incoherent explanation, "Perhaps if you tell me exactly what you want to know and why, then I will be able to determine if I can help you or not."

After a moment's pause, I regained composure. The Grand Duchess looked astonishingly like Anastasia.

"I need to know about the Leuchtenberg family," I said, finally.

"My husband, Maximilian's family?" the Grand Duchess asked.

"Yes, Your Grace," I answered.

"I see," she said. "And why? Does it have to do with this Anastasia you mistook me for?"

"In part," I said, softly. "I am looking for her. Her father is a Leuchtenberg."

"Jerry," the Grand Duchess Maria said, smiling, "you sound as if you are in love with her. In that case I will tell you everything I know about the Leuchtenbergs!"

She sat back in her chair and folded her hands gently in her lap. The diamonds glittered off her silk robe, sending a myriad of rainbows throughout the room while Glinka's *Ruslan and Ludmila* continued to play.

"My first husband, Maximilian Leuchtenberg, also had a noble heritage. Just as I am Tsar Nicholas I's daughter, Maximilian was the son of Prince Eugène de Beauharnais and Augusta, the Princess of Bavaria."

I nodded slowly, trying to recall the notes I had been studying.

"Eugène Beauharnais's father, Alexander de Beauharnais, perished during the French Revolution and his mother, Joséphine, remarried in 1796 with Napoleon. Thus, Eugene became Napoleon's stepson."

"And your husband was Josephine's grandson?" I asked, already confused.

"Exactly," the Grand Duchess answered. "And my husband's father was Napoleon's stepson and supposed heir."

"I think I understand," I said, suddenly wanting another drink. "Would you like a brandy?" I offered the Grand Duchess.

"Well," she smiled, "actually I would like a taste of wine."

"I'd be delighted," and I poured the best wine I had into the only crystal I owned.

After we were both settled, each with our own drinks, Maria continued explaining the Leuchtenberg's family history.

"One could say that the Leuchtenberg history, in some ways, began with Napoleon," said Maria, serious once more.

"With Napoleon?" I asked, confused again.

"Let me explain. After Napoleon became Emperor, he wanted to secure legitimacy for his brothers and sisters by having them marry, if not royalty, at least nobility and he included Eugène de Beauharnais, Josephine's son, in his plans. Napoleon selected the charming and well-educated Princess Augusta for his twenty-four year old stepson, not necessarily because of their love for each other — they had never met — but because Augusta was the daughter of Napoleon's close ally, Maximilian-Joseph, whom Napoleon made King of Bavaria."

"I see," I said, grateful for my brandy.

"Well, Augusta was outraged," Maria continued. "She was in love with her cousin, Prince Charles of Baden, and they were already engaged. Augusta's love interest, however, did not coincide with Napoleon's plan for the formation of the Great Alliance of Electorates and the principalities of Southern Germany, linked by a treaty with France! Napoleon decided to break off the angagement of Augusta and the Prince of Baden, appeasing the Prince by offering him Josephine's niece, Stephanie."

"That's horrible!" I cried, astounded that people could be treated as if they were some meaningless piece of property.

"Not only that," the Grand Duchess exclaimed, "but Napoleon and this niece of Joséphine, Stéphanie, were supposedly lovers! She was said to have borne Napoleon's son, Kaspar Hauser, the famous foundling of Nuremberg! Thus, Napoleon persisted in his demands that Augusta should marry his step-son Eugène."

"I'm surprised Augusta and her cousin didn't elope," I said.

"Perhaps they would have," Maria replied. "Except Augusta's father wrote his daughter a most despairing letter concerning Napoleon's wedding plans. It read:

> Remember, my dear child, that the fate, not only of your father, but also of your brother and of Bavaria, depends on how quickly this connection is established.

"Augusta, a dutiful daughter, finally agreed to the marriage. In a letter to her father she wrote:

> If the peace of mind of my dear father and the fate of the entire nation depend on my decision, I offer my sacrifice even if it means destroying my future.

Meanwhile, Eugène was completely unaware of Napoleon's negotiations with the King of Bavaria. Oh, Eugène must have been shocked when — nine days after Princess Augusta agreed to the wedding plans — Napoleon ordered him to proceed immediately to Munich and prepare for his wedding day. Then, upon Eugene's arrival in Munich, Napoleon ordered him to shave his rather formidable mustache so that he'll make a more favorable impression on his bride-to-be!"

Quite frankly, I couldn't understand why the Grand Duchess Maria was laughing so hard. She even had to set down her wine to keep it from spilling.

"But your Grace," I said, somewhat surprised. "You are speaking of your husband's parents."

"Oh, Jerry," she replied. "You have so much to learn about life."

It was hard for me to remember that this exquisite woman, dressed in silk and diamonds for her wedding day, had already lived a full life.

"Shall I continue?" she asked, now calm.

"Oh yes. Please," I said.

"Very well. Eleven days later, on January 14, 1806, Eugène de Beauharnais and Augusta, the Princess of Bavaria were wed. That same year, Napoleon wrote a letter to Augusta's father, the King of Bavaria, stating that in default of a direct heir, Napoleon would designate Eugène as his heir. The couple was overjoyed, obviously. Napoleon had been married ten years without producing a child. But, unfortunately for the young couple, the birth of Napoleon's son in 1810 dashed their hopes."

"How strange," I commented. Maria nodded her head.

"Yes, I'm sure Eugène was quite disappointed," she said softly. "But Napoleon at least named him Viceroy of Italy, and he and Augusta resided in Milan until Napoleon's fall and the dissolution of the Italian viceroyalty."

I was still thinking of the manner in which Eugène and Augusta were forced to wed. "Were they happy?" I finally asked.

"Supposedly, they fell in love shortly after their wedding and remained a happily married couple until Eugène's rather premature death. But that's not to say life was easy for them. An especially difficult time was during the year 1812, when Napoleon's army, including a contingent of Italian and German soldiers under Eugène's command, fought in Russia and were ultimately defeated. Following Napoleon's downfall, Eugène was deprived of his status in Italy and was denied another principality. Eugène and Augusta moved to Munich and purchased the Seeon Castle from Augusta's father for five million francs. That is how Eugène received the title of Herzog von Leuchtenberg."

"Do you mean to say that he bought his title?" I asked, before realizing my question's rudeness.

"In a manner of speaking," my guest answered, evading the question.

Not knowing how to respond, I poured the Grand Duchess another glass of wine. She lifted her head and smiled bravely.

"Such things happen, Jerry," she said. "History turns with astonishing speed."

"Please forgive me."

"Nonsense! There is nothing to forgive. Besides, Eugène was a charming young man. The soirées given by him and his Princess Augusta were quite popular among the Bavarian nobility."

79

Did I note a touch of defensiveness in the Grand Duchess' tone? I decided to change the subject.

"And Eugène's children?" I gently prodded.

"My generation?" Maria asked, brightening somewhat.

"Yes, exactly!" I said, relieved.

"Well!" Maria continued, nibbling on one of the macaroons I had just placed before her, "Eugène died in 1825 at the age of forty-three. He and Augusta had seven children. Their oldest son, Augustus, an heir to the title and to the Castle Seeon, died in 1835, one year after his marriage to the Queen of Portugal. Thus, Augustus' brother, Maximilian, inherited the title Herzog von Leuchtenberg and the Seeon Castle."

I suppose my face betrayed a hint of confusion for at that point, the Grand Duchess reached over to my desk, whipped out a piece of writing paper, and began to draw the Leuchtenberg family tree. When she was done, she handed it to me.

"Does that clarify matters?" the Grand Duchess asked.

"It does indeed," I answered, truthfully. "This is an exquisite rendition."

"It's only a family-tree, Jerry, not a Rembrandt. But thank you just the same," she said, laughing and obviously pleased. "Well then. Shall we continue?"

"By all means," I replied.

"Well, Maximilian von Leuchtenberg — my first husband — was a man of broad interests. Being brought up without a father from his childhood, he grow up under the influence of his mother, one of the most educated princes of that time. He received an excellent education, not only in the sciences, but in art, literature and music. He entered a military service later in Bavaria and took the same position as his father and brother before. In 1837 by the order of his uncle, the Bavarian King, he came to Russia. He was nicely received by the Imperial family and accompanied the Emperor to Odessa and then to Constantinople. He spoke and wrote Russian so fluently that he fooled many native

Russians into believing that he was born here, instead of in Bavaria. But not everyone appreciated his intelligence. One contemporary even had the audacity to describe him like this:

> The Duke de Leuchtenberg is a tall, well-made young man, but there is nothing distinguished in his features. His eyes are handsome, but his mouth projects and is not well-formed. His figure is good without being noble; a uniform becomes him and supplies that want of grace that may be observed in his person. He looks more like a smart sub-lieutenant than a prince.

Isn't that horrible! Obviously, the critic didn't have a brain in his head. Sometimes sensitivity and intelligence matter more to a woman than looks."

I laughed, noting Maria's straight features and large blue eyes. Earlier that evening I had been reading Anna Feodorovna Tiutcheva's memoirs, the daughter of the great Russian poet, Feodor Tiutchev. She described the Grand Duchess Maria as having 'a refined intelligence with real beauty and a warm heart.' I couldn't have agreed with the poet's daughter more, although Ms. Tiutcheva should have also mentioned the Grand Duchess' spunk.

"I remember the first time I met Maximilian," Maria continued, her eyes glowing with the memory. "My father was giving a ball at the Winter Palace in honor of my nineteenth birthday; my first dance was with Maximilian. I felt so glamorous and happy, moving across the floor in the strong arms of a Bavarian officer.

"My mother had ordered me a brand new, pink silk dress made just for the occasion, and it tied at the waist with a belt covered in pearls and rubies. I wore a diamond necklace that my father had given me that very afternoon. What an occasion! The sound of music, the sparkling of jewelry, the sight of bare shoulders, sweet feminine smiles and strong men... I do believe that Maximilian fell in love, not only with me, but with the entire Russian court! But why my father assented to Maximilian's request for my hand in marriage is still not clear. Perhaps those absurd rumors about my clandestine love affair with a young poet had something to do with it."

"So, it is true!" I exclaimed, before I could stop myself.

"What is true?"

"That you had a love affair with a poet, before marrying Maximilian von Leuchtenberg. May I ask his name?"

"Jerry! You are as incorrigible as my father's inquisitors. No, I won't tell you!"

"Forgive me," I said meekly. "Please continue."

"Oh, it's really quite all right. It all happened so long ago. But I will tell you that in the literary salons of St. Petersburg this poet's name was pronounced with great respect. He was quite handsome, young and tall, with a slim waist and dark, innocent eyes. His long fingers would move nervously up and down the buttons of his black jacket. His soft voice reflected his passion and he'd recite his poetry in a carefully modulated voice, penetrating all the women's hearts. He could have had any woman he wanted, but when he read his poems he'd fix his eyes only on me."

At this point, the Grand Duchess Maria pulled out an intricately embroidered handkerchief and started dabbing at the corners of her eyes.

"That's a beautiful story," I said, half-weeping myself.

"I know," replied the Grand Duchess. "And this beautiful young man, this gifted poet, committed suicide on the day of my wedding. A poem was found on his deathbed — a love poem dedicated to M.N."

"You?"

"Yes. Maria Nicholaevna."

Maria cleared her voice and lifted her chin. For a moment I thought I saw tears in her eyes — and she recited, by heart, the poem written for her so many years ago:

82

Don't call me. My voice won't answer the echo.
The masked-ball is about to end.
Every tremulous sound is just an affliction.
Every true word — just an unfinished bar.

A woman's cry. Silence. Royal trumpets.
Don't call me. The violin bow broke.
Its wind licking my withered lips, howling,
tying my emotions into one knot.

In timelessness fairy-tale images drawn.
In your kingdom — Royal procession again.
Every step leads to the abyss. Don't call me.
A courtier I am not.

In your kingdom another masked-ball begins.
Don't call me. A dancer I am not.
Into a quietude, lightly trembling,
from your masked-ball I depart.

My guest and I were both silent for awhile, the Grand Duchess sitting quite still. If it weren't for Anastasia, I might have wanted to court Maria. But such a relationship would have been quite awkward.

"Shall I continue?" Maria asked, once she had regained her composure.

"By all means."

"There were certain conditions imposed on Maximilian by my father," Maria explained. "Maximilian had to promise to live in Russia permanently and our children had to be baptized and educated in the Russian Orthodox faith. But after our marriage, my husband received the title 'His Highnesty' and Graf Romanovsky, he became a general-mayor of the Russian military service."

"All St. Petersburg celebrated the wedding, and the streets were full of dancing and festivity. Inside the Imperial chapel, representatives from all the sovereigns in Europe and Asia bore witness to our wedding vows. The Marquis de Custine described the wedding:

A marriage of inclination celebrated in broidered habiliments, and in a place so pompous, was a novelty which crowned the interest of the scene. The young bride is extremely graceful; her eyes are blue and her fair complexion has all the delicate freshness of early youth; openness and intelligence united form the predominant expression of her face. This princess and her sister, the Grand Duchess Olga, appear to be the two most beautiful persons at the Russian court — happy unison of the advantages of rank and the gift of nature. When the officiating bishop presented the married pair to the august parents, the latter embraced them with a warmth that was affecting. Everybody had fallen on their knees and, last of all, the Emperor; the lovers were united; the imperial family and the crowd arose; the priests and choir chanted the Te Deum, and discharges of artillery outside announced the consecration of the marriage to the city. The effect of exquisite music, mingled with the thunder of the cannon, the ringing of the bells and the distant acclamations of the people, was inexpressibly grand!

"And it was an honor for anyone to be invited to this wedding. Among the guests was the famous Russian composer, Michael Ivanovich Glinka, who dedicated two of his compositions — a waltz in G-major and a polonaise in E-major — to me. As I explained when I entered, my wedding inspired the overture to the opera you're playing now, *Ruslan and Ludmila.*"

"And were you in love?" I asked, thinking of the poet who had sacrificed his life for her.

"Oh Jerry. That is always a more difficult question than people realize," she answered, solemnly.

"Maximilian and I lived in Marinsky Palace in St. Petersburg, built for me by my father. The cost of the palace was more than 12 million rubles and was filled with unparalleled works of art. And my husband adjusted to his new life and position without any apparent difficulty. He was elected the President of the Imperial Academy of Arts in 1843, a position that he held until his death in 1852. His profound knowledge of art, especially Italian art, was remarkable. Maximilian was also interested in the sciences, particularly in a new field — that of electromagnetism. In 1839 he became an honorable member of the Imperial Academy of Science in St. Petersburg. He had a laboratory in the Winter Palace where he conducted his experiments, the results of which on August 7, 1840 he presented through the Academician Jacoby to the Imperial Academy of Sciences in St. Petersburg. Maximilian was also interested in bronze casting, mineralogy and mining. Nicholas I ordered him a position as a Head of the Institute of Mineralogy. Maximilian built a plant near St. Petersburg. The first Russian locomotive came out of this plant."

"Certainly this is all very impressive," I conceded, "But you still haven't answered my question. Were you happy?"

Without pausing for a beat, the Grand Duchess Maria continued.

"We were a tremendous social success. We were knowledgeable, interesting, charming..."

"Your Grace," I interrupted, knowing that she was hiding something painful, but something that she wanted to express.

"Alright Jerry," she said slowly, playing with the handkerchief that she still held in her hands. "I'll admit it. We were unfaithful."

Somehow, I was not completely surprised.

"Maximilian's delicate manners and shy smile made him very popular with women," Maria explained.

"I hope I won't be too presumptuous," I said softly, "but I read in Anna Feodorovna Tiutcheva's memoirs that he

liked to gamble and that he also 'had success with women.'
Is this true?"

Maria sighed.

"At the beginning of our marriage we were happy. But,
as with many married couples, the difficulties of child bearing, the mundane routine of family life.... Each year I gave
birth to another of Maximilian's children — seven in all —
and with every child, I grew less and less enchanted with
my husband's charms.

"I started to take lovers, even while Maximilian was still
alive. One of them was the pseudo Duke Alexander von
Hesse, whose sister married my brother, the future Tsar,
Alexander II. Alexander von Hesse was supposed to be sired
by Grand Duke Louis II of Hesse and Rhein. In reality his
father was Baron Augustus Sevarilens von Granny, Chamberlain to the Duchess of Hesse, Princess Wilhelmina von
Baden. The Duchess gave birth to Alexander three years after she was separated from her husband and when she lived
openly with her Chamberlain. My other lover was Grigorii
Alexandrovich Stroganov, the first man I truly loved, aside
from the poet I knew in my youth."

At this point the Grand Duchess became quite still.

"I am so ashamed," she whispered.

I reached for the bottle of wine and poured the Grand
Duchess another glass. After we sat in silence for a bit, I
decided to ask Maria if she would like me to read her some
memoirs I had found, written by her oldest son, Nicholai
Maximilianovich.

"You should know how you were perceived," I said. "It
will, I believe, reassure you."

Maria smiled bravely, lifting her chin in an expression
of pride.

"By all means," she replied.

I looked through the scattered notes I had lying about
and lifted the parchment paper of a particularly old
manuscript. I cleared my throat and began:

"It is difficult for me to describe my mother. "Beautiful" is not the right word. "Glorious" perhaps, but this, too, does not adequately describe her. My mother's face, her bearing, her walk bespoke of dignity. She knew she was the daughter of the Emperor of all Russia, but at the same time, she was humble enough to seek a man who would love her for herself, and not because she was the Grand Duchess Maria.

I do not remember my father. He died when I was a child, barely nine years old. I remember my mother's second husband and probably her real great love, Count Stroganov. I used to ask her, "Mama, how did you meet this handsome man?"

With a coquettish smile, she would manage to partially avoid my question, while seeming to answer.

"I met him at a ball. When your father was busy discussing mining, science, electromagnetism... the Count Stroganov asked me to dance."

"Then you knew the Count while you still lived with our father?"

Ignoring my question, mother would continue her story.

"While we were dancing," she explained, "this stranger started a conversation about art. It became quite clear that he was a connoisseur of Italian baroque art. He told me that he lived in Florence during part of the year. Something attracted me to him. Perhaps the way he was holding me when we were dancing – one arm around my shoulder pressing me to him.

87

'Grand Duchess,' he said, 'I am Count Grigorii Stroganov. May I call on you at your palace to continue our talk about art?'

Before answering I looked at my husband. He was deeply engrossed in conversation with another scientist. He seemed to have no idea that I stood alone, with a stranger, on the dance floor.

'Yes, Count Stroganov, you may call on me.' And the stranger kissed my hands and walked away."

Here mama paused.

"And then?" I asked. But she wouldn't continue.

My mother became Stroganov's lover while my father was still alive."

Still transfixed by the manuscript's words, I gradually became aware of Maria's low sobbing.

"Maria," I said, bending down beside her, "why are you crying?"

"I am a horrible woman. I was unfaithful to my husband and I didn't even try to hide the fact from my son."

"But you couldn't have hidden the fact. You are an honest woman, your son never blamed you, and your love for Stroganov was true. Besides, your husband was guilty of the same misdeed!"

I wanted to shake Maria to her senses. I wanted to convince her that her guilt was causing more harm to herself than her love affair had ever hurt anyone else. And still, she wouldn't stop crying.

"Grand Duchess Maria!" I said firmly. "What will you do? Carry your guilt with you for another century?"

"Jerry," she said, smiling through her tears, "if I weren't already deceased, I'd say you loved me."

I blushed a deep crimson and Maria continued her saga of the Leuchtenbergs.

"Maximilian died unexpectedly in 1852," Maria said after taking a sip of wine. "During one of his trips to Ural, he caught a severe cold and never recovered. He died when our last child, Georgii Maximilianovich, was due to be born. Georgii was our seventh child. He never saw his father."

"After Maximilian's death, I became the first woman President of the Imperial Academy of Arts in St. Petersburg. Even though Maximilian and I weren't the happiest of married couples, I was still sadly grieved. In order to forget my despair, I would go to the Academy, making sure the students were being treated properly, attending to the Academy's acquisitions. The Russian sculptor, N. Pimenoff, made a bust of me at the time, which was placed in the main hall of the Academy.

"But within two months of Maximilian's death, I married Count Grigorii Alexandrovich Stroganov. And as you said, Jerry, he was my true love."

"Yes, Maria," I answered. "Even your son knew that. And he didn't blame you."

Maria smiled at me, her eyes still holding traces of her tears. Then she leaned toward me and started to speak in a whisper.

"The marriage took place in Count Potemkin's private chapel and was kept a secret. If my father had ever learned that Stroganov and I had married, he would have banished me to a convent and sent Stroganov to Caucasus, where he would have served in the army fighting the Turks! The only person who knew about the marriage and approved of it was my brother, the future Emperor of Russia, Alexander II. I had to lead a double life, pretending to be Maximilian's inconsolable widow while traveling in secret, as if I were on a clandestine mission, when I visited Stroganov in Italy where he lived. Finally this conspiracy ended in 1855, when Nicholas I, my father, died."

"You traveled to Italy in secret? Afraid to visit your own husband?" I asked.

Maria nodded her head slowly and then gave a bitter laugh. I was charmed by her spirit and struck by the hard life she'd lived.

"Your Grace," I said, "may I read you another excerpt from Nicholai Maximilianovich's memoirs? I think it will interest you."

The Grand Duchess raised her arm, palm up, allowing me to do her the honor. I lifted her oldest son's manuscript once more and began to read:

> "I did not see Stroganov frequently during my mother's marriage to him. He spent most of his time at his palace in Italy and I had to complete my schooling in Russia. The first time I was able to actually become acquainted with him was when mama was dying in her Marinsky Dvoretz. I have never seen a more sorrowstricken man. Stroganov was holding mama's hand and sobbing quietly. He was still handsome, although slightly more stooped, with grey hair. His sorrow was more profound, and perhaps more sincere, than any of her children's. I was overwhelmed by Maria's death struggle and wept almost incessantly when she finally died, but during her death throes, it was Stroganov who stayed by her side.
>
> Stroganov was a broken man after her death. He survived her by only a few years."

At this point, Maria began weeping again, silently into her handkerchief. After a bit, she started to calm down.

"Tell me, my dear Jerry," she implored, "what happened to my dear Stroganov?"

"Are you sure you want to know?" I asked, thinking that we should start lightening the conversation.

"Yes," she answered. "I want to know everything that happened to him, and to my dear son who wrote these beautiful memoirs, Nicholai Maximilianovich!"

"Very well, Your Grace," I said, wishing that I were more gifted at telling humorous stories, "if you insist."

She nodded her head and what could I do?

"As you know, Stroganov was not very rich," I began. "The few paintings he possessed by the grand masters were kept in Tuscany, and when he died, someone in his family inherited his house and its contents."

"Why are you telling me what happened to the paintings?" the Grand Duchess asked.

"That's what I know. That's what I've been researching," I said, pointing to the piles of texts and notes on my desk.

"Oh," she answered with a shrug. "Then you should know that he and I had a fabulous collection of paintings."

"Yes," I answered, "that you hid from your father."

"Oh yes," she responded vaguely. "But I want to know about Stroganov."

"Of course, Your Grace." I said, taking a sip from my brandy. "Stroganov kept a scrupulous account of what was yours and what was his. After your death, Nicholai was supposed to inherit the bulk of your estate according to Russian law. But in spite of your apparent wealth, you died with no cash on hand."

"My dear sir," Maria whispered, as I now realized she was wont to do when she was somewhat angry, "let me remind you of whom you address! How can you say I left no cash?"

"Excuse me Your Grace, but the Marinsky Dvoretz, and many of your smaller villas required tremendous up-keep. And the paintings you had collected were kept under poor environmental conditions and started showing signs of wear. I'm afraid that your son was without cash."

Suddenly Maria paled, her blue eyes widened in disbelief. For a moment I thought she would faint.

91

"Jerry!" she exclaimed, "Is that true?"

I immediately came to my senses. What was I doing telling the Tsar's daughter that she left her children without enough money?

"Please forgive me," I said quietly. "I shouldn't have told you."

"I wanted you to," she answered, still slightly peeved. "Just try using some tact. Continue. I had no idea that my children were left destitute."

"I would hardly say destitute, Your Grace!"

"Continue."

"Of course. Your son, after realizing his financial situation, paid a visit to your brother, Tsar Alexander II, asking him for financial help. However, Alexander II had currently fallen in love with one of the Tsarina's Frejlins and was not interested in solving his nephew's financial problems."

"Alexander wouldn't help him?" Maria was clearly shocked. "But he had helped me hide my liaison with Stroganov from our father! He was my greatest ally!"

I shrugged my shoulders, nodding my head sadly.

"Go on Jerry," Maria said impatiently, "Tell me what happened to my son!"

"Your son talked to his sisters who were then married to well-to-do noblemen and they reached the decision that none of them had enough money for the upkeep of Marinsky Dvoretz. They decided to sell it."

"They sold the palace my father had built for me! My Marinsky Dvoretz!" The Grand Duchess was now holding her handkerchief in a tight fist.

"Please, your Grace," I pleaded, almost on my knees. "Let me read what your son wrote. He explains it better than I do."

Without waiting for a reply, I began to read, once more, from Nicholai Maximilianovich's tattered memoirs:

"I cried at the signing of the sale contract. I had spent the happiest years of my life at the

Marinsky Palace. I remember when my sisters and I, as small children, used to surround mama, shouting,

"Mama, dance for us!"

"Children," she'd reply, laughing, "children, don't you see that I am pregnant with another brother or sister of yours. And you want me to dance!"

"Don't worry, mama! The baby wants to dance too!" we insisted. Then we would form a circle around mama and start to dance. Mama couldn't resist us for too long, and soon she would join us, singing in her beautiful voice:

> There was a little bird who came to a rose in bloom. He kissed the rose in bloom and flew away. The rose in bloom was sad waiting day by day for the little bird who loved her and who never came again.

I sang this song to mama when she was dying. In spite of her suffering, she smiled her beautiful smile, one that I could remember from when I was very young."

"That was quite moving," Maria, now calm, whispered. "Thank you for reading that to me."

"You're very welcome, Your Grace," I said, pleased that I had finally been able to appease her.

I refilled our glasses and we drank in silence for a bit, somewhat worn by the evening's turmoil of emotions. Despite Maria's tears and anger, her face was radiant and serene as if we had merely spent the evening playing Parcheesi. She looked thoughtful, the diamonds on her gown sparkling off her pale skin.

93

"You know, Jerry," she said, still contemplative, "of all my children, Sergei was the favorite. Even though Nicholai was the eldest and principal heir, I used to give Sergei certain gifts during my lifetime. He particularly liked receiving gifts of art. I gave him a substantial number of paintings, quite valuable ones, before I died. Tell me, what happened to him?"

"Oh Your Grace," I said hesitantly, "Sergei was killed at the age of twenty-eight in the Balkans during the Turkish War. He died just one year after you."

Thankfully, the Duchess did not have another emotional outburst. She merely smiled sadly, shaking her head.

"Poor Sergei," she exclaimed. "He was a beautiful child."

We sat in silence, again, the Grand Duchess thinking about her children's fate.

"Did you know that Nicholai fell in love with a commoner, Nadezhda Annenkov, already a mother of two sons?" the Grand Duchess asked me. "He was advised by the Imperial Court to leave Russia even though I stood up for him. Do you know if they married or not, Jerry?"

"Grand Duchess, Nicholai and Nadezhda married in 1879, three years after your death. He and his bride left Russia and lived in Paris. He died in Paris in 1890 at the age of forty-eight."

"And did they have children?" Maria asked.

"Not of their own. But Nicholai Maximilianovich adopted Nadezhda's two sons, Nicholai Nicholaevich and Georgii. They returned to Russia and were in Baron Wrangel's White Army. They fought bravely against the Bolsheviks, but after the revolution they were exiled from Russia."

"My son sold my palace and my grandsons were exiled? Jerry, you are telling me horrible things!"

"Perhaps it was fortunate Nicholai sold the Marinsky Palace when he did. After the revolution, it would have been worth nothing. And your grandsons suffered the same fate all White Russians had to endure. Even my father suffered losses."

"Really, Jerry?" the Grand Duchess asked, suddenly looking frail. "Has life been so uncertain?"

"Georgii, Nicholai's youngest son, had to sell off certain valuables from the Seeon Castle."

"The Seeon Castle? Maximilian's home?" Maria asked quietly.

"At the beginning he sold only small items," I said, hoping to stay Maria's tears, "But he also had to sell some of the library, collected by Eugène de Beauharnais and his wife, Augusta."

"Poor Georgii!" Maria exclaimed.

"Yes," I nodded, thoughtfully. "The auction took place on April fifteenth and sixteenth, in 1928, but unfortunately, the money did not last long. By 1934 most of the Eugène de Beauharnais' archives were sold by Georgii's oldest son, Dimitrii Georgievich, at Sotheby's in London to Mr. de Coppet, a professor at Princeton University."

"Princeton?" Maria enquired.

"An American university," I answered. "One of my friends visited Princeton and found the Beauharnais archives, thirty years after their acquisition, in a deplorable state. Alexander I's letters to Josephine and Eugène had been sold separately and still cannot be traced. But some of the letters were published in a book entitled *The Romance of Prince Eugène*."

"This is tragic!" the Grand Duchess said softly. "To think that such rare and beautiful goods were sold at an auction and that personal letters were made public. To think that my grandsons were so destitute, they had to resort to such means."

"After the war, financial circumstances forced the Leuchtenbergs to grow vegetables in Seeon for sale at the local market. Georgii's son, Dimitrii, finally sold the Castle to the Brewery Stein."

"Maximilian's home was turned into a vegetable market? And then sold to a brewery?"

"I'm afraid so, Your Grace," I said sadly. "The remaining members of the Leuchtenberg family moved to France, Canada and the United States. They, like any other Russian nobles, would not have been allowed to survive in their motherland. But your grandson, Georgii Leuchtenberg, died in 1929 and was buried in the cemetery at Seeon, and his widow, Olga, continued living in the castle until her death. She is also buried in the same cemetery."

The Grand Duchess Maria's hands were folded in her lap, still as stone.

"Maria? Maria, are you all right?"

She slowly turned her head toward me and breathed a deep sigh of sadness.

"Jerry. I had the chance to know Georgiĭ when he was only a small child, before I died. As I said, Nicholai's marriage to Nadezhda was looked on with scorn, but I knew from experience that one must follow one's heart. I let the couple visit me, and Georgiĭ, my sweet and lovely grandson (I never thought of him as a step-grandson), was a wonderful comfort! Did you know that he looked like my father, Tsar Nicholas the First? Of course they were unrelated. He was a peculiar boy, though. He spoke rapidly in a high-pitched voice with a lisp, and in general, he gave the impression of a kind, but timid person. At least he didn't sell Seeon."

"Yes, Your Grace," I answered, realizing that absolutely everything I had just told the Grand Duchess must have come as a tremendous shock.

"I can just imagine him," she continued in that same emotionless tone, "Georgii Nicholaevich von Leuchtenberg, my adopted grandson, as a tall, handsome man with large dark eyes and a grey mustache... I imagine that, in spite of the fact that he and his family lived as exiles, they must have had large family reunions where everyone only spoke in Russian. Perhaps when this 'Grand Duchess' Anastasia made her appearance, all the members of the Leuchten-berg family gathered together. And perhaps this meeting was the last one. Then, in silence, they visited the small cemetery where my first husband's family was buried. And only after their last dinner together at the Castle, after a discussion of the latest events, Georgii Nicholaevich, my grandson, announced his decision to sell the rare collection of books and part of the family archives...."

Maria seemed lost to me, half in a trance, speaking as if she didn't know I was there. Perhaps she was trying to turn all the horrendous information I had given her into some form of good.

Suddenly she rose from her seat as if pulled up by a vi-sion. "The candles barely flickered," she continued, "even though the wind was blowing behind the high, narrow win-dows. And the whimsical shadows cast by tree branches on the walls of the Castle created an atmosphere of mystery. The candles, the shadows, the sounds of wind and rain and the occasional flash of lightning all had the effect of mak-ing the family feel united — with the same destiny and the same past..."

"They must have talked about you," I said, lifting my head to the woman who stood so sad and beautiful before me.

* * * * *

I awoke the next morning in my study, having slept in the large armchair I use for reading or for listening to music. My phonograph was still on, the needle pushed against the inside of the record, going around and around. I stood slowly, my back sore from sleeping in such a cramped position, and went to turn the phonograph off. When I saw that Glinka's *Ruslan and Ludmila* lay on the turntable, I remembered the previous evening's events.

I started laughing to myself, thinking that I was surely losing my mind. Who else would dream about a Grand

Duchess whose beauty was only matched by her sorrow? And my own role in the dream? A bumbling detective, trying to comfort the Duchess with wine and only succeeding in telling her more and more disheartening family news? Besides, only a fool wouldn't have used the opportunity of her visit to ask about the art collection she had saved from her father's destruction. And surely, I would never have passed up the opportunity to ask about Anastasia's father.

Without any help from this ridiculous notion of a ghostly intervention, I could only surmise that the painting of Charles I was owned by Eugène de Beauharnais, as an inheritance from his mother, Josephine — given to her by Napoleon. Upon Eugène's death, he must have bequeathed it to his son, Maximilian, and Maximilian's bride, Maria. Maria, in turn, must have bequeathed it to Sergei, her favorite son, and it was then inherited by Nicholai after Sergei's untimely death. This would explain Puyvelde's statement that the painting had belonged to the Grand Duchess Maria, Sergei and Nicholai Leuchtenberg.

Absorbed by these thoughts, I tripped over a pile of books in my study. From out of the back pages of Nicholai Maximilianovich's memoir fell a piece of very familiar looking writing paper. On it was a depiction of the Leuchtenberg's family tree, carefully written in a feminine hand. The rendition was exquisite. At the bottom of the page were the initials M.N.

Chapter 7

Triangular Formations

When the coin is tossed, either
love or lust will fall uppermost.
But if metal is right, under one
will always be the other.
— Gerald Brennan
Thoughts in Dry Season

My story would be incomplete if I didn't introduce you
to my close friends, Tom, Perdoul and Christina, each of
whom played an important, if somewhat different role in
the further development of my case.

Not too long after my ridiculous dream about the ghost
of Grand Duchess Maria, Tom and I were sitting in my
living room, absorbed in conversation and drinking a little
too much, even for a Saturday night. We had just returned
from a concert where we heard Shostakovich's seventh sym-
phony, performed for the first time in Leningrad in 1942
during the Second World War. At the time, Leningrad had
been besieged by German troops for 900 days. That sym-
phony was dedicated to the people of Leningrad.

Tom is an art historian at Oxford University and has
been my best friend since college, where we first met.

We have maintained an affectionate relationship for the past twenty years and we share all our problems, all our thoughts. He is tall and slim, with pleasant manners and a low voice. His eyes are almost black they are so dark, and they flash when he becomes excited. But it is Tom's hands that betray his surface calm — long-fingered and delicate, they seem to carve the very words he says and are always gesticulating and waving in the air. He becomes quite impassioned when he speaks, and his class lectures are known to be one-man shows. His talent as a teacher is more appreciated each year.

I could talk to Tom about almost anything in the world. We could argue the whole night long about Dostoyevsky, the role of Grigorii Rasputin in Russian history, or how to prepare Chicken Kiev. Like myself at the time, Tom was a bachelor who scorned marriage and cherished his freedom. He was a Don Juan, a lady-killer, always running from his mistress when it came time to propose. But we never discussed the women with whom we were involved. It was taboo.

Tom's knowledge of Russian art and history has always been extensive. After we returned to my house from the concert, I told him about the Charles I portrait in my possession and its possible ownership by nineteenth-century Russian royalty, even though I had no tangible information as to how the portrait became part of the Leuchtenberg collection. I informed him what Puyvelde and Anastasia had told me, as well as reiterated the threatening message I had received in Munich while visiting the Seeon Castle. Tom thought for a few moments and then began to talk in his usual circumlocutory way.

"You know, I was in Leningrad once. You probably remember my mixed feelings concerning the city and its inhabitants," he said softly, his hands, as of yet, still. "The city was almost destroyed during the war and rebuilt again very quickly. It was originally built on the swamps by Peter the First's serfs. Many people perished because of the unbearable working conditions, and parts of the city were constructed on their graves! Even so, Peter the Great was a remarkable man."

At this point, Tom's hands began to draw his sentences. I could see that he had already traveled backward in time and was actually seeing the words he spoke.

"Did you know," Tom continued, "that Peter travelled to England in sixteen ninety-eight? The English King, William the Third, Prince of Orange, presented Peter with a beautiful twenty-gun yacht. He also had Peter painted by Sir Godfrey Kneller, a pupil of Rembrandt and Bernini, and the most admired portrait painter of the realm. I saw an engraving of the painting."

"When Peter posed for this portrait he was only twenty-five years old. The portrait is full-length, and Peter is dressed in a rich robe. The crown rests behind him on a table. Far away, through the window, you can see a marine landscape with ships, painted by the well-known marine artist, W. van de Velde... You know, Peter was an exceedingly handsome man, almost seven feet tall, broad-shouldered, big-boned and heavily muscled. I have been told on several occasions that I look like him, especially when I was in Russia."

"Tom!" I said, somewhat impatient as well as amused. "This is fascinating, especially your resemblance to Peter the Great, but what is your point?"

"You're always so impatient, Jerry. Enjoy the story and you'll understand the point when it's relevant!"

I sighed. How could I argue with a veritable genius. If only he weren't such a long-winded, vain genius.

"Now, where was I?" Tom asked.

"W. van de Velde," I said, resigned to my fate.

"Ah good! Well, W. van de Velde came from Holland to the court of Charles the Second and died in England in seventeen oh-seven, and this portrait of Peter the First was considered to be one of his best. The original was placed in Hampton-Court in England in the King's residence. Now,

101

however, the location of the painting is not known and there is a story associated with this portrait."

"Tom!" I cried out. "You're telling me a story within a story, the point of which I still don't have a clue."

"I'll ignore that comment, Jerry," my friend said, but he was smiling. Tom liked to tease his listener, lulling them with anecdotes, announcing the point at the most surprising time.

"The famous traveller, Cornelius de Bruyn,' Tom began again, his hands eloquently poised, "visited Moscow in January of seventeen oh-two, and saw the Russian Tsar for the first time in his life at a small gathering in a well-to-do Dutch gentleman's private home (Hulst was his name). Cornelius de Bruyn recognized the Tsar and greeted him respectfully. The Tsar was surprised and asked how de Bruyn could recognize him. The traveller then explained that he had seen Peter's portrait, by Sir Godfrey Kneller, at the artist's house in London. The portrait impressed de Bruyn so much he always remembered it."

"Yes..?" I said, drumming my fingers on the arm of my chair.

"Now," Tom went on, "in the Hermitage there is a wax figure of Peter I sitting on the throne, surrounded by the Dutch and Flemish paintings which Peter brought back from his second trip abroad. It tells you that Peter not only posed for portraits, but was a passionate art collector himself."

"Russian aristocrats followed the example of their ruler, and the Russian court became a target for art sales by collectors, auctioneers and peddlers from all over the world. In order to get insight into these affairs, I really suggest that you go to the Hermitage and to Leningrad."

I was astounded by the way in which Tom expressed his ideas, but I immediately picked up on this one. The only way I could obtain information on art collecting in Russia would be to go there. The trip appealed to me greatly.

"Have you ever read a book called *The Castle of Otranto?*" Tom asked, now on a completely different topic.

"The title is familiar to me but I can't remember the story," I answered, hoping to disguise my ignorance.

"It is a Gothic story," Tom said. I smiled inwardly, knowing that my friend was about to interest me in yet another tale. "It was one of the first romantic novels written in England in the middle of the eighteenth century by Horace Walpole, the son of Sir Robert Walpole."

"Now, Sir Robert Walpole was a great Whig leader and had been the prime minister of England for twenty years in the early part of the century. He had one of the greatest art collections of that time, and his grandson sold it to Catherine the Second of Russia. This sale caused a tremendous scandal in the English Parliament. I know from another book by Horace Walpole, called *Anecdotes of Painting in England,* that his father's collection contained twelve Van Dycks, and, if I am not mistaken, there is a painting of Charles the First among them!"

"What?" I exclaimed, rather excited. "Walpole's collection contained a portrait of Charles the First and his grandson sold it to Catherine the Second of Russia?"

"Yes!" Tom answered.

No wonder his students loved him. He made you feel as if you had discovered the information yourself, instead of it merely being told.

"Maybe it's the portrait you're looking for," Tom said. "If so, your trip to Russia is a necessity! And the first place you should go is the Hermitage."

Just then, our conversation was interrupted by the doorbell. It was quite late, and I was surprised that anyone would be visiting at this hour. The thought flashed through my mind that there might be an emergency in the building, but at the door I realized my visitor was Christina, a friend whom I still have difficulty trying to understand. Christina must have guessed from my attitude that she was not exactly wanted at that moment.

103

"I'm sorry, Jerry," she murmured. "I can leave now and come back later. But I do need to talk to you sometime soon..."

"Oh, but please come in," Tom intervened in a most annoying way. "Jerry never told me that he had such a charming friend."

I turned around, trying to signal with my expression that this was not what I wanted, but Tom completely ignored my request. Instead, he stretched out his hand to greet my guest.

Actually, Christina is a very pleasant woman. We had been involved for almost six months before my trip to Berlin. I was never really in love with her; she was not my type of a woman. I did not think that she was very bright. By talking slowly and stretching each word, she made the sound of her raspy voice even more unpleasant. I liked Christina best when she was silent. What really attracted me to her was her body — her soft pink skin and radiant smile.

At that time, I hadn't seen her for almost a month, not since I'd met Anastasia. Tom never knew about Christina's relationship with me, just as I never knew about his affairs. He probably suspected my recent attraction to someone. In telling him about my Berlin trip I could not hide my emotions about Anastasia's mysterious disappearance.

Tom already liked Christina. His eyes were sparkling and his charming smile did not leave his face for even a minute. Christina accepted his invitation, after I shrugged my shoulders as if to say her interruption was alright, and she took off her coat. She was wearing a narrow black skirt that outlined her round hips and a bright silk blouse that was cut low enough to show her full breasts and pink skin — I had to admit that she looked very attractive that evening. I offered her a drink and Tom, of course, accepted it for her. He was seated at the edge of his seat, obviously eager to engage her in conversation. Once the three of us were settled, Christina took out a manuscript out of her bag.

"What is this, Christina? Have you begun to write romances?" I asked sarcastically.

"No Jerry, I'm serious! I want you to read this story for me. PV wrote it — your friend you introduced me to," she said, rather pointedly.

"You've heard from PV?" I exclaimed. PV was another one of my oldest friends. "I thought he was living in Russia!"

"He is, and this manuscript is supposed to explain why," she said in the same tone. I couldn't understand why she had such an edge to her voice.

"You have a friend who lives in Russia?" Tom asked excitedly.

For a moment I thought he was sounding animated only for Christina's benefit, until I finally realized that he was smiling broadly for me.

"Why didn't I think of that? I can stay with PV while I'm in Russia," I said.

"Russia?" Christina exclaimed.

Tom and I started to laugh joyously, almost as pleased with the burgeoning reality of my upcoming trip as with Christina's surprise.

"But why did he write you?" I asked, after we had told Christina about my hopeful trip.

Christina explained with some hesitation, blushing and not looking at either Tom or me, that after the date I had arranged between her and PV, they had become involved. When PV left rather abruptly for Russia, he dropped by the day before his departure to bid Christina adieu.

"I was surprised by PV's sudden departure," Christina explained. "It seemed as if he were running away from something that was troubling him. He promised to explain everything to me once he got to Russia, and instead, I have gotten this absolutely mystifying story that has nothing to

105

do with either him or me. I don't have the faintest idea what he is trying to tell me."

I took the manuscript and promised to get in touch with her as soon as I finished reading it. PV's departure to Russia had disturbed me as well, but I hadn't had time to examine why closely. Christina's concern troubled me as well.

Because of the late hour, Tom and I offered to see Christina home. The night was unusually warm and the full moon hung over our heads like a luminous halo of light, bright and beautiful. Tom and Christina became deeply involved in conversation and I felt lonelier than ever. Here was a perfectly charming girl that I was practically giving away, while I seemed to spend all my time chasing phantoms and conversing with ghosts.

It was 12:30 when I finally returned to my apartment. I took a hot shower and sat down in my study to read PV's story, entitled *The Night of Don Juan.*

* * * * *

The Night of Don Juan

They call me Carlin. I can't remember my real name. When I was still a young child, not even five, the King's men bought me from my parents because they mistook me for a dwarf. I remember being wrenched from my mother's arms, knowing that something horrible was happening, but the King's men took me, and I never saw my family or my home again.

They brought me down from the mountains and onto a magnificent road. We rode for four days and finally arrived in a city — the likes of which I had never dreamed could exist. Stone houses rose from the ground, hundreds of people walked through the streets, and vendors jostled passersby, hoping to sell their wares. I saw gypsies like myself, but they were ragged and had no dignity, begging from the multitudes who did not notice them. The King's men laughed when I started to cry.

"Don't worry, little one. You will grow up to be as famous as Fernando Lazcendo. And you will invent new jokes to amuse the Infante and His Majesty."

But Fernando Lazcendo was a dwarf, and I am a midget — small but proportionally built. And it is because I am delicate that His Majesty favors me even more than the dwarf. The King takes me everywhere.

And so, I am privileged to secrets that others would not be trusted to keep, to knowledge that could be misused if it fell into the wrong hands. Conde Villemediana, for example, was not what he seemed, as the following story should explain.

A few days before the beginning of each Lent, the Spanish Court holds a reception followed by a masked ball. Everyone is invited and the ladies dress with particular care. Fairy queens and mermaids are equally jeweled, and costumed Princesses flirt with devils drinking sangria in the dark. The great hall in the palace is always filled to capacity and the crowd becomes so dense that it is difficult to move. Because of my size, the legs of men and the long dresses of ladies provide formidable obstacles for me. This year there was an even larger crowd, with royalty coming to Madrid from as far away as Seville.

Sometime after midnight, I grew tired and decided to go home and rest. Just as I was nearing the exit, I spotted a large man wearing a devil's mask who cast a frightening glance at me. He started moving toward me, coming closer and closer, until he swooped me into the air, lifting me with one hand. He slid his other hand inside my pants and started to fondle me unabashedly. I let out a scream and the devil let me fall to the floor, disappearing into the night.

On my way home, I saw a human body lying face down, half in the gutter and half on the pavement. I carefully rolled the body over with my foot, and staring at me in the moonlight was a devil's mask on the dead man. Even though I was afraid, my curiosity consumed me. I looked both ways down the empty street and, with trembling fingers, removed the mask. Before me lay the face of Conde Villamediana.

I crawled to the steps of a nearby house, frozen in fear. Señor Villamediana was a famous poet and valiant knight. He fought bulls in the main square of our city, the motto *My Love is Royal* embroidered on his hat.

I do not remember how long I sat on those steps. Sometime before dawn a horsedrawn cart stopped at the corpse's side. Three heavily veiled women in black dresses descended and approached the cadaver. They knelt at Villamediana's side in silence and lowered their heads in prayer. One woman dropped her handkerchief in the already congealed blood that had flowed out from Villamediana's chest wound. When they finally rose, they motioned the coachmen to bring the stretcher from the cart. The women and the coachmen lifted the body onto the stretcher, carried it to the cart, and drove away.

The following day, I sought out the Grand Inquisitor, Confessor for all persons associated with the Palace. Although I am not an ardent client of his, he received me cordially.

"Benevolent Father," I said. "I came to tell you what happened to me last night."

I described the horrifying event as quickly as I could, feeling terribly responsible for Villamediana's death.

"Father," I said, my voice low and grave, "perhaps if I hadn't screamed, or if I hadn't resisted his advances... Then Conde Villamediana wouldn't have left the palace and his life would have been spared."

The Grand Inquisitor laughed gently.

"The events of last night were decided some time ago. You could have done nothing to save Villamediana," he said firmly.

But I was not satisfied with his reply, and I pressed the matter further.

"He was wounded shortly before I found him. If I had run for help as soon as I saw him lying in the street, then..."

"My son," the Grand Inquisitor said, "the wound inflicted upon him was intended to kill."

"No hay plazo que no se cumpla ni deuda que no se pague," I murmured under my breath. "There are no debts that will not fall due, and no debts that will not be paid."

The Benevolent Father looked at me for a long while, his penetrating eyes searching my face. Then he rang a bell. A Dominican friar immediately appeared at the door.

"I do not want to be disturbed," my Confessor said.

As soon as the door was closed, the Inquisitor turned to me.

"You have committed no sin, my son, but you have been badly frightened by last night's events. Whether Villamediana's death frees me from the oath of secrecy which I, as his Confessor, am bound to observe is debatable; God alone can decide. But I will tell you all I know about Don Juan de Tassis Conde Villamediana."

The following account is the story the King's Confessor told to me. Only God and Villamediana know whether or not it is true.

Don Juan Villamediana was the son of a respected courtier, but in spite of being raised according to the strict rules of courtly etiquette, Villamediana had always shown a certain recklessness, particularly in his relations to women. This quality did not escape the notice of Villamediana's neighbor, Don Gonzalo de Ulloa, Commander of Kalatrav, a proud nobleman known for his fierce temper. Gonzalo's daughter, Doña Ana, had reached the age when a budding beauty changes into a splendid flower. The young Don Juan Villamediana often spied upon Doña Ana when she walked with her duenna in the garden, and he fell violently in love with her.

Villamediana bribed the duenna to take Doña Ana a poem he wrote that expressed his ardor, and a miniature of him riding on a splendid white horse. Although Dona Ana did not reply, Don Juan Villamediana persisted in his courtship and eventually convinced the duenna to bring Doña Ana out on the balcony while he was passing by so that they could talk. Months passed, the bribes were doubled, and finally Don Juan asked the duenna to let him into Doña Ana's bedchamber.

"But I can't allow that, Don Juan Villamediana," the duenna replied, nervously pushing back her graying hair with the palm of her hand.

Apparently, Don Juan was very persuasive, or perhaps Doña Ana was ready to receive Don Juan. Within a few days, the rendez-vous was arranged.

"Doña Ana," Don Juan called to his beloved, entering her room through the balcony. "Are you there, my love?"

The bedchamber was pitch black, but Doña Ana called from her bed. "Over here," she said in a soft, quavering voice. Don Juan walked carefully to where Doña Ana lay and entwined her in his arms. Immediately, the doors of the chamber flew open and Don Gonzalo entered with four of his squires. The duenna had double-crossed Don Juan, informing Don Gonzalo about the clandestine visit. Upon seeing her father Doña Ana fainted, and Don Juan was seized, stripped and dragged onto the sofa where he was thrown face down.

Don Juan Villamediana expected to die. Instead he felt the beginnings of a torture that was as degrading as painful and he let out a scream.

"After this you will never have pleasure with a woman," Don Gonzalo shouted, riding the man who had attempted to shame his own daughter as if Don Juan were a woman receiving him in love. And indeed, after the initial pain, Don Juan Villamediana felt a strange sensation of pleasure despite Gonzalo's violent and hateful thrusts.

Finally the squires released Don Juan who tumbled onto the ground, shamed. With the sureness of instinct, Don Juan grabbed a sword from one of the squires and thrust it deep into Don Gonzalo's chest. The squires fled as Don Juan stood over his aggressor, naked and desperate. Gonzalo looked into Don Juan's eyes, emitted a single laugh, and died.

Don Juan Villamediana fled the country and lived in exile until Our Majesty granted the young man a pardon. During his time abroad, Don Juan wrote poems and sonnets, always about the nature of love, and when he returned to the Court many ladies were awaiting the appearance of this handsome nobleman. His skill as a swordsman and a bullfighter, his elegant appearance, and his manners dazzled the Court. Soon he became known as a notorious seducer of women, and even the Queen was rumored to have been his lover. Perhaps Villamediana encouraged this rumor, for he had his hat embroidered with the words *For Royal Love* and wore it whenever he fought the bulls.

Villamediana's arduous pursuits always resulted in victory, but when a lady was ready to receive him in her bed, Don Juan was unable to perform. Her feminine odor affronted him, for Don Juan secretly longed to share his bed with a man. The curse of the slain Don Gonzalo prevented Don Juan from consummating his love affairs with women, and being reckless as he was, Don Juan Villamediana became the leader of a circle of noblemen and commoners who defied God and Nature, and enjoyed committing this abominable sin.

"The existence of this ring of sinners was discovered only recently through relentless efforts on the part of our Dominican brothers. We are conducting a trial of this abominable group shortly," my Confessor explained.

"But who killed Don Juan Villamediana?" I asked.

"I don't know," the Inquisitor replied.

"What about the mourners I saw on the side of the road?" I asked. "Who were they?"

"One was Doña Ana de Ulloa; she remained faithful to Don Juan even after her father's death by his hand. The other two are unknown to me."

Indicating the end of our talk, the Grand Inquisitor rose from his chair. I left his room still very perplexed. I was somewhat annoyed by the Confessor's attitude toward Villamediana's supposed "abominable sins". Such happenings were being conducted in the Court and I never had a clue to them.

A week later, the Inquisition court began their proceedings. The court was presided over by the Grand Inquisitor himself, with two Dominican friars acting in the capacity of prosecutors and associate justices. The names of the accused were called one by one, and at the end, the Grand Inquisitor added the leader's name, Don Juan de Tassis Conde Villamediana. A hush fell upon the audience. Many of the Court ladies who attended the trial and who mourned Don Juan now understood why their seductions were never completed.

The faithful servant of Villamediana was not among the accused. He fled the city immediately after his master's murder, and by assuming different names, was able to escape the violence of the Inquisition.

On the last day of the trial, anyone accused who was also of noble origin was no longer in the courtroom. I asked the man next to me what happened.

"They were allowed to flee the country," he replied. "You know how kind our gracious Majesty is."

All the accused commoners were condemned to death, executed on the same day of the verdict.

Returning to the Palace, I passed some street urchins who were singing in low voices:

> *Mentidero de Madrid,*
> *Decidue, quien mato al conde?*

(Gossip of Madrid,

Decide, who killed the Count?)

La verdad del caso ha sido
Que el matador fue Bellido
Y el impulso soberano.

(The truth of the case is
That the killer was Bellido,
Under order of the Sovereign.)

The King? I thought. The King?
(Author's note: The choice of Juan de Tassis Conde de Villamediana as a model for Don Juan Tenorio was first made by Gregorio Marannon in his book *Don Juan,* Collection Austral, Madrid, 1940.)

* * * * *

PV and I had been friends since we were students at Oxford. He graduated with first-class honors in ancient history, and then obtained a teaching position at one of the better-known public schools. His colleagues considered him eccentric and he had the reputation of being something of a clown, but I thought of him as one of the most innocent human beings I have ever encountered. But PV was a bit foolish.

PV's full name is Perdoul Vsevolodovich Begunkov. He was supposedly named after the city, Pieria, in ancient Macedonia, the birthplace of the Muses. Why he was named after the Muses' birthplace was unclear, except that his grandfather, the Tsar's Ambassador to the Court of St. James, wanted it so. Unfortunately, Perdoul's name also sounds like the Russian word for "fart". After hearing the snickers and seeing the looks of surprise whenever anyone called his name, PV's friends took it upon themselves to change it to its present abbreviation. Imagine being called "fart" all your life — PV had put up with it for years.

113

We had stayed in contact, seeing each other occasionally, and I was surprised when he announced he was returning to Russia. He had inherited some money from his parents, and he thought that the income from this capital would be sufficient to live well in the USSR.

"You're crazy, PV," I told him. "Consider your grandfather's anti-Bolshevik stand. You'll either be shot or, at best, sent to the Gulag."

But PV was convinced nothing harmful would happen to him. Several weeks later, I received a long letter in which PV described the events following his return to Russia. He was indeed interrogated on several occasions by the KGB, but his innocent behavior impressed even the policemen and he was dismissed as a *yurodivyĭ*. In Russian, this term refers to someone who is half-saint and half-idiot. Such people are both protected and highly regarded, particularly in Russian villages. If being a *yurodivyĭ* secured PV's freedom from the KGB henchmen, let him be considered as such for as long as he lives.

I went to sleep feeling somewhat perplexed. I could understand why Christina was so confused after finishing PV's story. I didn't see any correlation between Carlin the midget and PV, except for their mutual naivety, and PV was certainly no Don Juan. But the manuscript was written in an earnest tone, and I knew that PV was trying to address some issue through it. I felt suspicious of PV's move to Russia, a relocation that had previously seemed very innocent.

It was only seven o'clock in the morning when Tom called. He woke me from a ghastly dream in which I saw myself walking with Charles I on the streets of modern day Leningrad, discussing the Grand Duchess Maria's love affairs and Van Dyck's technical prowess in his portraits, when we were suddenly captured by KGB agents and condemned to death. Tom's phone call saved me from the execution.

Tom was highly impatient. Not only did he want to know what PV's manuscript contained, but more importantly, he wanted to know what my involvement with Christina was and if Christina was serious about PV. At seven a.m. I am almost always groggy. But after last night, with the excitement concerning my possible trip to Russia as well as the late hour I stayed up reading PV's story, I was decidedly gruff. When Tom told me that he wanted to become further acquainted with Christina, I told him he could marry her today for all I cared.

"Jerry," Tom persisted, "are you sure you don't mind? I know the situation can be a bit touchy — two and possibly three friends all dating the same woman."

"Do what you want, Tom," I answered. "Just try not to call me so early on a Sunday morning."

Tom apologized, sounding quite pleased. In a way, I guess I was too. Christina deserved a man like Tom, and I was certain that her relationship with PV and me had been less than satisfactory. I felt a twinge of sadness though, losing a woman who adored me, and I wondered if I stood a chance of ever finding Anastasia.

After I dressed I called Tom back, more willing to discuss PV's story. Tom was silent for a bit before asking me about PV's personality traits. He advised me to look into the Scotland Yard records for data on PV before asking for his help in Russia. I promised to inform Tom about PV's dossier at Scotland Yard — if there was one.

To my surprise PV did have a file at Scotland Yard as a homosexual who met with other young men in a rather inappropriate fashion in Hyde Park. The reason PV fled England was to avoid prosecution. Suddenly everything made sense — his story, his relationship to Christina, his decision to move to Russia. I wondered what Tom and Christina would say when they found out.

My next task was to check if Van Dyck's *Charles I* was still exhibited in Russia. My telephone call to the Witt

Library was answered by a librarian who, after a few minutes of searching, told me that in the most recent listings of paintings from the Hermitage, there was indeed a portrait of Charles I by Van Dyck. With those words, I knew I could convince Sir Alex to send me to Russia — the motherland of Afanasiĭ Gromotrubov and the place where my parents met and lived until they were obliged to flee. The thought of this trip was very appealing.

However, when I talked to Sir Alexander about my plans, he was not at all enthusiastic.

"Since you are a member of Scotland Yard, the KGB may consider you a British spy," he argued.

I persisted until finally Sir Alexander wrote an official letter to the USSR Embassy in London, assuring them that my activities in Russia would be limited to researching the origin of Van Dyck's painting. In return, Sir Alexander requested an official letter assuring him about my safety during the sojourn in Russia. Ten days later he received such a letter from the Ambassador. In addition, the Embassy enclosed a letter signed by the Military Attache, requesting all concerned individuals to extend their courtesies in my endeavors. They also advised me to travel on an ordinary British passport, rather than a government passport, since this would make the Russians less suspicious.

Armed with my passport, a letter from the Embassy, and a courtesy visa, I was ready to go to Moscow. My final task was to write PV. I consulted Tom and Christina and they both encouraged me to do so.

"Who cares about what he did in Hyde Park," they both said, "he's your friend!"

I soon received an enthusiastic answer from PV, inviting me to Russia as his honored guest. Not only had he arranged meetings with the Director of the Hermitage and one of the foremost Russian art historians and art critics, he was also in the process of establishing other contacts that could help me in my search. PV's letter reassured me and I felt safe asking him to accompany me through my Russian travels. In contrast to Burgess, PV's only encounter with the law was the offense of homosexuality – and not working as a spy.

Just before my departure, I called Tom several times but he did not answer the phone or call me either. Unable to reach him, I sent him a note two days before leaving for Russia. I boarded my plane for Moscow the next day thinking about all recent events in my life involving PV, Christina, Tom and Anastasia.

Grand Duchess Maria and Maximillian Leuchtenberg

Chapter 8

The Russian Adventure

Be as cautious as a stranger wherever you may be,
but do not desire your word to have
power before you, and you will have rest.
— Thomas Merton
The Wisdom of the Desert

After the plane landed at the Sheremetyevo airport in Moscow, we were instructed to remain seated while each passenger underwent a thorough inspection by two uniformed men. The minutes passed by with tremendous slowness. Descending the stairway, I heard a familiar voice calling my name. It was PV, standing a few yards from the base of the plane's staircase, shouting and waving his hat. I yelled his name in return and once I reached ground, started to walk quickly towards him. At that moment a heavy hand clamped down on PV's shoulder, and a particularly sober-looking official dragged PV away.

"I just came to greet my friend,' PV tried to explain.

"No civilian is allowed on the landing strip. You're breaking the law," came the official reprimand as PV was packed in a car and whisked away, accompanied by several uniformed guards.

The event was disconcerting. I knew I was unable to do anything until my passport had been stamped and my luggage inspected. This incident, however, provoked a good bit of suspicion among the customs officials and I was treated somewhat roughly. As I was interrogated about the origin and purpose of my trip, I quickly produced the letter from the Military Attache of the Russian Embassy in London written for me. The interrogations stopped abruptly, and I was escorted through customs without further complications. At the airport exit I met PV, much to my surprise.

"What happened to you, PV?" I whispered, checking the area for officials.

"Nothing," he said. "They all know I'm a *yurodivyĭ*. They were more amused by my behavior than worried about it."

I embraced PV and felt my anxiety gradually begin to slip away. We looked at each other and began to laugh.

"By the way," PV said, throwing his arm around my shoulder, "would you mind calling me by my real name? Everyone here calls me Perdoul Vsevolodovich. If you call me PV, I might not know you're referring to me."

"Perdoul Vsevolodovich?" I responded, somewhat uncertain. "That's quite a mouthful. Would you mind if I just called you Perdoul?"

"All right with me," said PV, grinning his innocent grin.

I noticed later that whenever I called him Perdoul the Russians immediately turned their heads — no wonder.

Perdoul had reserved a room for me at the Ukraine Hotel. We hailed a taxi and were halfway there before he told me we had reservations on that evening's night train to Leningrad.

"Tomorrow is the only time the Director of the Hermitage can see us," he explained.

"The Director? That's terrific," I said. "But then why do I need a room?"

"Don't you want to rest?"

I knew there was no sense arguing with PV — or should I say Perdoul — and so we continued to the Ukraine Hotel. There was a long line at the registration desk, and while I waited, Perdoul took my passport and disappeared behind the desk. He returned in a few minutes with a piece of paper.

"This is your registration and the receipt for your passport. We can go to your room."

"How did you do that?" I whispered to my friend, as he rose a finger to his lips and shook his head.

We went to the tenth floor of the hotel, and at another reception desk in front of the elevator, we received my room key from a woman who looked like a typical Russian babushka with the exception of a few missing teeth. While she examined my registration certificate, a very serious and solemn expression shadowed her otherwise kindly face.

Perdoul left me in the room to arrange for our dinner and went to get the train tickets to Leningrad. Prompted either by Perdoul's suggestion or because I was emotionally exhausted, I slept until dinner time. Perdoul arrived exactly at six o'clock and we had a leisurely dinner at the Ukraine Restaurant. Finally, we took a taxi to the station and boarded the Leningrad train. We shared a large and a relatively well-equipped compartment which, as Perdoul explained, was designed especially for foreigners. As we prepared for bed, Perdoul asked if I had my passport with me.

"Of course not," I answered. "It's with all my other papers at the Ukraine Hotel."

"But you can't travel in Russia without a passport," Perdoul said, obviously distressed. "They won't register you at the hotel in Leningrad! Oh, it's all my fault."

"Stop, Perdoul," I said, even though I was annoyed. "At worst, we'll return to Moscow at once."

Finally, we both fell asleep, awaking only as the train pulled into Leningrad. In the city, Perdoul had made reservations at the Europeiski Hotel. Of course, when we tried to register there, I was asked for my passport.

"I don't have it," I tried to explain. "I left it at the registration desk at the Hotel Ukraine in Moscow. Perhaps you should call them."

"Why should I phone Moscow?" the clerk replied. "They should phone us if they retained the passport by mistake."

Finally Perdoul intervened. "We understand your dilemma," he began with heartfelt empathy, "but we're extremely tired from our travels. Couldn't you, perhaps, permit us two rooms for three or four hours? And then we will return to Moscow."

To my surprise, Perdoul's ridiculous plan appealed to the clerk, and he gave us keys to our rooms and bid us a good rest. When we left our suite after several hours, nobody at the hotel desk paid the slightest attention to us.

Perdoul was obviously quite skilled in ways I had never perceived.

The sun was shining and this austere city, which was usually covered by fog, looked bright and cheerful. We walked along the Nevsky Prospect, past the Palace Square and to the banks of the Neva River. When we reached the statue of Peter the Great, once the symbol of imperialist St. Petersburg, Perdoul began to recite some lines from Pushkin's *The Bronze Horseman.*

> On a lonely windswept shore
> He stood, filled with lofty visions
> And gazed afar...

Even though I was embarrassed by my friend's dramatics, I also enjoyed them. And the monument was a sight to behold with Peter I on a rearing horse, crushing the enemy of the Empire as represented by a snake under its hind hoofs.

"You know," Perdoul said, his eyes still dreamy, "when the Germans laid siege to Leningrad in the Second World War, the Russians considered lowering this statue to the bottom of the Neva River, in order to prevent its possible destruction. They discarded the idea, protecting it with large sandbags instead."

To this day I can see Perdoul reciting Pushkin's poem by his *Bronze Horseman.*

Now we returned to Nevsky Prospect. There I would pass the Anichkov bridge, on which two pairs of horses stand, sculpted by the famous artist, Peter Karlovich Klodt. The concept of man struggling to tame a wild animal is represented by each of these sculptures. In the first pair, man lies defeated under the horses' hooves. In the second pair, man triumphs by taming the animals. In the middle of the nineteenth century, two of the sculptures were sent out of Russia as a gift to the Neopolitan Court. The plaster cast of the original was preserved in St. Petersburg. A few years later, the two missing statues were recast in bronze from these plaster models. During the casting, however, the workmen forgot that the horses were to wear shoes. Today, the horses in one of the sculptures have horseshoes, and in the other are without.

Not far from the bridge, in a small garden, stands a tall column with a sculpture of Catherine the Great at the top and seven figures at the bottom. This monument was erected by Tsar Alexander II in honor of his great-grandmother. Six of the seven statues are men, one is a female. The woman is Catherine's best friend, Countess Dashkova, who was one of the best educated women in Russia and the first President of the Imperial Academy of Sciences. The men represented Catherine's lovers and faithful councilors. The sculptor, malicious tongues have said, intended to commemorate Catherine's sexual temperament by measuring it to the length of her lovers peos. Each male statue proudly carries a large sword.

After our walks, Perdoul insisted on dragging me to see the opera Eugene Onegin. I knew there was no sense in arguing that seeing one great performance in a day is sufficient and so I reluctantly agreed. The opera was performed in Kirov's Theater of Opera and Ballet, formerly the Marinsky Theater. Almost as soon as I sat in the comfortable seat amidst the fabulous decor, I closed my eyes for a moment and dreamt that I was here over a hundred years ago.

I saw the Grand Duchess Maria sitting near me. She was still an attractive woman, although now in her fifties. Of course she was elegantly dressed, wearing a deep decolletage characteristic of her time and almost as exquisite as when she was nineteen, dressed for her wedding day. I could smell her perfume and when she turned toward me, I saw a most mischievous smile pull at her lips.

"Jerry," she whispered somewhat conspiratorially, "it's good to see you again." And then the Grand Duchess winked.

When the music roused me from my dream and I opened my eyes, the old woman in the seat next to me was glaring angrily. She addressed her husband, saying "These young men nowadays just come to the opera to sleep!"

"Pardon me, *grazhdanka*," I said, trying to make up for my apparently rude behavior. All I could hope was that I hadn't winked at the matron, mistaking her for the Grand Duchess Maria. "Why is the theater named after Kirov? Was he a famous singer or a ballet dancer?"

The woman looked at me with such disdain that I did not dare attempt further conversation. Besides, Perdoul was kicking my left leg under the chair with tremendous force.

"What is it, Perdoul?" I hissed.

"Jerry, if you want to ask a question, please ask me first. Everyone knows that Kirov was a famous party boss in Leningrad. He most certainly did not sing or dance. He started the revolution. When Kirov was shot by Leonid Nicholaev, his death marked the beginning of Stalin's era of terror and mass murder. Many years later it became known

124

that Kirov's assassination had been arranged by the secret police itself, with the connivance of Stalin!"

Apparently our whispering began to attract the attention of other neighbors, and they started raising their fingers to their lips, making loud shushing sounds. The performance was not first class and I was very glad to leave the theater after the opera had ended.

That night, I was awakened by a terrible noise. I jumped out of bed almost certain that a device had exploded in my room — but it seemed to be intact. And yet, when I opened the bathroom door with extreme difficulty, I found that the ceiling had fallen and nearly a five-inch layer of plaster covered the floor, bathtub, sink and toilet. I lay awake until morning and at eight o'clock sharp, as soon as the reception desk started to function, I reported the accident and requested another room.

"We don't have any free rooms," the clerk snarled. "But as of today, we won't charge you for having a room with a bath. We'll only charge you for the room."

Did the room clerk honestly think he was doing me a favor? I started to argue rather angrily when Perdoul appeared on the scene.

"Jerry," he reminded me, in a low voice, "you are staying here because they forgot that your passport is still in Moscow. Don't provoke them! Go and eat breakfast and I will arrange something."

I was still fuming with anger as I stood in line for the hotel breakfast. Within half an hour Perdoul reappeared.

"You have another room. I have personally transferred your belongings," he said with a large grin.

We went up to inspect my new quarters. It was not a room; it was an apartment apparently kept intact from before the revolution, equipped with *fin de siècle* furniture and an antique grand piano.

"It's wonderful, Perdoul! I feel like the old Gromotrubov."

Perdoul beamed. But we had to leave immediately in order to keep our appointment with the Director of the Hermitage.

At the Hermitage, we were received by a pleasant and extremely good-looking secretary who ushered us into a magnificent room originally used as a meeting place for the Tsar's cabinet. Now it was the office for the Director of the Hermitage who presented himself as a courtly gentleman with an engaging smile. I told him the purpose of our visit and he put me in contact with the Curator of Flemish and Dutch paintings. The Curator suggested that I return the next day, when he'd be happy to show me the Hermitage's "Room of Van Dyck's".

Since we had the day free, Perdoul insisted on showing me the important sights of Leningrad. We walked to a square where a large Sobor, or Russian orthodox cathedral, was located. On the other side of the square I saw a most splendid building.

"Nicholas I built that palace for his beloved daughter Maria," informed my guide.

"Yes, I know," I said softly. "The Marinsky Dvoretz."

Perdoul glanced at me quizzically. Then he showed me the Astoria Hotel where the great Russian poet, Yesenin, committed suicide. My friend even offered to take me to the rooms where Yesenin hanged himself, but I refused this honor and prodded Perdoul to show me the other sights of Leningrad worth visiting.

We took a bus and after a thirty-minute ride, reached a dirty place which looked almost like a medieval village.

"Here at the Chernaya Rechka — the Black Rivulet — Pushkin was mortally wounded in a duel with Dantes," Perdoul explained. "He died a day later in his apartment in the center of the city."

"That's wonderful, Perdoul," I said. "Now where will you take me? To the morgue?"

"Actually, I thought we'd go to the Necropolis where all the famous Russians are buried," Perdoul answered innocently.

At the cemetery, Perdoul refused to show me the tomb of Tchaikovsky, Dostoyevsky, or Turgenev. Instead, he dragged me to a tomb with the monument of an army officer sleeping on a bench.

"This man," Perdoul explained, "was on duty at the Tsar's palace at night. Once he was so tired that he fell asleep. As was his bad luck, Tsar Nicholas I decided to check on his guard that night. He came upon the sleeping officer and shouted at the top of his voice, 'How dare you sleep while standing guard!' The officer woke up, saw the Tsar and died of a heart attack."

"Perdoul, do you actually believe what you're telling me?" I asked.

I had forgotten Perdoul's gullibility, at least somewhat more endearing than his incessantly morbid curiosity.

On the same day, we visited the Russian art museum. By bribing the guards with rubles, we were shown all the Malevich, Kandinsky and other paintings of the same great period of Russian avant-garde that were carefully hidden in the cellars of the museum.

Perdoul was a most interesting guide.

* * * *

That night, I was rather tired and sleepy and shortly after dinner went to my suite. Around ten o'clock I heard a timid knock. I opened the door and saw a young, pleasant-looking girl who, with a thousand apologies for her intrusion, asked whether she could talk to me for a moment. I invited her to come in and learned that she and her girlfriend were unceremoniously thrown our of these very rooms with the excuse that the suite was to be vacated for an important *inostranetz,* a foreigner. Her girlfriend had found a place to stay that night, but she had not and therefore dared to approach me, asking permission to sleep on the floor.

I looked her over and found her to be pleasant, not beautiful, but with a good, although slightly plump figure. I decided that she did not need to sleep on the floor.

"You can share my bed," I said.

She did not object.

In the morning she was gone, leaving a piece of paper on my night table with one word written on it. *Spasibo* — thank you.

Shortly thereafter Perdoul appeared and it was time to go to the Hermitage.

* * * *

We met Mr. Pavlowsky, the Flemish and Dutch art curator at the Hermitage. He was a kind, modest man who spoke quietly and moved softly. It almost seemed as if he were trying to appear invisible. He was slovenly dressed, wore old-fashioned spectacles, and his thin, gray hair circled his head like a faded wreath. In spite of his appearance, however, I noticed that his colleagues treated him with great respect. Later, I learned that this somewhat timid man was responsible for reconstituting the Hermitage's history and had devoted his entire life to researching and gathering material pertaining to its collections. I did not gain access, unfortunately, to this extremely significant file.

Mr. Pavlowsky led us through a veritable labyrinth until we reached the room containing twenty-five Van Dyck paintings. My eyes lit up when I saw the portrait of Charles I hanging on the far wall. I realized at once, however, that it was not the same painting I was looking for. Even though this portrait, like the one found on Berg's yacht, was a 3/4 length portrait of Charles I in armor, and even though the facial expressions on both renditions of the King were strikingly similar, this painting included a steel glove on Charles I's right hand, the left hand being bare. I was, of course, disappointed.

"Van Dyck only painted the face of the King," the curator explained. "The rest was done by his assistants."

We walked toward the painting, examining it in greater detail.

"Look at the glove that is lying on the floor," Mr. Pavlowsky continued. "It is for the right hand, but that hand is already wearing a glove. If Van Dyck had painted the entire picture, he would have never permitted himself to paint two gloves for the same hand."

I nodded, appreciating the painting's flaw and noticed a portrait of Charles I's wife, Queen Henrietta Maria, whose face was already familiar to me. I wondered how the largest collection of Van Dyck's paintings came to be established here, in Russia.

"What is the history behind this collection?" I asked.

"Five paintings were bought by Catherine the Great from the Baron Crozat collection in Paris," Mr. Pavlowsky began. "Two paintings are from the Stroganov collection, which he purchased in Paris between the years 1769–1779. One painting was bought from Gotzkovsky in Berlin and another was originally in Le Luve de July's collection. Eleven paintings belonged to the Walpole collection, also bought by Catherine, three of which are of unknown provenance and two of which were painted in Van Dyck's workshop, but not by him."

I walked among these masterpieces in a daze. I could not say which painting I liked most since all of them were beautiful. But if I had been compelled to make a choice, I would have given preference to the portrait of the Flemish painter, Jan Wilden, with his wife and child. Van Dyck painted Wilden's portrait when he was twenty-two years old. I also liked the painting entitled, *Head of an Old Man,* painted at the same time, as well as one of Van Dyck's self-portraits from the years 1627–1632.

129

"Do you, or did you have any other portraits of Charles I that are not exhibited?" I asked.

"No," Mr. Pavlowsky answered, thoughtfully shaking his head. "This is the extent of our collection. Perhaps at one time there were more portraits, but I wouldn't be able to tell you what happened to them."

I asked the curator for other references where I might find information concerning Van Dyck's portraits of King Charles I. He mentioned two books that I had already read and suggested I contact an eminent art historian, Mr. Levinberg, in Moscow — with whom Perdoul had already arranged an appointment.

We thanked Mr. Pavlowsky for the time he spent with us and returned to the hotel. Even though my time in Leningrad hadn't been altogether fruitful, at least I had managed to spend two nights in a room with a piano — and all without a passport, under the pretense that Perdoul and I were staying for only a few hours in order to rest.

* * * *

"Your passport, please," demanded the clerk. Perdoul and I were once again in Moscow, at the Ukraine Hotel — but the issue of passports never seemed to change.

"My passport is already in your possession. Here is the receipt," I told him.

"You were travelling in the USSR without a passport? Why weren't you arrested?" The clerk was visibly perturbed.

"Don't worry about my travels," I told him. "Please, just assign me a room."

The clerk complied with ill grace and gave me a slip of paper with my room number written on it in a small, cramped hand. After retrieving the key from the same babushka on the tenth floor, Perdoul and I dropped off our suitcases. We didn't have much time before our appointment with Mr. Levinberg, the art historian Mr. Pavlowsky

130

had mentioned. I didn't bother to unpack, leaving my suitcase unlocked since I had lost the key some time ago.

Perdoul and I took a taxi to Mr. Levinberg's apartment where we were greeted by a pleasant man in his early sixties. Our host had a good sense of humor and spoke in a dignified manner, his pale blue eyes twinkling at the jokes he made. As is the custom in Russia, a small reception awaited us when we came in. We drank tea and ate Russian sweets and cakes provided in abundance by our host's wife.

After we were seated and the usual pleasantries exchanged, I asked our host the same question I had now asked so many others: What do you know about the sale of Russian art after the Russian Revolution?

"This particular topic pains me," Mr. Levinberg replied, "but nevertheless, I will provide you with some information. Russian art was first sold through galleries and auction houses in Germany. Then two American brothers, Armand and Victor Hammer, entered the scene.

"Armand and Victor's father, Dr. Armand Hammer Sr., was one of the founders of the Communist Party in the United States. Lenin invited Dr. Hammer to Russia shortly after the Revolution and he took Armand Jr. with him. (The son spoke Russian almost fluently and had received an MD from Columbia University.) After Dr. Hammer left Russia, Armand stayed behind and brought his brother, Victor, to Moscow. Lenin, who had now befriended the son just as he had the father, authorized Armand Jr. to sell vast quantities of Russian art abroad in order to obtain the hard currency that was sorely needed by the newly established revolutionary government, and the brothers sent Russian art treasures by the shipload to the United States. Supposedly, Victor Hammer loved everything Russian — food, songs... everything."

"What about the private collections," I asked. "Or the various museums' collections?"

Our host sighed and shook his head, refilling our tea cups as if stalling for time.

131

"After the Revolution," Mr. Levinberg answered, "all private art collections were taken by force from their rightful owners and stored at the Hermitage. The number of masterpieces kept there was extremely high and anyone who knew art was working there, cataloging the confiscated items. However, even the Hermitage was stripped of many treasures. The best 'Russian' Tiepolo is now in France, the best Rembrandt in the Netherlands. These sales of the Hermitage art objects would have gone on forever if not for Arbelli's angry letter of protest written to Stalin. Arbelli was the Director of the Hermitage in 1936. You see, when the government officials wanted to sell the priceless collection of Sassanid Persian silver bought by the Empress Elizabeth, Arbelli protested the projected sale and won his case. Stalin declared a moratorium on the sale of art objects from the USSR."

"So, after 1936, Russia no longer exported its art?" I asked. "Officially, that is correct. But Stalin did not intervene in 1937, when an American Ambassador's wife started buying art that once belonged to the Tsar's family. There were many opportunities for any given painting to be sold or 'removed' abroad during the eighteen years after the Revolution."

Mr. Levinberg was clearly disturbed by his government's actions and I wondered if he had been working at the Hermitage during those years, or if he had been a collector. But these questions were much too personal, and I shifted the subject on to more practical ground. "I am looking for a Van Dyck painting of Charles the First," I said. "I believe that the Grand Duchess Maria, and then two of her sons, Sergei and Nicholai Leuchtenberg, once possessed it. Would you know where I might find records of their paintings?"

Mr. Levinberg thought for a bit, and then replied that there were two catalogues of the Leuchtenberg collection — one prepared by Passovan in 1851 and one by Somoff in 1884. He also mentioned a book written by N. Vrangel on the legacy of the Grand Duchess Maria. "Is any mention of Van Dyck's portrait in one of the catalogues?" I asked.

"I can ask one of my students to find out," the art historian offered. "But if the only existing copy of any of the catalogues is in a museum it may be very difficult to see it. Our curators are now extremely possessive of their guardianships. Also, my students are presently working on one of the collective farms, digging up potatoes, of all things. But they will be back at the end of this month and I can most certainly ask one to help you in your search."

"What if I pay one of your students a salary?" I suggested. "Would he be able to stop digging potatoes now?"

Mr. Levinberg began to laugh. "Unfortunately, this is impossible," he said. "First of all, a Russian student can't accept pound sterling; he could be arrested for this. I would pay him for his work in rubles and you would reimburse me sometime in the future. Secondly, each and every Russian citizen must spend one month a year on a collective farm. It is, practically speaking, a law."

"Every year? For an entire month?"

Our host continued laughing and nodded his head.

"What is worse is that the peasants expect it," he said in a lower voice, suddenly serious. "And they've gotten damned lazy." At this point I felt compelled to change the subject and I decided to ask him about the Stroganov collection, since the Grand Duchess Maria had married Pavel Stroganov's cousin. I wondered if Maria had possibly acquired the painting through her second husband's family, as opposed to her first husband's or her own.

"Part of the Stroganov collection was kept in Italy and sold after World War II at an auction by Christies. Stroganov also kept part of his collection at his palace in St. Petersburg. This collection was confiscated, taken to the Hermitage, catalogued, and sold with many other paintings in 1931 by Lepke in Berlin."

At this point, our hostess who had been silent until now, reminded her husband of the old Leuchtenberg who used to consult him about art. They started to talk quite rapidly in Russian and I could not pick up the subject of their argument. In the end they wrote down Leuchtenberg's address for me, mentioning that the man was quite sick and lived in very poor conditions. Perdoul and I thanked our hosts for their hospitality and they promised to contact me should they hear of any information pertaining to my case.

* * * *

Leuchtenberg lived on the periphery of Moscow near the metro station Vodny Voksal — the Water Station, in an old six-story building. "This is it," Perdoul whispered in mock fright, and he opened the heavy door to the building.

We found ourselves in a dark hallway, the smell of cat urine permeating its very walls. I could hardly breathe. Apartment number seventeen, Leuchtenberg's apartment, was on the second floor and we ran up the stairs in order to escape the smell. But on the wall outside Leuchtenberg's apartment were seventeen hand-written names, scratched into the wall besides the door bell. Every name had a number besides it, and Leuchtenberg's name was the last, again number seventeen.

"It looks like number seventeen is our lucky number," Perdoul said. "Do you think the number by the name means you have to ring the bell that many times?" And as he asked me this, Perdoul proceeded to ring the doorbell seventeen times.

We waited for quite some time but no one answered the door. Finally, as we were turning to leave, an old woman appeared on the steps behind us. She looked like the authentic Baba-Yaga — a witch from a Russian fairy tale.

"What are doing here?" she asked us rather rudely. "And why are you continuously ringing my doorbell?"

"We are looking for Comrade Leuchtenberg," answered Perdoul.

"You mean old Count Leuchtenberg? Are you his relatives?"

We shook our heads and the old woman seemed considerably relieved.

"Good! As far as I know there are none!" she said in her cracked voice. "But if they exist, I wouldn't be surprised if they started swarming around here like some old buzzards, hoping to inherit some of his possessions."

"And why is that?" I asked in my most polite tone.

"The old man is almost ninety years old now and he is dying from cancer," she said, glancing at us with her narrow, suspicious eyes. "But all of his neighbors are looking after him in turn." The old witch cackled at her own joke. "I will take you to him."

She opened the door and preceded us into the apartment.

"Grazhdanka, could you explain why Leuchtenberg's apartment has so many names on the door?" Perdoul asked.

She looked at us as if we had fallen from another planet and did not answer.

Inside, the apartment looked like a prison. Through the doors on either side of the long corridor, I heard children cry, dogs bark and people whispering in muffled voices. At last we reached a door adjacent to a small kitchen from which emanated the smell of cooked cabbage. The woman knocked at the door, looking us over once more. "He's in there," she barked. We waited at the door while she went into the kitchen, presumably to share her suspicions about us with the others.

"Come in," we heard a weak voice from behind the door.

Opening the door very carefully, we found ourselves in a magnificent room, furnished with heavy antique furniture, lush Persian rugs, and Renaissance paintings covering the walls. An antique clock, painted in gold, chimed the hour — its statuette, banging at the clock's gold dome with a tiny hatchet.

135

"Who is it? Who's there?" said the same weak voice. Behind the curtain, a very old man was lying in bed. Wrinkles covered his pale face, but his eyes were young and peered at us with curiosity. I introduced Perdoul and myself, telling the old man that although we were Russians we were both Oxford graduates now practicing art history. I told him that we came specifically to him in connection with a portrait of the English king, Charles I, painted by Van Dyck and supposedly once owned by Grand Duchess Maria. The old man became quite alert.

"You mean King of England and Scotland. Charles I was a Stuart descendant of the Scottish Kings!"

I was caught by surprise. To hide my embarrassment I changed the subject, asking him about all the names and numbers on the front door and about the long corridor and the many doors that we had to pass. Leuchtenberg smiled and explained that this apartment, along with all the others in the building, belonged to his family.

"After the revolution they were given to the plebs!" he practically shouted. "And I was left with the only one room." Leuchtenberg raised his shriveled hand, gesturing to the room. "There are seventeen families living in this place with only one kitchen, one toilet and no bathroom. People who go to the toilet put their names on the list and use the facility in that order."

Perdoul almost started to laugh, but I shot him a look in warning.

"The problem that existed originally," the old man said, "was that there was only one issue of the *Pravda* to be used as toilet paper, and the toilet users at the end of the list were jilted. Now the problem is solved because all the tenants have chipped in to buy two daily subscriptions to the *Pravda.*"

Perdoul chuckled after hearing this, despite my earnest glances. "It's absolutely true," Perdoul whispered to me. "If you could choose one item of luxury in the USSR, it would be a roll of soft toilet tissue."

136

At this point, the old Leuchtenberg gestured for us to sit down, and we pulled two exquisite chairs toward the gigantic bed.

"So why are you here?" the old man asked.

After making a polite inquiry as to our host's health, I stated the purpose of our visit. Leuchtenberg looked straight at me with his sparkling eyes and a soft smile began to play on his lips. He started talking as if he were dreaming, forgetting that Perdoul and I were there. Sometimes he would ask a question that had nothing to do with his story, or he would repeat himself, saying the same sentences several times. At one point it seemed as if he had drifted off to sleep. I started to think of leaving when he suddenly laughed and opened his eyes again, his words beginning to make sense.

"I heard this story from my beloved mother; a story about the portrait of Charles the First which could be the one you are looking for," Leuchtenberg stated, his words slightly slurred. "According to family legend, it first belonged to Catherine the Second and was presented to her by the English Ambassador, Sir Charles Hanbury-Williams."

"Sir Charles Hanbury-Williams," I asked, quite excited.

"Shh!" Perdoul whispered emphatically. "Don't disturb his thoughts.'

Perdoul was right and I sat back in my chair ready to listen. "Sir Charles arrived in St. Petersburg in seventeen fifty-five," the old man continued, apparently still lucid. "Before coming to Russia, he had been the Minister at the Court of Saxony and a friend and boon-companion of Sir Robert Walpole..."

"He went to Russia, anxious to ensure Russia's support in the event of a conflict between England and France. But his attempts to approach the Empress Elizabeth failed. He then turned to the 'young court' and immediately noticed the beautiful and witty wife of Grand Duke Peter, Catherine, who at that time was madly in love with twenty-two year old Poniatowski, the future King of Poland. Sir

Charles, who at first dreamt of becoming her lover, realized that this approach would fail and stepped back..."

"Sir Charles was in love with Catherine?" I said, finding it hard to believe that the woman had so many paramours.

"...Charles found another way to approach Catherine, however," the old man continued, not even hearing my question, "by lending her money, which she always seemed to need, and giving her presents. Among the presents he gave her was a beautiful portrait of the unfortunate English King, Charles the First, by Van Dyck. Sir Charles became her confidant and he and Catherine carried on a clandestine correspondence for almost a year. The first draft of Catherine's autobiography was written for the English Ambassador."

At this point Perdoul and I were grinning like madmen, listening to old Leuchtenberg speak. Here was my information, I kept thinking, straight from the horse's mouth!

"About ninety years later," Leuchtenberg continued, still completely oblivious of our presence, "the portrait, now hanging in the Hermitage, was noticed by Tsar Nicholas I. The Tsar disliked everything that was connected with Catherine, his 'immoral Grandmother,' and he particularly disliked portraits of her lovers. Looking at this portrait, Nicholas decided that this was just another of Catherine's lovers and demanded that Bruni, the Curator of the Hermitage, immediately remove it from the gallery and destroy it."

"The portrait was destroyed?" I practically shouted, forgetting my vow of silence.

"'Burn it!' ordered the Tsar," Leuchtenberg shouted back in a particularly authoritative voice. "But Bruni winked at the porters. They understood the signal and placed the portrait in a storage room, the existence of which was unknown to Nicholas the First. A few days later, Maria Nicholaevna, the Tsar's daughter, came to the storage room and took the portrait to Marinsky Dvoretz. She had organized a hiding place for all the paintings that had been ordered destroyed by her father's caprice."

So, Maria was responsible for saving the painting, I thought to myself.

"A few days later, the new English Ambassador presented his credentials to the Tsar. During the polite chit-chat following the ceremony, the Ambassador asked the Tsar,

'Your Majesty, could I see the famous portrait of Charles I by our great court painter Anthony Van Dyck?'

'Call Bruni,' the Tsar ordered."

"...When Bruni arrived, the Tsar asked him about the portrait.

'You ordered it to be destroyed, your Majesty, a few days ago thinking it was the portrait of one of your grandmother's lovers,'

Bruni replied.

'You ass!' the Tsar spat, forgetting he should use a more diplomatic language in the presence of the Ambassador. 'Why didn't you identify the portrait for me?'

'You didn't give me a chance,' replied the unhappy Bruni.

The English Ambassador was quite amused by this exchange and said to the Tsar,

'I thought Your Majesty did not like revolutionaries. The King, whose portrait you ordered to be destroyed, was the victim of a revolution and is our only martyr King. His head was cut off by the order of Cromwell, the leader of the 'round-head' revolutionaries.'

The Tsar became red-faced and turned to Bruni. 'Bring the portrait back!' he screamed.

This put Bruni in a terrible dilemma. If he admitted that the painting existed, he would betray his and Maria's scheme, revealing them both as insurgents. If he said the painting was destroyed, he'd be lying. In either case, he could be put to death.

Bruni decided to lie.

'Your Majesty,' he said, 'I do not have the power to restore the portrait of his Majesty King Charles I of England and Scotland from ashes, as if the painting were a phoenix.'

139

'Go away!' the Tsar said to Bruni. And he terminated the audience with the Ambassador."

"What an excellent story!" Perdoul remarked. I had to agree. But the Leuchtenberg still hadn't finished talking.

"In the first dispatch sent by the new English Ambassador to the government of George II of England," the old man continued, "the Tsar was described not only as a martinet, but also as a barbarian who engaged in the destruction of priceless art objects."

"Indeed," Perdoul and I both said, nodding our heads.

Leuchtenberg stopped talking and closed his eyes. I thanked him kindly for his story and before we were even out the door, the old man was snoring. Perdoul and I rushed out the building, not wanting to linger amongst the smell of cooked cabbage and cat urine. Once we were on the subway I turned to Perdoul and asked, "Do you think Leuchtenberg was telling the truth, or do you think he is completely deranged?"

Perdoul shrugged his shoulders, unable to answer.

"All I know," Perdoul finally said, "is that the man reminds me of my grandfather, the Ambassador, who lived to be ninety-five. He retained his mental faculties until the very end of his life. He died trying to catch his parakeet that had escaped from its cage and flown through an open window."

"He died chasing a parakeet?" I asked, not quite believing what I had just heard.

"He died falling out the window," Perdoul replied.

Perhaps Perdoul's comparison was apt. I could see the same thing happening to old man Leuchtenberg from apartment seventeen. Back at the hotel, I asked Perdoul to help me compare Leuchtenberg's story with the notes I had pertaining to the case. But when I tried to open my suitcase I discovered it was locked.

"Perdoul, I know I didn't lock my suitcase. I don't have a key." I was quite upset.

140

"Probably the KGB searched your room," Perdoul said in a whisper. "The KGB?"

"Yes. They must have searched your belongings and accidentally locked the suitcase."

For some reason, perhaps because of all the other strange occurrences that had happened to us that day, we both started to laugh.

"Let's go to the reception desk," Perdoul suggested.

At the reception desk, Perdoul created a scene. He spoke frantically in a high-pitched voice, angrily pounding the counter. The clerk was terrified as were the onlookers.

"You should be ashamed of yourselves, treating an important foreign visitor with such indignity. Why it's an absolute disgrace!" he shouted, pounding for emphasis. "I demand that you unlock this man's suitcase immediately! At once! Or I shall report your moronic actions!"

The terrorized clerk disappeared behind the door and returned with the manager of the hotel. After nervously apologizing for the inconvenience, the manager explained that he could not open the suitcase without authorization from the officials on the first floor of the hotel. He asked us politely to go there ourselves, reporting our inconvenience directly.

It took Perdoul and myself all of two seconds to realize that the first floor of the hotel contained the local headquarters for the KGB. Every room was occupied by an agent. All the agents pretended not to notice our presence, bending over their desks as if they were thoroughly absorbed by their work. We haphazardly chose one room and entered without knocking. Even though the man occupying the room was ready to leave for the day, already wearing his green Fedora hat and a heavy greatcoat, we decided to detain him. He was somewhat annoyed but when Perdoul started telling him about the suitcase he took off his hat and sat behind the desk, listening politely to our complaints. "What is your name?" the man asked me.

"Jerry Gramtrub at your service," I replied.

"Where do you live?" he asked.

"London, sir," I said.

The agent opened a file, searched for a long time, then looked for another file, found it, became interested in the contents of one page and turned to me.

"Your real name is Gromotrubov, not Gramtrub, and you are an agent of Scotland Yard," the man said.

"My real name is Gramtrub although my parents' name was Gromotrubov," I explained, trying not to appear too contemptuous. "I am an official, not an agent, of Scotland Yard and I am here on a mission unrelated to the Yard's activity."

I pulled out the letter from the Military Attache of the USSR Embassy in London. After reading the letter, the agent's attitude changed completely. He became extremely solicitous and pleasant, and finally, with a big smile he said,

"Ashyblis. We made a mistake. I am sending a locksmith to your room who will open the suitcase immediately."

Perdoul and I rose from our seats, our smiles as false as the agent's, and returned to my room. But as we entered we heard someone in my bathroom.

"Perdoul," I whispered, "get the floor key clerk, immediately."

Perdoul did as told and I cautiously crept toward the bathroom. Steam was drifting through the half-open door. As I peered inside, I saw a man taking a bath in my tub.

At that moment Perdoul returned with the clerk who wore a look of innocent surprise once she saw who was taking the bath.

"What is the trouble?" she said.

"Who is that man in my bathtub?" I asked somewhat upset.

"But that is Volodya, our plumber," she answered.

"How dare he use a guest's bathroom facilities!" Perdoul said indignantly.

142

"But he was dirty. Why shouldn't he use a bathroom if it isn't occupied?" the clerk asked.

"Get him out of here!" Perdoul said, even more indignant. "At once!"

By then Volodya, who was already dressed, unobtrusively removed himself from the scene of his apparent disgrace. "Who was that?" a KGB official asked, entering my room with a locksmith.

Perdoul started to laugh uncontrollably and the key clerk left shrugging her shoulders as if nothing were wrong.

* * * *

I spent the next day in the Pushkin Museum of Art, known for its collection of Western European Art. The museum was founded in 1894 by Professor Ivan Tsvetayev, head of the Department of Art History at Moscow University and the father of the Russian poetess Marina Tsvetayeva.

Before talking with the curator, I decided to see the Flemish art collection. This collection included seventeenth-century paintings by such artists as Rubens, Jacob Jordaens, Franc Snyders and Van Dyck. In my opinion, the best of the Museum's three portraits by Van Dyck was the portrait of Jan Ven den Wouwer which showed Van Dyck to be a subtle and sophisticated portraitist. There was no portrait of Charles I.

The curator was not very helpful. She provided me with minimal information and said that some paintings from the Leuchtenberg collection came to the Museum after the revolution, but that most of them were Italian. She did not know anything about a portrait of Charles I by Van Dyck, and suggested I see their Rembrandts. I finally realized that her favorite subject was not Van Dyck, but Rembrandt. The Museum possessed six of his paintings.

"Rembrandt was able to convey with unprecedented profundity and force an entire world of human emotions — the inner beauty of man," she explained.

143

"What do you think about Van Dyck?" I asked, later wishing I hadn't.

"I think that he was more a craftsman than a profound artist," she said. "But his ability as a portrait painter was remarkable. He also had a good sense of color. However, he did not research the collision of light and shadow, and he did not play with its combinations as Caravaggio did. Van Dyck loved the luster of material, its shine. Unfortunately, sometimes in his paintings you'll find the unneeded brush stroke or false background — as in music when you see a false score. Sometimes, Van Dyck's own taste betrayed him," she answered.

For some reason, this woman's tone bothered me. She acted as if she were the only expert on Van Dyck, denigrating his work as if she could do better. I wanted to argue with her.

"Don't you think the flaws, if any, are accounted for by the fact that he painted too quickly? He was always in a hurry to finish one portrait in order to start the next one immediately. If you look at his early religious compositions, and some of his landscapes or even at the portraits from his Italian sojourn, you will notice that they are not so purposely decorative or theatrical as the paintings he executed in England," I said.

But she continued in the same superior tone.

"Yes, one cannot deny that he was a man of great talent. And he certainly could present his models at their best. But my favorite artist, as you may have noticed, is Rembrandt. I don't think there any other portrait painter who compares with him."

After I left the Museum, I realized I hadn't learned anything more about the portrait of Charles I by being in Moscow. I didn't believe old man Leuchtenberg, but he had increased my curiosity concerning the fate of the Leuchtenberg's and the Grand Duchess Maria's collections. What had happened to their paintings? I decided to ask Perdoul if he would return to Leningrad with me, so that

I could continue my research at the Hermitage. Perdoul complied and even telephoned the secretary of the Director of the Hermitage, asking her if we could have another appointment with Mr. Pavlowsky, the Curator of Flemish art, for the next day. The Director's secretary remembered us well and convinced the Curator to see us promptly. We returned to the Europeiski Hotel after another ride on the overnight train. This time I had my passport and there was no difficulty in obtaining our rooms.

Perdoul and I met Mr. Pavlowsky and he asked me whether I had accomplished anything in Moscow. After explaining that I had heard only gossip and fairy tales, the curator smiled.

"I am afraid, Jerichon Afanasievich," he said, "that you have a major task before you. You cannot take a piecemeal approach to your search and expect to uncover an unknown painting's provenance. You have to know the history of Western art collection from the time the first item was brought to Russia until the time of the revolution or even thereafter."

I had mixed feelings about this suggestion. Even if I extended my stay in Russia, how could I hope to learn what he was suggesting? I was a policeman not an art historian. The curator, however, did not see any reason why I would be incapable of undertaking this task.

"The libraries and our museums are places where you will find art journals and books on Russian collections of Western art," he explained.

When I thanked Mr. Pavlowsky, he smiled in such a way that I couldn't tell if his advice was suggested out of kindness or some type of sadistic pleasure in watching me suffer. I realized such a task was beyond my capabilities, but since I was enjoying my rather madcap visit in Russia, I decided to ask Sir Alexander for permission to postpone my return for a few days. Sir Alexander granted my wish — mentioning that I should continue pursuing my search for the elusive Charles I. This was the last thing I had in mind.

I returned to Moscow with the intention of spending a few more days with Perdoul, sightseeing and theater going.

I arrived in Moscow quite late and I lodged, again, at the Ukraine Hotel. When I went to bed I could not fall asleep. Either the excitement of the day or the quantity of vodka I had drunk with Perdoul during our evening meal at the Caucasian Restaurant *Aragwa* kept me awake until the wee hours of the morning. When I was finally able to immerse myself into a state of slumber, I was awakened by what I can best describe as a scratch at the door. Now completely awake, I listened more carefully and realized that somebody was knocking. My policeman's instinct told me to be very cautious when answering a knock at the door in the middle of the night in the Soviet Union, but the noise persisted and I finally decided to open the door.

Before me stood a disheveled, poorly dressed man with a week's growth of beard and deep-set, penetrating dark eyes staring at me from under bushy brows. I was scared and started to close the door when he mentioned the names of Leuchtenberg and Levinberg.

"Mr. Levinberg told me about your search for provenance of the Van Dyck's portrait of Charles I. He also mentioned your interest in the art collection of the Leuchtenberg family. Mr. Levinberg recommended that I come and see you. I think that I can be useful to you. My English is much rusty from disuse of practice," whispered my midnight visitor.

I decided to let him in. Although he looked poor and abandoned, he had the face of an intellectual. I seated him in an armchair but after a few moments he got up from his chair and silently asked me to follow him into the bathroom. After he had seated himself on my toilet seat, he motioned for me to close the door. I did so and took a seat on the edge of the bath, whereupon my visitor began speaking in his broken English.

"You can talk Russian with me," I said. "Both my parents were Russian and I speak and understand the language very well."

146

He was relieved and told me, in Russian, that my room was bugged, but that the KGB had great difficulty placing microphones in this particular hotel's bathrooms.

"Did you ever come across the Leuchtenberg collection and portrait of Charles I by Van Dyck?" I asked him. I was still uncomfortable in his presence.

"Spare me half an hour and hear my story," said my guest.

"Alright," I replied, "but I am still slightly groggy from lack of sleep and too much vodka."

He disregarded my remarks and started to tell me his story.

"I am an art historian," he began, his voice soft and earnest. "My name is, or rather was, quite well-known to scholars in this field here and abroad. I am a specialist, so to speak, in European paintings of the sixteenth through the eighteenth centuries. Since the Hermitage once had the largest collection of Western paintings of this epoch, I decided to write a treatise on the history of Western paintings in Russia.

These paintings were largely collected by the Russian monarchy and I researched the art collected by Peter the Great and continued with his successors. The museum at the Hermitage was primarily the depository of these collections and by the end of the nineteenth century, it contained the largest number of outstanding paintings by Western artists.

I had a list of the Hermitage paintings which I had been compiling since 1915. I made a catalog of these paintings and when I compared them to what is now in the museum, I was shocked by the number of priceless paintings which had 'disappeared' from the Hermitage. I realized that many may not have been lost, but sold. Soviet rulers, starting with Lenin and continuing with Stalin, literally robbed the Hermitage of many items in its collection and ordered them to be sold abroad in order to replenish Russian coffers with

147

'almighty' dollars. I started to inquire about specific individuals who were directly involved in these unsavory deals and encountered a wall of silence. Nobody informed me, nobody admitted anything. But I, stupid as I was, persisted in my investigations until one day, two individuals in green fedora hats came to my apartment and introduced themselves as KGB officials. They arrested me in spite of my repeated pleas of innocence, and took me to Lubaynka prison.

I was put in solitary confinement and the next day was interrogated by an official. He told me that because of my unnecessary and politically abject research, I was accused of being a spy for American art collectors. I protested my innocence, claiming that as an art historian I had the right to inquire about the lost art from the Hermitage.

'Don't you know that if people don't want to tell you something, you should stop asking!' I was told by my interrogator.

I was finally brought to trial and accused of... treason. If convicted, I would be executed.

Luckily for me, the prosecutor was a young woman who had graduated from the same university as I had and who had a surprisingly intelligent face. She told the court that there was no legal basis for accusing me of treason and advised me to admit to a more minor crime — a misdemeanor. The court accepted my pleas and condemned me to five years in a gulag."

At this point, I felt compelled to offer my visitor a glass of water. Taking a glass from the sink, I poured some tap water into it and gave it to him. He took it rather appreciatively and I returned to my seat on the bathtub's edge, allowing him to continue.

"My first months in the gulag were terrible," he whispered sadly. "I was deprived of books, writing material, the most common utilities necessary for survival. I was also in the company of thieves and assassins. At first, my 'companions' were hostile towards me, considering me a stupid

148

intellectual who didn't know how to avoid prosecution and jail sentences. Gradually they became accustomed to my presence chiefly because my sister sent me a considerable quantity of cigarettes, which I shared with them.

Finally, one of my fellow prisoners took me in his confidence and, taking me aside, explained how I could bribe the commander. I was astounded.

'Ask your relative,' he said, 'to send you rubles, which they have to deliver to you, and then tell the guards that you want to see the commander because you are sick. This is a known password. It means you will give him something.'

I was very much afraid of following this scheme and postponed the plan for weeks. But the conditions of my confinement became so unbearable that I finally asked my mother for money and proceeded with the plan.

'What do you want!' the commander yelled, once I was brought to him after claiming sickness. He was looking directly at the fat envelope I had in my hand.

'I want paper and writing implements,' I replied.

He extended his hand and took the envelope containing my mother's money. After counting its contents, he said,

'You can have it.'

'But I intend to write a long article, and I need a large supply of materials.' I was surprised that I was bold enough to make this statement.

'You will have enough paper to write another volume of *Crime and Punishment,*' laughed the commander.

From that time on, I was writing daily, from memory, the history of Western art in Russia. When I was released from the gulag, however, I had become a nonperson. Only a few friends recognized my existence and sheltered me in their apartments, houses or dachas. Nobody ever dreamt of offering me a job. This is my present state of vegetation — it does not merit the word 'existence.' But I managed to write my treatise and I would like to have it published outside the country."

I looked at my visitor with pity and admiration. He had risked his life and his integrity for his work. I finally realized to what extent intellectuals were persecuted in Russia, and that no matter what the Russian government presents to the West, the officials of the Soviet Union are barbarians who, like Nicholas I, are both stubborn and prejudiced.

"I have the treatise with me," my visitor said after a moment's pause, "and I would like you to take it outside Russia and have it published."

"Why have you chosen me for the task?" I was quite sincere in my astonishment.

"Old man Leuchtenberg and Mr. Levinberg told me that you are a policeman and an art historian and you are interested in the history of Western art. In my manuscript you may find answers for your questions. You can also help me and because of your qualifications, you should have no difficulty in smuggling the manuscript out of Russia.

In response to this praise, I laughed. "What will happen if they catch me at the airport, smuggling this out of Russia? They'd put me in jail!"

"Then you will have to bribe the warden as I did and he will give you paper and pen to translate my chapter into English." Seeing that I was not amused, he hastily added, "You are too shrewd not to be careful."

I smiled at the flattery.

"You understand," I said, "that I must read the manuscript before I risk smuggling it out."

"I understand," he replied.

My visitor got up suddenly from the toilet seat on which he was sitting during our tete a tete and mentioned that it was time for him to leave. He thrust a dirty envelope into my hands, containing the manuscript, and noiselessly disappeared.

After he left, I inspected the treatise he had given me. It was handwritten but legible, and I spent the next few hours reading it through. I found his account fascinating and I decided then and there to smuggle it out of Russia.

150

I felt unusually sad saying goodbye to Perdoul. Not only had he been very helpful, but I had gotten accustomed to his ways. Perdoul was also quite emotional, kissing me goodbye on the cheeks for a goodbye.

"Will I ever see you again?" he said with tears in his eyes.

"Perdoul, you will visit me in London," I replied.

"Perhaps," said Perdoul. His smile was sad as he waved goodbye.

London looked strange to me when I got off the plane. The passport and customs officials were so polite and un-suspicious in comparison with their Russian counterparts. I went to my apartment, poured myself a large whiskey – the first after days of indulging in vodka and cognac. Then I started translating the treatise on Western Art in Russia which I have decided to include in this book of memoirs.

Grave of Herzog Georgij von Leuchtenberg (1927–1963).

Chapter 9

Centuries of Art Collecting in Russia

by W.S.S.[1]

> My task, which I am trying to achieve, is,
> by the power of the written word, to make you
> hear, to make you feel — it is, before all,
> to make you see.
> — Joseph Conrad

The Time of Peter the Great

The collecting of Western art, particularly paintings,
was first initiated in Russia by Peter the Great. Before his

---

[1] W.S.S. was a dissident who did not want his name to be divulged.
He died about six months after I saw him in Moscow. I do not hesi-
tate now to tell his real name — Vsevolod Semeonovich Strakhulsky,
revered today in Russia as an outstanding art historian and connoisseur. — J.A. Gramtrub

time, native Russian art reflected a Byzantine influence notable in the religious paintings, architecture, frescoes and mosaics produced during this period. Although French tapestries were first collected by Russian ambassadors to France during the fourteenth century, these were the only art objects brought to Russia from the West. Alexei Michailovich, the second Tsar of the Romanov dynasty, is also known for collecting Western art — a tradition maintained by his descendants until shortly before the Russian revolution. But the grand era of collecting paintings by European artists really began during the reign of Peter the Great. In Pushkin's words, Peter 'opened the window into Europe.'

In 1703, a new capital called St. Petersburg was built by Peter I on swamps near the banks of the Neva River. Thousands of Russian serfs from all over the country died during its construction as a result of the unbearable living conditions. But during the centuries since its foundation, the beauty of this northern capital has been glorified by many poets. St. Petersburg has been referred to as 'proud and majestic' by Alexander Pushkin; 'misty and mysterious' by Alexander Blok; 'touching, big and fearful' by Osip Mandelstam.

In the first years after the city was built, St. Petersburg looked like a typical Dutch city with its endless canals, light bridges and rows of small grey houses. The interior of Peter's St. Petersburg residence was also reminiscent of the Dutch aesthetic, and the heavy furniture and copper light fixtures reflected the Tsar's desire to live comfortably, not luxuriously.

Thus it is not surprising that of all the countries visited by the Tsar during his reign, Holland impressed Peter the most. There he collected animals which had not been seen in Russia, sending back monkeys and parrots. He actually took one monkey that he especially liked to England and did not part with it even during his visit with King

William III. Peter also studied mathematics, shipbuilding and printing in Holland.

During his first trip abroad (1697–1698), Peter visited Jacob de Wilde's museum in Holland. De Wilde's daughter, Maria, commemorated the event by engraving a picture of his meeting with her father. During this time, Peter bought several paintings and had two boats built, the ceilings of which were painted by known Dutch artists.

The first portrait of Peter was very probably painted by the Polish artist, Theodore Lubinitski. It is now lost. But the second portrait was painted by the Dutch painter Michael van Muschen. This work was recorded for the first time in an auction catalog in 1706 and for the second time in 1717. According to these catalogs, the portrait depicted an allegorical representation of Peter but, unfortunately, the original of this portrait is also lost. At the request of King William III, a third portrait was executed in England by Godfrey Kneller. It soon became a tradition for Russian nobility to have their portraits painted by fashionable foreign artists such as Dawe, de Grooth, Angelica Kauffmann, Vigee-Lebrun.

Peter's first trip to Holland is also notable in the unforeseeable political role it played. The jewels he bought for his wife there eventually saved his life.

In April 1711 Peter was persuaded by the Hospodar of Moldavia, Demetrius Cantemir, to launch a military campaign against the Turks. Three months later, in July, the Russian contingent's situation became desperate. They were surrounded on the Pruth River by a superior Turkish army. Peter knew that within a day or two his army would be defeated. Furthermore, as a captured enemy of the Sultan, Peter himself would be paraded down the streets of Constantinople in a cage.

Peter decided to negotiate with the Grand Vizier and he chose Vice-Chancellor Shafirov as his envoy. Shafirov offered the Turks Azov, dismantling Taganrog and returning all the territories won by the Russians during the last twenty years. The negotiations were successful and the siege was lifted, enabling Peter to escape Turkish captivity. But some say that the Tsarina Catherine had Shafirov offer the Turkish Vizier large sums of money and her own jewels, bought for her when Peter first visited Holland. When the Sultan learned that Vizier betrayed him through greed, he condemned him to death by pouring molten gold down his throat.

During his second European trip in 1717–1718, Peter went to Amsterdam where he partook in a great many auctions. His favorite painters at that time were Rubens, Van Dyck, Rembrandt and Jan Steen, and he bought many of their paintings. In a letter to the Tsar, Kologrivov, one of Peter's agents, documented the purchase of 117 paintings — twenty-seven bought in Brussels and the rest in Antwerp. The paintings were brought to St. Petersburg and placed in the Peterhoff Gallery and in the Monplaisir Palace. Among them were Van Ostade, Jan Steen, Rembrandt, Bruegel and Teniers Jr. The Peterhoff Gallery now contained 200 paintings. Peter's collection would eventually exceed 400 paintings in all.

Peter also sent Kologrivov to Florence, Venice, Rome and other cities to buy not only paintings, but also antique marble statues. These statues were later placed in Peter's Summer Garden, built on the banks of the Neva River. Kologrivov also bought numerous French tapestries and more paintings during his visit to Paris.

In addition to buying Western art, Peter the Great invited foreign artists to work for him. One such artist was a friend of his whom he met in Amsterdam, the landscape painter and art dealer, Xsel. Xsel was engaged by Peter in 1717 and sent to St. Petersburg with his family. He worked first for the Russian court, and then for the Academy of Sciences. One of his daughters became the wife of a Russian brigadier-general, while the other one married a famous physicist. Xsel died from a stroke at an old age in 1741 while still in St. Petersburg.

Xsel recorded numerous anecdotes concerning Peter's method of art collecting. In one such story, he describes Peter's infatuation with a painting that depicted a woman, her lover, and a trumpet player. Peter commissioned a similar canvas in order to make fun of one of his servants whose wife was unfaithful. This servant, instead of keeping quiet about his wife's affairs, announced them to anyone who would listen. Peter conceived of the idea of having himself painted as the wife's lover and the husband as the horn player, trumpeting the affair to everyone around.

Art collecting soon became popular amongst the Russian nobility, as they followed the precedent set by their ruler. One such collector, Count Menshikov, was Peter's close friend. During the reign of Elizabeth, his collection was transferred to a specially built gallery in Oranienbaum. Among those who later became known as collectors were Peter Semenov-Tianshansky, the famous geographer, Delorov, Galinishchev-Kutuzov, and Shuvalov. Their collections of Flemish and Dutch art became the pride of St. Petersburg. In fact, Dutch paintings in Russia were so well-known abroad that in 1905, when the American art collector John P. Morgan wanted to purchase a Rembrandt, he sent his representative not to Holland but to Russia.

Unfortunately, not all the collectors during Peter's reign exhibited such good taste as those mentioned. Paintings were often hung without any indication of the work's origin or date of execution.

In 1724, Kunstkamera, a small art gallery and the first art museum was opened in St. Petersburg. Kunstkamera primarily exhibited paintings by Dutch and Flemish artists. In 1882 twenty paintings were transferred from this gallery to the Hermitage. Among them were Rembrandt's *David Parting from Jonathan* (bought by Peter in Amsterdam), Jan Steen's *The Marriage Contract,* and landscapes by J. Van Goyen.

Peter the Great is also known to have collected "the eighth wonder of the world." During his visit with the

Prussian King Friedrich Wilhelm I, Peter expressed his admiration for the Amber Room in the Palace Man Bijou in Berlin. The room consisted of twenty-two amber panels. In 1716, when the treaty of alliance with Russia was signed, the Prussian King presented the Amber Room to Peter the Great as a gift.

The amber panels were initially mounted in the Summer Palace and were later transferred to the Winter Palace. When Peter built the Catherine Palace as a present to his wife, the amber panels were relocated again. The yellowish brown spectrum of amber mosaics with its warm transparent golden hues was enhanced the addition of skillfully carved amber frames, garlands, heads of ancient gods, and whole scenes from the Bible.

During World War II the Catherine Palace was almost destroyed and the Amber Room was taken by the Nazis to the former capital of East Prussia — Königsberg, Germany. The amber panels have either been demolished or so carefully hidden that any attempts to locate them have, to date, ended in failure.

Peter's contribution to the creation of the first Russian galleries, museums and private collections is remarkable. After Peter's death in 1725, his immediate successors were much less interested in art collecting. In 1730, however, Empress Anna Ivanovna, the daughter of Peter's feeble-minded half-brother, Ivan V, ascended the throne. She ruled the country for almost ten years and during her reign, she compiled a list of paintings hanging in Monplaisir, the Summer Garden, and in Peterhoff. This list was drafted by J. von Staehlin, the foreign art expert who worked for the Russian court and for the Academy of Sciences. The inventory is of great value as it is the first record of paintings in the possession of the Russian Court.

With Elizabeth's accession to the throne in 1740, the second daughter of Peter I and Catherine I, did cultural life in Russia thrive again.

Elizabeth, Empress of Russia

It is difficult to describe Elizabeth's reign. Historians most often consider this Tsarina as merely a transition between two great personalities: Peter the Great and Catherine II. And yet in her own right, Elizabeth was a remarkable person.

Elizabeth was widowed at the age of thirty-one. Her husband, the young Prince Karl August of Holstein-Gothorp, died of smallpox shortly after their wedding. She was also suspected by the Empress Anna Ivanovna as being an usurper and was kept at arm's length. Because of her precarious position and, for those times, advanced age, Elizabeth had no suitors. When Anna Ivanovna died in 1740, a coup d'etat put Elizabeth on the throne. The new Empress gave up any ideas of marriage

It is rumored that Elizabeth had numerous lovers, but only one close romantic attachment is considered definitive — Alexei Razumovsky, Ukrainian peasant who sang in the church chorus. In addition to having a beautiful voice, Alexei was also a very handsome man. Elizabeth, who was very fond of choral music, asked him to sing in her private chapel and then took him to bed. They remained devoted to each other until Elizabeth's death. The grateful Tsarina bestowed on Razumovsky and his family the status of nobility.

Elizabeth was an insomniac, perhaps because she feared for her life. In order to soothe her nerves, she would often wander into her private chapel at night and call for the chorus to perform. Members of the chorus were talented young boys from all over the country and they had to stay awake every night in order to be at the Tsarina's service. Among the boys was seven year old Dimitrii Bortniansky who fell asleep during a performance for the Empress. Elizabeth took pity on him, brought him to her palace, and after realizing the enormous talent of the boy, supported him in his musical education. Bortniansky went to study in Italy and returned to Russia a famous composer.

During the twenty years Elizabeth reigned, cultural life in Russia flourished and the first Academy of Arts was opened in St. Petersburg. Elizabeth's largest purchase of paintings occurred in 1745 when 115 paintings were bought in Prague and Bohemia, through the intermediary of the artist George Christopher Grooth, for the sum of 12,000 roubles. The paintings were hung in Catherine's Palace, in the magnificent hall designed by Rastrelli. Among the paintings were landscapes by Jan Both, architectural compositions by Emanuel de Witte, realistic genre scenes by Adriaen Van Ostade and David Teniers the Younger, and still lives by Jan David de Hem and Jan Feit. The *Allegory* by Theodore van Thulden, *Storm of the Town* by Palamedes, and the seventeenth century copy of Rubens' *Rape of the Sabine Women* were also purchased as part of this collection. Italian masters, such as Luca Giordano and Antonio Balestra also hung in Catherine's Palace, as well as French artists like Jacques Blanchard (called the *French Titian* for his unusually rich palette) and Pierre-Denis Martin (whose paintings *The Battle for Lesnaya* and *The Battlefield of Poltava* were executed especially for Peter I).

The first public auction of art objects took place in St. Petersburg during Elizabeth's reign, in 1751. About 800 items were sold at the auction including Italian marble tables, statues, and "empty bottles." From that time on, art was sold in Russia at auctions, stock markets, through art dealers, lotteries and at the Academy of Arts. Art was also sold in bookstores: the most famous of these was owned by the German dealer, Klosterman.

Elizabeth had one major weakness — her love for her nephew, Peter, the son of her deceased sister, Anna Petrovna. This poorly-educated German prince was brought to Russia at the age of fourteen and declared heir to the Russian throne. Peter was not good-looking, but his face became even more disfigured after he had smallpox at the age

160

of sixteen or seventeen. Since being unable to choose his own bride, Elizabeth did so for him. She decided on an impoverished German princess from the house of Anhalt-Zerbst, whose father was a Major General in the Prussian army and whose mother was a cousin of Peter's father. Elizabeth must have had uncanny foresight in choosing Sophie for Peter's bride. This fifteen-year-old girl who came to Russia with three dresses assumed the Russian name, Ekaterina. She became known as Catherine the Great.

Her marriage to Peter may have never been consummated. Her firstborn son and the future Tsar, Paul I, was fathered by the handsome courtier, Sergei Saltykov. Her daughter, Anna, by the future Polish King Stanislaw August Poniatowski. Her youngest son, Alexei Bobrinsky, by Grigorii Orlov — the great love of her life.

Elizabeth died in 1761 and her nephew was proclaimed Tsar as Peter III. He occupied the throne for no more than six months. Catherine's lover, Grigorii Orlov, engineered a coup d'etat with his brothers, some members of the nobility, and two regiments of soldiers — all with Catherine's connivance. Peter III was obliged to abdicate the throne whereupon he was imprisoned. A few days later he was killed — strangled to death by Grigorii's brother, Alexei Orlov.

Catherine probably did not know about the plans for her husband's murder. Even if she did, it is doubtful that she would have been able to prevent it.

Catherine the Great

Catherine was crowned in Moscow on Sunday, September 22, 1762, by the Novgorod Metropolite, the head of the Russian Orthodox Church. She was dressed in a gold silk gown, the Imperial double eagle embroidered on her skirt. Over this she wore an ermine mantle crafted from four thousand pelts. Her crown weighed five pounds and was studded with tremendous precious stones, thousands of diamonds, numerous pearls, and a 415-carat ruby that Tsar Alexis had bought from a Chinese Emperor a century before.

Catherine was thirty-four years old at that time, full of energy and ideas to remake the country that had become her own. Her wit, intelligence and charm, combined with her superior organizational abilities, made her popular not only in Russia but also in Europe.

Catherine, who had no formal schooling, was self-educated. She was particularly interested in philosophy — especially Voltaire. Because of Catherine's influence, Voltaire became so fashionable that no one could call himself an intellectual if he did not possess the philosopher's books. (Sixty volumes of Voltaire's books were translated into Russian. Almost all of them were published during the reign of Catherine II.)

Catherine, who learned French fluently during her childhood in Germany, was also a Francophile. Not only did she read many French writers but she also invited, in 1759, the gifted Frenchman Jean-Baptiste de la Monthe to occupy a chair in the newly established Academy of Fine Arts in Moscow. Catherine was also acquainted with the writings of Diderot, whom she later befriended. Diderot was instrumental in introducing Catherine to Baron Friedrich Melchior von Grimm, a literary figure and a savant. Grimm met Catherine only once, but he became her correspondent and it is known that she wrote him 1,500 or more letters in which she expressed her thoughts and often asked for his opinions. Grimm also acted as Catherine's principal advisor when she purchased art in France.

Catherine's interest in collecting art is marked by her construction of an annex to the Winter Palace. She named this addition the "Hermitage" — place of seclusion. Collecting art became Catherine's obsession, not only as an aesthetic pleasure but also as a strategy to strengthen the prestige of her country. She begrudged neither money, time nor efforts; the most brilliant era of art collecting in Russia started with Catherine II.

The first major collection of paintings Catherine bought for the Hermitage was one originally owned by King Frederick the Great of Prussia. The King was a passionate art collector but the expenditures incurred as the result of the Seven Years' War emptied his coffers and he was obliged to part with 225 paintings from his collection, most of which were Flemish and Dutch. Frederick's intermediary, Johann Ernst Gotzkowsky, offered the paintings to the Russian Court. Catherine was delighted to accept the offer. Not only did the collection give her a good start with the Hermitage, but she was happy to deprive the arrogant, self-assured Grosse Fritz — as King Frederick was nicknamed — of his prize possession. As it happened, the Prussian King's taste in painting was not very remarkable. Only a few paintings in his collection were exceptional, such as Steen's *Loafers,* Rembrandt's *Doubting Thomas* and van Baburen's *Concert,* mistakenly attributed at that time to Frans Hals.

Catherine herself was not an art connoisseur. She relied heavily on the advice of her friends and agents. One of her agents was Prince Dimitrii Alexeevich Golitsin, the Russian ambassador in France. He was instrumental in inviting the well-known sculptor, Etienne Maurice Falconet, to Russia. Falconet lived in Russia from 1766 to 1778 and sculpted the famous statue of Peter the Great in St. Petersburg. After returning to France he was elected to the Academy of Fine Arts and nominated the Director of Sculpture at the Sevres factory through the influence of Madame de Pompadour.

Golitsin also traveled to the Netherlands where he studied Rubens, Teniers, and Van Dyck. He was an expert on Italian art and wrote numerous books, the first of which described the work of Falconet and was published in 1772. Golitsin started to translate Descamps' *Vie des Plus Illustres Peintres Italiens, Flamands et Francais,* 1753–1764, but it was never completed. He also purchased for the Empress Rembrandt's *The Return of the Prodigal Son* for 6000 livres. Golitsin himself possessed a remarkable collection of paintings.

In the years 1750–1780, Paris became a center for art sales — but the fashion for Flemish and Dutch paintings determined the demand at these sales. Catherine always had a representative at Paris auctions and through their bids was able to acquire several collections. One of these was owned by Jean de Julien, an art expert and friend of Watteau. The auction took place at the Louvre and brought 392,000 livres. Among the paintings in this collection were Dou's *Old Woman Reading,* Tenier's *Wedding,* and Rembrandt's *An Old Woman with a Book.* When Le-Live de July's collection went for sale privately, Catherine's obtained Van Dyck's *Family Portrait,* which is still exhibited in the Hermitage today. Three Van Dycks were also known to exist in the collection and were sold by Prince Charles Joseph de Ligne.

Another noteworthy collection purchased by Catherine the Great, was one that belonged to the late Count Heinrich von Bruhl, the minister of King Augustus II of Saxony and Poland. Von Bruhl was in charge of buying paintings for the Dresden gallery and it was rumored that he acquired quite a few paintings through fraud in order to add to his own collection. Eventually, his collection became one of the finest in all Europe, rivaling even that of his King.

Catherine II, ignoring any rumors about Bruhl's dishonesty, asked her Ambassador to Saxony, Prince Alexander Beloselsky, to offer a sum of money large enough to outbid any competition for the Bruhl collection. The collection was delivered to the Hermitage and among the paintings were numerous works by Watteau, Rubens and Rembrandt.

I have several copies of Diderot's *Rameau's Nephew* in my library. This masterpiece was among the manuscripts obtained by Catherine when she purchased Diderot's entire library. The transaction took place years before Diderot's death, but the Tsarina permitted him to keep possession of his library until she required it. Thus, only after Diderot's death in 1783, did his books and manuscripts arrive in St. Petersburg.

It is not known who discovered the manuscript of *Rameau's Nephew* or how it was smuggled out of Russia at the turn of the eighteenth century. But the fact is that the manuscript fell into the hands of Schiller who showed it to Goethe. The latter translated it into German and had it published in 1805. Subsequently, many French versions of the work appeared in print and I have several of these editions. The text of this masterpiece differs from edition to edition and none represent the true original. Luckily, in 1891, a manuscript in Diderot's own hand was discovered and the authoritative edition was published in 1950.

In a preface to one of the bowdlerized editions of the work, the unknown author refers to Diderot as an intermediary in arranging the sale of a French art collection to Catherine. This aroused my interest and I decided to investigate Diderot's contact with Catherine.

I knew from other sources that Diderot had been described to Catherine as a famous writer and philosopher, but whether Catherine and Diderot started to correspond with each other prior to 1770 is not clear. Certainly Diderot's relationship with the Tsarina must have been known to a wide circle of French aristocracy; for when the heirs of Baron Crozat decided to sell his art collection, they turned to Diderot to serve as an intermediary in selling the collection to the Tsarina.

Of all the collections established in Paris during the eighteenth century, none could surpass that of Pierre

Crozat. Pierre Crozat made a fortune on financial operations and devoted his life to collecting art. A refined connoisseur, he chose his paintings not only in France, but in Italy. His house was built especially to store his collection and to display it in a proper manner, and he kept the door open, not only for artists but for those who wanted to acquaint themselves with his treasures. At the time of his death in 1740, Crozat possessed 400 paintings, 19,000 drawings and 15,000 engraved stones — as well as relief carvings, marbles and bronzes of antiquity or renaissance, and pottery from Urbino. He died without immediate issue and part of his collection, mostly paintings, was willed to his nephew, Marquis du Chatel. Part was sold by his executor, Mariette, for the benefit of the poor.

Marquis du Chatel died in 1750 and his collection was divided into three lots. Part was sold at an auction and another part of lesser value was inherited by Chatel's daughter, Louise-Honorine, who was married to the future Duke of Choiseul.

The largest and most valuable part of Chatel's collection, however, was inherited by Louis-Antoine Crozat, Baron de Thiers. He kept the collection in his palace at Place Vendome in Paris. Baron de Thiers died in 1770 leaving three daughters to inherit his art treasures. One was married to Marquis de Bethune, General of the Cavalry; the second to Victor-Francois Broglie, Marshall of France. The third was a widow of the late Count of Bethune, Sieur of Bordes, Lieutenant Governor of Artois.

The heirs of Baron de Thiers were apparently more in need of money than of art and decided to sell the collection. They were not keen to dispose of their heritage at a public auction, however, and decided to contact Diderot. Diderot, in turn, asked Francois Tronchin to help him estmate the value of the Crozat collection. (Tronchin had, himself, sold his art collection to the Tsarina in 1771.) Two more experts were called to help with the task. Remy was chosen by the heirs, and Menageot was chosen by Diderot. 158

pieces of the collection were priced at 460,000 livre and this price, apparently acceptable to the heirs, was recorded in a contract signed in the presence of a notary on January 4, 1772. The actual sales contract was signed by Diderot in the name of the Tsarina and by the three daughters and two sons-in-law of Baron de Thiers.

Diderot arranged the transport of 400 paintings, packed in seventeen cases, by barge to St. Petersburg. There were difficulties and delays, but finally on November 6, 1772, General Betsky, President of the Imperial Academy of Arts, advised Tronchin, in the name of the Tsarina, of the paintings' safe arrival at St. Petersburg. The paintings were in perfect condition. Tronchin received several sable pelts as a token of gratitude from the Tsarina.

When the other part of Crozat's heritage was offered to Catherine, fifty-five pieces were sold for 400,000 livres. This enraged the two sons-in-law of Baron de Thiers. They accused Diderot of losing 200,000 livres in their own transaction. In a letter to Tronchin, Diderot stated that the allegations were, "neither completely true nor completely false."

Diderot managed to acquire yet another important collection for Catherine the Great — de Choiseul's, Louis XVI's powerful minister who ruled France for twenty years. The abrupt end of de Choiseul's political career brought him to the verge of financial bankruptcy and he was obliged to sell his art collection at an auction. Diderot bought eleven paintings at this auction, including Van Dyck's *Susanne Fourment With Her Daughter* (see Appendix), Wouverman's *Deer Hunt,* Murillo's *Young Peasant and Young Peasant Girl,* David Teniers' *Village Fete* and Jan Steen's *A Sick Old Man.*

Out of the twenty-four Van Dycks on exhibit at the Hermitage, five are from the Crozat collection: *Portrait of a Young Man* painted in 1620–1621; another *Portrait of a Young Man* painted in 1623; a portrait of Marc-Antoine Luman Banker in Lyon painted during Van Dyck's stay

167

in Italy during 1621–1627; a self-portrait painted during Van Dyck's second Antwerp period from 1627-1632; and a *Portrait of Eberhart Jabach,* painted in 1636. But what had happened to the other nineteen paintings? The original Crozat collection included eight Rembrandts, a Raphael, four Veroneses, a Giorgione, a Tintoretto and two Annibale Carraccis.

Either because of her gratitude for arranging the purchase of the Crozat collection or because she genuinely admired Diderot, Catherine invited him to St. Petersburg. When they met in October 1773, Diderot was sixty years old and Catherine was forty-five. Diderot stayed for almost half a year.

He arrived in Russia at a most difficult time for the Russian Empress — when she was being subjected to two impostors. One was a Cossack, Emelian Pugachev, who proclaimed himself to be Peter III. He said he had survived the assassination attempt and he wanted to reclaim the throne. The other impostor was the so-called Countess Tarakanova, a mysterious and beautiful woman who claimed to be a daughter of Tsarina Elizabeth. She too claimed to be a more legitimate heir to the Russian throne than Catherine. Ultimately, Pugachev was captured and imprisoned in an iron cage. The cage was placed on a horse cart and driven throughout Russia in order display the false emperor. Afterward, he was beheaded. Countess Tarakanova was put in prison in the Peter and Paul Fortress in St. Petersburg where she eventually died of tuberculosis.

Aside from exposing impostors, Catherine was waging a war against Turkey. But in spite of all this, Diderot was warmly welcomed by the Empress.

They first met at the Hermitage, in front of two masterpieces from the Crozat collection, Giorgione's *Judith and Holofernes* and Rembrandt's *Danae.* The Russian Empress and the French philosopher spent many days together — discussing art, literature, music, education, politics and obviously, philosophy. When Diderot told Catherine that she

168

had "the soul of Brutus in the body of Cleopatra" or in another version "the soul of Caesar with all the seductive qualities of Cleopatra," these remarks became known all over Europe.

Gradually, their relationship changed from a formal one to one of great mutual respect and friendship. The Empress asked Diderot to help her set up a university in St. Petersburg and they talked about publishing an edition of Diderot's encyclopedia in Russian. Diderot also offered his advice on such matters as serfdom and laws of succession — matters of which he knew next to nothing. Catherine listened with one ear and pacified the garrulous philosopher with platitudes. After Diderot's death, she was less merciful. Catherine classified his critique on her edict of Great Instruction as "a piece of twaddle."

Diderot left Russia in March 1774. Catherine asked him not to say goodbye since she hoped they would see each other in the future. This did not happen.

Aedes Walpolianae

The sale of Crozat's art collection created quite a storm in France, but this was nothing compared to the public outrage over the sale of the Walpole collection in England. Dr. Johnson even went so far as to organize a campaign in Parliament against the sale, asking people to sign a petition in order to buy the collection as a national treasure. His efforts were in vain, however, and the collection was delivered to St. Petersburg. Catherine enjoyed the scandal and informed Grimm that she had her claws in the Walpole paintings and would "no more let them go than a cat would a mouse."

In 1779 the Russian ambassador to England, Baron Musin-Pushkin, notified Catherine that one of the most outstanding art collections in England belonged to Sir Robert Walpole and that it would be available on the art

169

market soon. Catherine immediately ordered him to buy the collection which was valued at 40,000 pounds sterling.

Sir Robert Walpole was the minister to George I and George II during the early part of the eighteenth century and one of the greatest art collectors in England. He collected his art for a long time — from 1715 until his death in 1745. Some of the paintings he bought at private sales, some he received as gifts and the Van Dycks he probably inherited from the Wharton family, who possibly bought them directly from the artist. Walpole also purchased art in France, Italy and Holland.

He had three sons, but only the youngest, Horace, inherited his father's passion for art collecting. In 1742, Horace Walpole, the author of one of the first romantic Gothic novels in England, *Castle of Otranto,* published a catalog of his father's collection. But Robert Walpole left his collection and title, the Earl of Orford, to his oldest son, also named Robert. This son died only six years after his father and, unfortunately, the collection went to Robert's son, George. George, being a weak person and erratic spendthrift, sold his grandfather's collection to Russia for 36,000 pounds. When Horace succeeded the title as the fourth Earl of Orford in 1791, he was already seventy-four. By then the house and estate were ruined and the paintings were gone. Horace Walpole described the sale of the Walpole collection as "the most single mortification to my idolatry for my father's memory, that it could receive."

Among the paintings George Walpole sold to Russia were twelve portraits — all Van Dycks.
1) King Charles I in armor (w.l.)
2) Henrietta Maria of France (w.l.)
3) Archbishop Laud
4) Philip, Lord Wharton
5) Sir Charles Wandsford sitting
6) Lady Wharton, sitting
7) Jane, daughter of Lord Wenmann
8) Sir Thomas Chaloner

170

9) Inigo Jones (head)
10) Lord Wharton's two daughters
11) Henry Danvers, Earl of Danby in his Garter robes
12) Sir Thomas Wharton (w.l.)

This list of paintings, with the exception of two — that of Lord Philip Wharton and Lady Wharton, was presented in a book written by Horace Walpole called *Anecdotes of Painting in England.*

* * * *

The last significant collection of Flemish and Dutch art that Catherine purchased was owned by a brigadier in the French Army, Count de Baudouin. Grimm recommended the purchase by verifying Baudouin's taste and mentioning that these paintings were well-known to Russian art lovers who had visited Paris. Within the collection were nine Rembrandts, four Ostades, three Ruysdaels and six Van Dyck portraits — some of which had been attributed to Rubens until recently.

I must mention that Catherine was also interested in collecting Italian art as well as Flemish and Dutch art. The Italian architects Rossi, Rastrelli and Quarenghi, all took part in building St. Petersburg and Russian artists often went to study art in Italy. Russian portraitists in particular were influenced by the Italian school. Count Shuvalov, who lived in Italy and possessed a rich collection of paintings by Italian artists, had established friendly relations with many influential people in the Italian art world in Rome. He helped Catherine acquire some of the best Italian paintings by Titian, Reni, and Andrea del Sarto.

According to legend, one day when Catherine was in a bad mood, she saw some illustrations of Raphael's famous loggias in the Vatican. She was so enchanted by what she saw that her mood improved and she decided to construct a replica of Raphael's loggias at the Hermitage. She sought the help of her old confidant, Grimm, to fulfill her dream.

She wrote, "I will not have rest or peace until everything is finished," referring to the loggias.

Reiffenstein, a Prussian by birth, was living in Rome at the time. Reiffenstein was an expert in ancient Roman art as well as a patron for Russian artists studying in Rome. He was chosen to oversee building a replica of the loggias for Catherine and an Italian architect, Giacomo Quarenghi, was chosen to construct the rooms. Catherine was delighted by their work. She wrote, "I like the replicas of Raphael's loggias very much; God knows what is going on in my mind when I am looking at them, and can't stop looking at them."

Orlov's, Potemkin's and Other Collections

Grigorii Orlov was an extremely handsome man, described as being tall, "with Herculean strength and an angelic face." He began his career as a soldier and during the battle of Zorndorff was recognized for his bravery. But he is best known for being Catherine's lover.

Before his love affair with Catherine began, however, he was involved with Princess Elena Kurakina — the Field Marshall Apraxin's daughter and the beautiful mistress of his military superior, Count Shuvalov. Shuvalov's death in 1762 saved Orlov's neck.

Catherine had already been married for nine years and was still in love with Stanislaw August Poniatowski (the young Polish prince and father of Catherine's second child) when she became attracted to Orlov. Catherine and Orlov's relationship lasted for almost twenty years and when it came to an end he lost his mind. He wore the diamond-studded-locket that Catherine presented to him, with her own portrait inside, his entire life. He appreciated this gift as much as some of the palaces and estates and the 6,000 serfs also given to him by his lover. In his turn, the Count gave Catherine one of the biggest diamonds in the world — 193 carats. According to legend, it had been stolen by a French soldier from the eye of an Indian idol. Catherine had this diamond set into the Imperial crown.

Although Orlov owned many portraits before Catherine chose him as her lover, her generosity enhanced his collection considerably. He kept his paintings spread between two palaces, also given to him by Catherine — the Gatchina and Marble palaces. After his death in 1783, these palaces and their belongings were bought back by Catherine, and the famous Orlov collection returned to the Empress. This collection consisted of 206 paintings.

But Catherine's favorite lover, and perhaps even the man she secretly married after Peter's assassination, was not the handsome Grigorii Orlov, but the ugly and extravagant Count Grigorii Potemkin — a veritable soldier, poet, politician, womanizer and artist. His eccentricity and debauchery made him known all over Europe. It is said that when a woman's evening slippers were soiled during his dinner party, he sent a hussar on a very fast horse all the way to Paris to get her another pair.

Potemkin was only twenty-three, ten years younger than Catherine, when they met at the time of the coup d'etat and disposal of Peter III. Apparently he made impressed Catherine sufficiently that his image stayed in her mind until later, when they became actual lovers.

Potemkin endured serious difficulties by taking on the role of Catherine's lover. He was blinded in one eye when the Orlov brothers violently attacked him. He then left St. Petersburg and entered a monastery with the intention of becoming a monk. He probably would have become a monk if it hadn't been for Catherine's letters. In a year and a half he quit the monastery and returned to St. Petersburg under the patronage of the Empress. She made him the Minister of War and Grigorii Potemkin became the most powerful man in all of Russia.

173

Under Catherine's guidance, Potemkin also became something of an art expert and collector. In 1792, after his death, Catherine repossessed his beautiful Tavrichesky Palace along with its furniture and paintings. The art collection was transferred to the Hermitage.

* * * *

Catherine the Great's influence on cultural life in Russia was tremendous and it became quite fashionable for Russian nobility to start collections of their own. Among those who collected Western art were the Golitsins, Stroganovs, Shuvalovs, Demidovs and Beloselskys. Their homes became private museums. One could not be considered an aristocrat without speaking French or having a display of Dutch and Flemish paintings on the walls of one's home.

The Russian nobles also gave numerous literary and musical salons that were simply the "talk of the town." The satirist Dimitrii Ivanovich Fonvisin wrote extensively about such soirees and of the people who gave them. Mitrofanushka, the hero in Fonvisin's play Nedorosl, became a common nickname for laziness and stupidity. And Fonvisin's statement that geography is not a science for the nobility to know; a horse carrier will take them whereever they want to go, became a famous proverb.

What moved Fonvisin to collect art is not known. Maybe his friendship with Count Orlov influenced him. Or perhaps during his readings for Russian nobility, he too became enamored of Western art. In 1777–1787 he traveled to Holland, France, Germany, Poland and Italy, where he enhanced his collection immensely.

During the reign of Catherine, Russia became the newest state in the world in art collecting. According to an inventory dated 1797, the Hermitage Gallery contained 3,993 paintings, 7,000 drawings, 79,784 engravings, 38,000 books and 10,000 engraved stones. Unfortunately, toward the end of her reign, Catherine's revenues were at 20 million roubles and her expenditures were over 80 million roubles — mainly because of the costly war with Turkey. The art-buying frenzy had to stop.

Although the collections were cataloged later on by Labensky, I realized that many lists of the paintings purchased by Catherine were either unavailable or lost. Numerous paintings, originally part of Catherine's collection, cannot be traced anymore.

From Paul to Alexander I

When Catherine died from a massive stroke in 1796, her son and heir lived for fear of his life in the Michailovsky Palace near St. Petersburg. Paul was quite knowledgeable about art and was keen to adorn his ugly palace with paintings and art objects mostly acquired from the Tavrichesky Palace, once owned by his mother's most famous lover, Potemkin.

Paul also placed some of his paintings in the Pavlovsky Palace, the construction of which began in 1780 and was completed in 1825. Part of the collection included Luca Giordano's *Expulsion from Paradise*, Rubens' *Lamentation for the Dead Christ*, as well as paintings by Ter Borch, Van Ostade, Jan Van Goyen and other Flemish masters. Paul himself acquired Rubens' *The Union of Water and Earth* and Fragonard's *Farmer's Children*. He was also responsible for organizing the inventory of paintings at the Hermitage.

The thick brick walls of the Michailovsky Palace did not save Paul from assassination. Death overtook him in his bed chamber when a group of conspirators, fed up with the half-mad Tsar, assassinated him. Paul's minister, Count Peter Pahlen, and the officers of Semenovsky Regiment were involved in the conspiracy. Paul's son and heir, Alexander, was nineteen-years-old at that time. He had been told of the conspiracy but did not intervene to save his father's life.

175

Alexander was born in 1777 and was the oldest child of Paul and Maria Fedorovna, the Princess of Wurtenberg. At the time of his birth his grandmother, Catherine the Great, was under the influence of the French philosophers and writers, such as Diderot, Voltaire, Montesquieu, and Rousseau. She took it upon herself to raise her first grandchild follwing the principles of nature and the laws of reason. The Tsarina also imposed a Spartan regime on her grandson. This vigorous upbringing may have helped prepare Alexander for the military campaigns against Napoleon. Catherine was undoubtedly disheartened by the limited capabilities of her own son and was possibly grooming Alexander for the throne.

Two educators, La Harpe, a Swiss, and Michael Nikitich Muraviev, a Russian, were Alexander's tutors. Alexander acquired a real interest in the arts and he converted the Hermitage from a private gallery into a museum. He also took part in buying art. His first purchase was Caravaggio's *Young Man with a Lute,* still considered the pride of the Hermitage collection.

The Hermitage collection was significantly enriched when Alexander visited Empress Josephine in her Palace *Malmaison* in 1815. The palace, apart from its beautiful surroundings, housed a tremendous collection, most of which had been confiscated under Napoleon's orders — stolen from museums, galleries and private collections in those lands conquered by the Grand Army. In 1796, after Napoleon's victory in Italy, he sent home paintings by Correggio, Michelangelo, Leonardo, Titian, Raphael, and Veronese. After the victory at Jena, the French General Lagrange sent Josephine forty-eight paintings hidden in Germany, belonging to the elector of Hesse-Cassel. Among those paintings was one Rembrandt and four small paintings by Claude Gelee (Lorrain). Giovanni Bellini, Andrea del Sarto, Giorgione, Perugino, Poussin, Greuze and many sculptures including those of the fashionable Canova could also be found in the Palace of Malmaison.

Alexander remained friends with Josephine until her death. He also remained close to her children, Eugène de Beauharnais and Hortense Bonaparte, the ex-queen of Holland and mother of the future Napoleon III. These friendships continued until Eugène's death in 1824. Unfortunately, their correspondence was sold at an auction in Paris in 1930 to different buyers and is now, for the most part, lost.

In 1815, when a campaign was started to return the Malmaison treasures to their legitimate owners, Josephine's daughter, Hortense, quickly managed to sell thirty-eight paintings and four Canova sculptures to Alexander for 940,000 francs. When the news about Alexander's purchase reached French official circles, a delegation went to the Russian Tsar asking him to return the art treasures. The Tsar agreed to return the paintings as long as he was reimbursed, but the French delegation refused to negotiate under such terms. The paintings remained in Russia.

Fourteen years later, Tsar Nicholas bought, for 280,000 francs, thirty more paintings that Hortense Bonaparte had inherited from her mother. Eugène de Beauharnais probably received half of his mother's collection. Among the paintings were three Van Dycks: a portrait of Charles I, and two portraits of his wife and children, priced at 15,000 francs each. The fate of these three portraits is not known at the present time.

During the reign of Alexander I, an English painter, George Dawe, came to Russia. He was a prolific worker who exhibited 150 of his paintings at the Imperial Academy of Arts. His portraits of the Tsar's sister, Duchess Maria Pavlovna, Count Volkonsky, and of the Russian heroes of the War of 1812 are still considered to be some of the Hermitage's best. Dawe met with great success in Russia and one of his admirers was Alexander Pushkin who wrote a poem, *To Dawe, Esq.* Dawe, in turn, made a drawing of the poet which, unfortunately, is now lost. Dawe's art supposedly inspired Pushkin to compose some of his most famous poems such as *Portrait* and *Commander*.

177

It was also known that Dawe became involved in the *Reynolds Affair*. Catherine the Great ordered three paintings by Sir Joshua Reynolds for the Hermitage. Among those was the famous *Infant Hercules Strangling Serpents*. Reynolds was supposed to have been paid for the painting and in addition, the grateful Empress sent him a cameo box with her portrait on the cover. But neither her gift nor the payment reached Reynolds during his lifetime. Reynolds' agents were successful in obtaining some money from the Russian Court only after his death.

Dawe knew that Reynolds had never received payment for his painting. In a moment of irony, Dawe asked the royal court if they would pay him with his compatriot's painting instead of with cash. Dawe assumed that the painting held little value for Russia. The Russians thought otherwise. The Hermitage custodian, Labensky, not only valued the painting itself, but also described it as an allegory of Russia at the time of Catherine the Great. The painting remained in the Hermitage.

Private collections also flourished in Russia during Alexander's reign. Count V. Trubetskoi and A. Korsakov both had noteworthy collections. Private collectors, such as Count Besborosko, Shuvalov, and Stroganov, usually made their acquisitions outside Russia. And everyone had their own tactic of buying art. For example, Count Besborodko purchased his art objects in a rather indiscriminate fashion, letting the members of the Academy of Arts select the paintings for him — whereas Stroganov bought every piece himself.

Alexander's Mysterious Death

In 1927, *The Mystery of the Emperor* was published in Paris and dedicated to Grand Duke Georgii Nicholaevich Leuchtenberg. It was based on the mysterious death, or disappearance, of Emperor Alexander I.

Alexander I, the favorite of his grandmother, Catherine the Great, was disliked and often humiliated by his father, Paul. When the conspirators told Alexander that they planned to assassinate his father, the boy made no attempt to inform his father that his life was in jeopardy. The murder took place on March 11th, 1801 and left Alexander with haunting memories of this crime. This event, and the enormous task of defending his country against Napoleon's invasion, may have helped transform Alexander into a deeply religious mystic after 1812.

Alexander's strange behavior provoked loose talk concerning his state of mind — and the crown was becoming a burden to him. He began to express a desire to abdicate.

On September 1, 1825, Alexander left St. Petersburg for Taganrog in Crimea. He explained his prolonged stay there as being necessary for his sick wife, who needed a 'change of air.' In October he wrote a letter to Count Volkonsky saying "I will move soon to Crimea and will live as a common person," and on December 1, 1825, he supposedly died in Taganrog. But did he die? A few days before Alexander's supposed death, a courier carrying dispatches from St. Petersburg to Taganrog died from pneumonia. It is rumored that the Tsar ordered the courier's body to be placed in a coffin and have it recognized as his own. Alexander then had himself carried out in a bath tub to the British Ambassador's yacht, anchored at Taganrog. Shortly thereafter, the Empress died on her way from Taganrog to St. Petersburg and it was impossible to find out whether she was included in Alexander's scheme.

The news concerning Alexander's death reached St. Petersburg only two weeks after the event. At the funeral, the Emperor's coffin was not opened for the general public — only for the family members. The courier's relatives were certain that their relative had been buried instead of the Emperor. The courier's widow received a rather large pension from the Tsar for the rest of her life.

Years later, there appeared in Siberia near the city of Tomsk, a monk called Feodor Kuzmich. His appearance dramatically resembled that of Alexander I. Kuzmich was extremely popular among the Siberian inhabitants and his reputation as a holy man spread far. When the future Tsar Alexander II became engaged to the Duchess Maria of Hessen, he and his bride traveled all the way to Siberia to visit Kuzmich. They wanted to be blessed by him. When Kuzmich died in 1862, a tombstone was placed on his grave by the order of the Tsar.

The mystery of Alexander's death deepened in 1926, when Alexander's coffin was opened in the Peter and Paul Fortress and found to be empty. Research concerning these strange events is hampered even further by the fact that all documents having to do with the death of Alexander I were carefully destroyed by members of the Tsar family. The log on the English Ambassador's yacht was made available in 1960 but it hasn't thrown any additional light on the peculiar circumstances surrounding Alexander's death or disappearance.

Nicholas I, Art Destroyer and Collector

When I think about Nicholas I, it is difficult for me to decide if this Tsar had any redeeming qualities. His taste, thought and behavior reveal a militaristic personality. His favorite form of entertainment, according to Countess Volkonsky, was to play the drum.

Contemporaries described Nicholas I as a man of strict morals (although he had a mistress) and of narrow mind, but with a wide range of fulfillment. He was inflexible in his quest for power and never doubted that he was right. He knew what he wanted but he always wanted too much. He tried to adopt non-Russian ideas to Russian reality and he considered himself an expert in everything. He was a true autocrat.

Nicholas' reign began during the rebellion of the Decembrists, which he cruelly suppressed. He executed most of the conspirators and he held a mock execution for the others, such as Dostoyevsky, whom Nicholas ultimately exiled to Siberia. Russian literature flourished during Nicholas' reign but two of the greatest luminaries, Pushkin and Lermontov, perished tragically at an early age. In a poem Lermontov wrote after Pushkin's death, the Tsar and his Count were blamed for the death of the greatest Russian poet.

I am perplexed by Nicholas' attitude towards art. It is clear that he appreciated good art but unfortunately, because of his rotten character, he treated it in the same arbitrary fashion as he treated everything else. Nicholas was more of an art destroyer than a patron.

Nicholas I was determined to remove everything that reminded him of his grandmother's immoral past. The numerous portraits depicting Catherine the Great's lovers were all banished from the Palace, returned to the lover's descendants or, preferably, destroyed. Fortunately, most of these paintings were preserved, away from the Tsar's sight, and ultimately returned to the collection at the time of Alexander III. Nicholas also ordered the melting of Catherine's priceless silverware, and the famous china sets *Ekaterininski* and *Kharkovski* belonging to Orlov vanished from the palace. The destruction of such priceless art can only be explained as a pathological prudishness. Nicholas hated his grandmother, whom he could scarcely remember, because he was ashamed of her amorous past.

Nicholas was indignant of anything that reminded him of the Decembrists. He ordered that all portraits depicting Decembrists, including the heroes of the Napoleonic War, be removed from the Hermitage. Fortunately enough, these paintings were hidden away in the Hermitage storage room and in 1903 they were exhibited again.

Sometimes Nicholas' reason for wanting a piece destroyed was based on mere capricious whim. When a statue of Voltaire caught his eye, Nicholas is known to have said, "Destroy this monkey!" and the "monkey," a work by Houdon, was removed from the gallery. There was a danger that the statue would have perished forever if not for the intervention of Count Andrei Shuvalov, who ordered its secret placement in the basement of Tavrichesky Palace. Only many years later was the beautiful statue of Voltaire returned to the Hermitage.

In 1830, the Poles revolted against the Russian occupation and it took most of Nicholas' army to crush them. From then on his hatred of Poles and anything Polish reached pathologic proportions.

Almost every year after 1830, Nicholas would expropriate estates and palaces of Polish nobility and confiscate the art and decorative furniture found in their homes. Once these objects were confiscated, they were usually destroyed. In 1832, for example, a collection of paintings which had arrived from Grodno and belonged to the Polish Count, Eustachy Sapieha, was destroyed by order of the Tsar. And in 1834, when a large crate of paintings was delivered to St. Petersburg from Warsaw, the Tsar ordered all those paintings that reminded him of Poland, whether they were landscapes or portraits of Polish nobility, to be burned. Only one portrait from this entire collection — that of the famous Polish patriot, Julian Nemtsevich — escaped destruction. This portrait was painted by the Polish artist, Brodovski, the pupil of David. Vasili Zhukovsky, the Tsar's favorite poet, pleaded with Nicholas not to destroy it. The rest of the collection was burned.

When such paintings weren't destroyed, Nicholas would sell them, pricing the paintings himself. Lampi's portrait of Count Sapieha was evaluated as being worth 1 rouble; Vigee-Lebrun's portrait of Countess Sapieha dancing with a tambourine was valued at 5 roubles. Some portraits were priced as low as 25 kopecs. Not all of this work sold however, and during Alexander II's regime, they were returned to their rightful owners.

Perhaps the most atrocious act Nicholas committed in connection with the Hermitage collection was ordering a massive sale of invaluable paintings purely because he did not like them. He knew from the catalogues compiled by Ernest Minich for Catherine that these pieces were of priceless value — but a total of 1,219 canvases were exhibited for the last time at the Winter Palace and a decree for their disposal was issued on August 31, 1853.

Included in this collection were artists such as Guido Reni, Annibale Carracci, Carlo Dolci, David Teniers, Van Dyck, Rubens, Giorgone, Van Ostade, Henrich van Baalen, Caravaggio, Veronese, Angelica Kauffmann, Rembrandt, Tintoretto, two paintings by Lucas van Leyden and many others. After the paintings were removed from the Tsar's Palace in January 1854, they were stored in the Tavrichesky Palace until the late fall of 1856. Because of unsatisfactory storage conditions, many paintings were ruined. The art dealer, Prevo, offered to auction these paintings and the auction was well-advertised in three languages: Russian, French and German.

The paintings sold for a total of 23,956 roubles and 25 kopecs. After expenses were deducted, only 16,447 roubles 30 kopecs were left. In other words, each canvass was sold for an average price of 14 roubles.

Many of these paintings found their way back to Europe and were bought by Chevlier Meazza. Count Andrei Pavlovich Shuvalov purchased another bronze statue of Voltaire by Houdon for which, in 1855, Count Morin offered him 50,000 francs. Kaufmann purchased two canvasses by Lucas van Leyden for 30 roubles. At the time of Alexander II, these two paintings were brought back to the Hermitage for 8,000 roubles.

For no reason at all Nicholas considered himself an art connoisseur but behaved in the same stubborn, autocratic manner that he did in other spheres of his interests. He went to the Hermitage every day between one and two in the afternoon, always accompanied by the Hermitage curator. During his walks through the museum, he used to express his opinions about the origin of various paintings in the most arbitrary manner. If he decided that a painting belonged to one or another school of art, nothing could change his opinion.

"This is Flemish", he would say to Bruni, the art curator.

"Your Majesty, I think..."

"No, no, Bruni. Don't even argue. This is Flemish."

Nicholas thought the Hermitage had too many works of Dutch and Flemish art and not enough Italian or Spanish. He refused, however, to buy several Goyas from the collection of Manuel De Godoy, the Minister of Charles IV of Spain, because he did not like Goya. (He had a weakness for paintings depicting battle scenes as did a much later monarch, Kaiser Wilhelm II of Germany.) Nicholas I, however, did approve the purchase of five Titians, among them the beautiful *Mary Magdalene* and *Virgin and the Child*. In 1845 the Russian ambassador in Vienna, Tatishchev, bequeathed his small, exquisite collection to the Tsar. It contained the Van Eyck diptych *The Crucifixion* and *The Last Judgment*.

In an ironic twist of fate, one of the best collections fell into Nicholas' hands by chance. This was the collection of his brother-in-law, King William II of Netherlands. In order to reconstruct this story I have to return to Paul I and his family.

The youngest daughter of Paul I (he had 10 children), Anna, was born in 1795 two years before her father's coronation. She was described by her contemporaries as "tall and well-built, with beautiful eyes; although not a beauty, her eyes were full of kindness." She was well-educated, as was almost every member of the Romanov dynasty, and had a better education than many members of the royal families in Europe. She was especially close to her elder brother, Nicholas, the future Emperor, and Nicholas was always very generous towards his sister — giving her valuable gifts, supporting her financially, and never refusing her requests. This relationship persisted throughout their lifetimes.

Anna was only fifteen when Napoleon asked for her hand, after his divorce from Josephine. Napoleon was looking for the bride of royal blood to bear for him an heir to the throne. But Paul's widow, Maria Fedorovna, and her brother Emperor Alexander I, did not accept Napoleon's offer. This made Napoleon quite angry but he soon consoled himself by marrying the Austrian Princess Maria-Luisa. In 1816, Anna Pavlovna married William, the Prince of Orange, who was the eldest son of King William I and who in 1840 after the death of his father, became the King of the Netherlands. His reign lasted only nine years. He was a charming, generous and extremely popular king. He and Anna had five children and were a happy couple. From her correspondence with Nicholas, one can conclude that she was devoted to both Russia and the Netherlands and wanted to serve both countries. Her husband loved art and spent time and money collecting paintings. After her husband's death, she inherited 1,500 paintings and his large debts. She was desperate that all the royal real estate would be sold to settle her husband's debts and, therefore, turned to the only person who could help her, her brother, Nicholas. A pathetic letter of Anna to Nicholas is preserved.

"... (the debt) amounts to a total of four and half million florins! It will be necessary to sell all our landed property, estates and houses in the country and therefore my eyes turn to you, dear brother and friend, to ask you under these cruel circumstances to acquire William's gallery of pictures that you set such store on owning and which is already mortgaged to you." Nicholas acted quickly to help his beloved sister and sent his curator, Bruni, to the Netherlands. At the auction, Bruni purchased William's paintings for 173,823 guilders, selecting paintings of only Dutch and Flemish artists. The purchase saved Nicholas'

185

sister from ruin but for the Netherlands it was a tremendous loss. The collection of William II included three Van Dycks: a portrait of Philip le Roy, a portrait of le Roy's wife, and a portrait of Martin Pepin.

The last large collection of paintings purchased by Nicholas was that of the Barbarigo Gallery in Venice in 1850–1854. Nicholas paid 525,000 roubles for the collection. The paintings included sixteenth-century masterpieces by Titian, Veronese and others. Except for two, all the Titians at the Hermitage were acquired through the Barbarigo collection.

In spite of his barbaric attitude towards art, Nicholas must also be considered a patron of the arts. When the Winter Palace burned down in 1837 it was quickly rebuilt, and after the reconstruction, Nicholas I decided to make the Hermitage a public museum. In 1849 a new catalogue of 4,500 pieces was compiled for the Tsar by the curators — and on February 5, 1852 the Hermitage opened its doors to the public.

In 1849 another important event took place in the artistic life of Russia. Privately-owned art works were collected for the first time at the Imperial Academy of Arts in St. Petersburg. The exhibition, containing 400 items of Russian and Western art, was opened to the public for two weeks. Herzog Maximilian von Leuchtenberg initiated two more exhibitions opened to the public of privately owned art — one in 1851 and the other ten years later.

The Leuchtenberg Collections

Nicholas's daughter, Grand Duchess Maria Nicholaevna, and her husband, Herzog Maximilian Leuchtenberg, possessed one of the best art collections in St. Petersburg. Maximilian's father, Eugène de Beauharnais, started the art collection in Napoleonic times when he was Viceroy of Italy. Later, living in Bavaria, he continued to add to his collection. The contents of his archives lists paintings bought for him by his agents in France and Italy. After his death, his eldest son, Augustus, inherited his collection, but after Augustus' premature death, the paintings came into the possession of his younger brother, Maximilian Leuchtenberg. The catalogs of the Leuchtenberg collection were published in Munich. The catalogs list such artists as Vanloo, David, Bellini, Reni, Annibale Carracci, Bernardino Luini (a pupil of Leonardo), Raphael, Titian, Veronese, Correggio, Carlo Dolci, Lorenzo Lotto, Andrea del Sarto, Leonardo Da Vinci, Poussin, Canaletto, Velasquez, Murillo, Rubens, Holbein, Teniers, Van Ostade, Ruysdael, Steen and Van Dyck.

Maria Nicholaevna had a great passion for art and was an avid art collector. Almost every day she visited auction houses, bookstores or other places where she might find paintings to exhibit in her beautiful palace. In 1852, after the death of her husband, she was made the President of the Imperial Academy of Arts in St. Petersburg. In addition to her own collection, she also inherited her husband's, which had been transferred from Münich to St. Petersburg and placed in the Marinsky Palace. How many paintings of the Beauharnais collection reached St. Petersburg is not known.

Maria Nicholaevna had another collection of paintings in Florence, Italy where she often lived with her second husband. The Hermitage curator, Liphart, compiled the catalog of her Florence paintings but I could not find it.

After the death of Grand Duchess Maria in 1876, her eldest son and heir, Nicholai Maximilianovich Leuchtenberg, had to sell the Marinsky Palace. In 1884, he placed her collection of 254 paintings and five sculptures in the Imperial Academy of Arts where they were exhibited until the Russian revolution. In 1884 a catalog of the Leuchtenberg collection was published by the Academy of Arts, but again, I had no access to it.

187

Nicholas inherited the major part of the collection. The other part was divided between other children and grandchildren of Maria Nicholaevna, such as Count Sheremetiev, Princess Kotchoubey, Count von Daehn, Princess Eugenia Maximilianovna Von Oldenburg and Maria Maximilianovna von Baden. After the death of Nicholai Maximilianovich, part of his treasures were divided between his sons, Nicholai Nicholaevich, who inherited mostly French and Flemish schools of art, and Georgii Nicholaevich, who received the Italian paintings.

Several art magazines published in the nineteenth century reported that various members of the Leuchtenberg family sold their paintings from time to time. In 1917, on the order of Kerensky's government, part of the collection exhibited in the Imperial Academy of Arts in St. Petersburg was sent to the Hermitage and the other part was transferred to Moscow. The paintings were kept in crates until the time of the revolution and because of poor storage conditions, several were damaged. After the revolution, some of the paintings were placed in the Pushkin Museum of Art in Moscow and some were sent mysteriously abroad to Germany and Switzerland.

It is impossible to obtain definitive information concerning the fate of the various paintings from the Leuchtenberg collection, dispersed in Russia and abroad.

Other Private Collections

Count Yusupoff's collection is one of the most interesting private collections of that time. Yusupoff is known to have participated in Rasputin's murder and was exiled by Nicholas II. Part of his collection was taken to the United States by Prince Felix Yusupoff before the revolution, and the other part of the collection went to the Hermitage after the revolution.

Pavel and Grigorii Stroganov's collection is also well known. Part of the collection was kept in their beautiful palace on Nevsky Prospect, designed by Rastrelli in St. Petersburg. The other part was kept in Rome where Grigorii Stroganov spent the second half of his life. Grigorii died in 1910 in Italy and his collection was sold in Paris the next year. Pavel Stroganov died in 1912. The Italian estate of the Stroganov's was sold at auction by Christies after World War II. Another part of their collection was sold in Germany in 1931 by the Rudolf Lepke Auction House.

The other well-known pre-Revolution collection was that of Count Gorchakov. It contained works of Flemish and Dutch painters of the nineteenth century. N.A. Kushelev-Bezborodko is still another respected collector. He inherited a large number of paintings from a relative who was a contemporary of Catherine the Great. This collection was given to the Imperial Academy of Arts in 1862 after the early death of its owner. The famous collection of the well-known Russian geographer, Peter Semenov-Tianshansky, of mostly Dutch and Flemish art, was donated to the Hermitage.

The palace of Princess Kotchoubey, who inherited the art work of her grandmother, Grand Duchess Maria Nicholaevna, was located on the banks of the Neva River and was filled with art: furniture, tapestries, decorative statues, china, and, of course, paintings. Among those was a miniature portrait of Princess Augusta. There also was a portrait of Catherine I and a wax figure of Paul I that is signed by the sculptor, Leberecht. The collection of paintings included: *Pieta* by Perugino; *Image of Jesus Christ* by the so-called "Spanish Raphael," Juan Juanes; landscapes by David Teniers; two landscapes attributed to Jacob Ruysdael; portraits by J.B. Greuze; and the portrait of Alexander de Beauharnais by the French artist M.J. Vien, David's teacher. The Kotchoubey Palace was one of the most beautiful palaces in St. Petersburg.

Under the reign of Alexander II, the Hermitage became a large and important institution. A new catalog was published and the pictures were hung according to the various schools they represented. In 1866 the curator of the Hermitage, Gedeonov, bought Leonardo Da Vinci's beautiful *Madonna Litta* for 100,000 francs from the Duke of Litta in Milan. Alexander Benois, a well-known Russian artist and collector, sold another Leonardo da Vinci to the Hermitage, the *Madonna Benois.* Both of these paintings are still in the Hermitage collection. Gedeonov also purchased a small *Madonna* by Raphael and another early work of this master from Count Conestabile in Perugia, Italy.

After Alexander II's murder the new Emperor, Alexander III, continued to purchase paintings for the Hermitage. S.S. Gedeonov's successor, A.A. Vasilchikov, bought a magnificent Fra Angelico, *Virgin and a Child,* along with his *St. Dominic* and *St. Aquinas* that had been painted for the Convent of San Domenico in Fiesole. Curators of the Hermitage also made some important purchases such as Guardi's *View of Venice* and the charming composition of Fragonard's *Stolen Kiss,* once owned by King Stanislaw August Poniatowski of Poland. Vasilchikov was an able diplomat who persuaded Alexander III to transfer several masterpieces from various Imperial Palaces to the Hermitage. These included Rembrandt's *David Parting from Jonathan,* which had been in Monplaisir, and Tiepolo's *Maecenas Presenting the Arts to Augustus,* formerly in Gatchina.

At this time, the Hermitage obtained seventy-three paintings from the remarkable collection of Count Golitsin, the descendant of the Ambassador to France at the time of Catherine II.

The End of the Empire

Alexander III died in November 1894 at the Crimean Palace in Livadia. Ten days after Alexander's funeral, his son, Nicholas, married Alix, the German Princess of Hesse. Alix (Alexandra) was known as "the funeral bride." Some were convinced that she was the one who had brought misfortune to the country. Russia was rapidly approaching catastrophe. With the murder of Nicholas II and his family the purchase of art came to its end.

In 1908, the Russian art magazine *Starye Gody* tried to organize an exhibition of various private collections. The exhibition never opened but it was known that among the paintings which were to have been shown were nine Italian paintings from the Grand Duchess Maria Nicholaevna's collection from her villa "Quarto" in Florence.

At the end of the nineteenth century and the beginning of the twentieth, some private collections were put up for sale but according to law, they had to be offered to the Hermitage first. These purchases enabled the Hermitage to double the number of its art works to over 8,000 paintings, over 40,000 drawings and half a million engravings.

At the time, it was popular for private collections to exhibit at the Hermitage. An exhibition which was opened on April 30, 1913 was a tremendous success. It represented the art work from the private collection's of S.V. von Daehm and S.V. Sheremetiev. They had both inherited their collections from their grandmother, Grand Duchess Maria Nicholaevna. Included in their collections were paintings by Sandro Botticelli, Tiepolo, and Titian. The Flemish school was represented by six paintings and the Dutch by five; among those was an early portrait of Rembrandt's mother. There was also a beautiful portrait of Count Georgii Stroganov painted by Vigee-Lebrun. It was the lats big exhibition before the revolution.

Although some art historians claim that Russian private art collections were sold abroad even before the Russian revolution, it was actually the new Soviet government that was most instrumental in the massive sale of Russian art works. The Soviet government authorized at least three trade organizations to dispose of Russian art abroad. The most active of these was the Allied American Corporation of the Hammer family. The Hammer brothers greatly helped the Soviet government to exchange *objets d'art* for hard currency. They also bought tons of Russian Tsarist jewelry and sold it through American department stores at very low prices.

Another major buyer was the American collector, Andrew Mellon. He wrote in one of his letters that the purchase in 1930–1931 of twenty-one masterpieces from the Hermitage collection was the turning point in his passion for art. The walls of Andrew Mellon's house in Pittsburgh were covered with paintings and his house attracted a large number of visitors and art lovers. On the walls of his living room were Van Eyck's *The Annunciation* which he bought for $502,899; Raphael's *Madonna Alba* which was bought in 1836 by Nicholas I and sold to Mellon for 1 million dollars in 1931; Titian's *Venus with a Mirror;* and Poussin's *Birth of Venus.* These paintings were subsequently donated by Mellon to the National Gallery of Art in Washington except for *Birth of Venus* which is now in Philadelphia's art museum.

Each purchase of art work from Russia became a sensation in the United States and the purchase of *Madonna Alba* made the front page of *The New York Times.* Russian art was also sold by the Soviet government at auctions in Berlin and Leipzig. Attempts to sell part of the Stroganov collection at the Rudolf Lepke Auction House in Berlin in 1931 ended in a scandal; prices offered at the auction were low and various relatives of Stroganov living outside Russia made claims for the ownership of the paintings. It is doubtful if they would have won their case since a similar suit — in which Princess Paley, the widow of the murdered Grand Duke Pavel, also wanted to have the paintings she once owned returned to her — ended in dismissal. Some of

the Hermitage collections were decimated; the one originally owned by Peter Semenov-Tianshkansky, which consisted
of 700 Flemish and Dutch paintings, was reduced to thirty.

This massive art auction continued for the next six years
and sporadic sales continued until 1936, when Stalin put an
end to the sale of Russian art work abroad. It is doubtful
whether the hard currency gained by these sales justified
the massive exodus of priceless art objects from Russia.
In any case, the fact that the dispersal of art was often
kept secret and that very few records were maintained by
the Soviet government, makes it impossible to trace exactly
which paintings were sold when. Except for the relatively
few pictures I've mentioned in this treatise.

This was the last chapter of the manuscript by W.S.S.
I believe that his investigation of the fate of the paintings
sold by the Soviet government landed him in trouble and
ultimately in the gulag.

Grave of Grand Dutchess Anastasia (1901–1984)

Chapter 10

A Party and Another Mystery

> They learn in sufferings
> what they teach in songs.
> — Shelley

I gave my report to Sir Alexander documenting why I was unable to trace the provenance of the Charles I portrait. According to Mr. Levinberg and my dissident friend, the illicit sale of Western paintings in Russia during Stalin's reign prevented me, or anyone, from ever tracking down who sold the portrait and when it was done. I knew that Sir Alex would be disappointed with my findings, but there was nothing I could do. Sometimes we search for wisdom only to realize that the venture has been futile. As my father would have said, sometimes the search itself has to be enough. What upset me most, however, was not my inconclusive report about the painting, but that I still had no clue to the mysterious disappearance of 'Mr. Berg' and, more importantly, where I could find Anastasia. After a long discussion with my boss about the results of my trip, and another case which demanded more time and work, I decided to take a few days off to put my thoughts together and get some rest. I left London for a quiet suburban "dacha", not letting anyone know where I was going or when to expect me back. The only person I called was Tom, but still no one answered the phone. I postponed my meeting with Tom until my return.

Coming back to London, I felt as if nothing had changed while I was away. I was met with the usual fog and drizzle. The colors were muted, the details subservient to my mood. It was only four o'clock in the afternoon when I reached my apartment. The place looked like an abandoned child, dirty and sad. I opened the curtains but it did not brighten the room.

When I turned the light on, the first thing that caught my eyes was the telephone and I knew exactly what I needed to do next — to call Tom. After I dialed, the answering machine clicked on, reminding me that I had reached the apartment of Tom Harlow and asking to leave a message. I decided to call him back later that evening as I proceeded on with my routine unpacking.

After a much needed nap and dinner alone at the corner restaurant, I opened my mail. There was a letter from Christina inviting me to her birthday party the following evening. She ended the note by saying how much she missed me and begged me to come.

"What a strange girl she is," I thought. "First, she neglected me and left with Tom; now she has missed me and wants to see me again."

I decided to see her tomorrow as she asked — and perhaps, Tom, — and eventually find out what happened while I was away.

Before Christina's party, I bought her a box of chocolate and three pink roses. I knew she disliked fresh flowers because she hated to see them die, but the color reminded me of her. My new grey suit matched my hair, and I felt I looked irresistible.

Picking up the flowers and the box of candies, I locked the door and headed out to my car with a splitting headache.

Admittedly, my personal life was never peaceful like lives of ordinary people of my age, I thought on my way to Christina. Many of my friends had already settled down, had a respectable house, a wife and at least two children. But then, some of my supposedly "happily married" friends were asking me for advice on how to solve their marital problems. Did they seek my help because I was, as a detective, a solver of puzzles? I often thought that I should one day open a marriage counseling agency to teach these men and women how to get away from "married life" problems and keep their marriages alive. At least after ten years of marriage, they should not be idealistic and should admit that they cheated on each other, instead of pretending they could be in love. Games, games, games... and lies, constant lies.

Oscar Wilde wrote that every married man lives as a bachelor and every bachelor as a married man. Perhaps he was right. I also remembered a verse written by my favorite poet, Oliver Goldsmith:

When lovely woman stoops to folly,
And finds too late that men betray,
What charm can soothe her melancholy?
What art can wash his guilt away?

Goldsmith lived in the middle of the eighteenth century — and nothing changed since then.

Who knows what love is anyway, or how long it can last? Ivan Turgenev was in love his whole life with a famous opera singer, Pauline Viardo. He followed her everywhere, never married, and was treated like a household pet rather than a lover. In one of his stories, he wrote that love is a disease, an incurable madness. Madness? Perhaps, yes, that could describe love. Or could love be just a momentary state that holds your mind and body, disappearing as soon as your partner leaves?

With these thoughts on love, I imagined Anastasia... could I still be in love? The case with Anastasia was different, I thought. She was shrewd enough to disappear from my life when I desperately wanted her. Now I realized that her move was right. We were both left with beautiful memories.

When the first burst of passion dies, lovers awake to smoldering ashes. It is often hard to say goodbye, but harder still to remain together. We seem to forget pain, once recovered, and fall in love again.

If God created the nature of human beings to love and to be loved, then are we supposed to learn from this cyclic pattern? Initially, love is pleasurable, even euphoric at times, but it ultimately turns to suffering and loss. Yet, from this darker side of the emotion, we need to suffer, to commiserate our losses.

Upon hearing someone blissfully say they are "in love", I pity these poor souls. Disappointment is bound to snatch away their happiness. Some have gone to the extreme reaction of suicide to escape seeing their lovers gazing at someone else.

In my love affairs, I have always stopped myself at the crucial brink between casual companionship and committed relationship. Tom, and I both work by this trusted method. And yet, I am not sure who loses more in the game of love — my married friends or me. Loneliness is a haunting parameter.

Others have often called me a cynic, but they do not realize I take this criticism as a compliment. Cynicism, in my opinion, knows the true value of things, not their overestimation; it provides my protective, solid defense against a cruel world of ruthless individuals. Those poor souls who trust innocently open their hearts to be easily hurt by the aggressive weapons of jealousy, fear and greed. Although my core is well-barricaded, it still leaks in my own pain and

198

swells with empathy for my closest friends, now especially for Tom.

"Friendship is a disinterested commerce between equals; love, an abject intercourse between tyrants and slaves..." who said that? I guessed again at my favorite, Oliver Goldsmith. If Goldsmith was still alive, we would certainly forge a great friendship out of similar thoughts.

Leaving my thoughts on love and friendship, I parked my car, approached Christina's apartment, and prepared for the party atmosphere. Smiling at the door, Christina embraced me passionately.

"I am so happy, Jerry, that you came! I was not sure if you had returned to London. I tried to call you many times but never got an answer... please stay after the party. We need to talk. It is important, Jerry." She stretched the words in her usual manner, but I noticed an underlying nervousness quivering beneath this.

Christina moved in front of me into the apartment, turning to look over her shoulder, inviting me to follow her. I realized how attractive she was in a low cut, short black dress with silver high-heeled shoes, her long, dark, curly hair covering her neck.

The room was crowded with people I did not know. First glancing around the main room, I noticed two older, quarrelsome men in a heated debate. Nearby, two young women lounging on a sofa appeared already well-intoxicated. In the corner of the room, a very striking man was passionately kissing someone, behind two men with long hair dancing the tango... or was one of those dancers a woman?

I momentarily closed my eyes to block out what looked like a surrealistic painting. The room was filled with smoke, and I began to sneeze. Laughing, Christina turned to me. Her laughter seemed different that night, bitter, not gay and lighthearted. As I touched her hand, she stopped laughing and looked at me seriously.

199

"We need to talk," she repeated again, and disappeared to another room.

Puzzled by the urgency in her voice, I was touched with pity for her stricken emotions. Looking in the direction she had gone, I caught my reflection in a mirror near the doorway. Through the smoke, I too looked surreal, ghost-like, transfixed with roses and candies.

Breaking from the trance with my ghastly reflection, I hurried after Christina, intent on bestowing my gifts. In the kitchen Christina was chatting with an older lady who had Christina's radiant smile. I introduced myself to her as she snatched the flowers from me. With swift timing, the old lady flippantly tossed the flowers on the table and headed me into another room. I had just met Christina's mother.

"Nothing is more important, young man, nowadays but love. And I am talking about real love — with passion, murders, suicides," she said superiorly, "...I hope you understand what I am talking about, such intense passion."

"Well," I thought, "what am I in for now...?" I kept quiet, not certain of this woman's motives, or that I would agree with them.

Pleased with her captive audience, she continued, "I remember my youth, my happy marriage — well, almost happy marriage. We had to separate when Christina was just two years old. He claimed I was "too boring" to be with for the rest of his life. You do not have to know all of this, young man, but... after all, I was only twenty-four years old. And my tears dried as soon as I met Larry. No, sorry, Jerry. Or was Jerry after James? You see, I've begun to forget the order of it all, but that's not really important at the moment," she paused for a moment, drawing her breath with a sigh, "It's Christina's love for you — that's what is important and now, perhaps your love for her."

With this announcement, she smiled knowingly, but her grisly wrinkles eradicated her attempts to be coquettish.

"Important is not what is important, but important is what is unimportant," I thought to myself, but did not want to confuse the lady. This conversation was beginning to entertain me.

"Do you mean to be speaking to Jerry, or you mean Tom?" I asked with an equally charming, false smile.

She seemed not to care if she addressed the wrong man, stating, "I am forgetting names, young man, but I know Christina is crazy about you, and, it is time for a girl of her age to have a husband. She needs to get married! After that ugly accident, she almost lost her mind...and this, most definitely, is all your fault."

"What you are talking about?" I asked, astonished by this blame. Annoyed with her accusation, I was curious enough about this "accident" to let her continue.

Our téte-a-téte, however, was deterred as a man appeared in the doorway. Moving toward us, he asked, "Am I interrupting anything? It is too hot and smoky in there. Do you mind if I join your conversation?" I recognized him as the man who had been passionately involved with someone in the other room; their lips must have grown tired of each other.

Aggravated by the interruption, Christina's mother crossed her legs nervously and tossed back a stray hair from her face. Her determination to corner me overruled any chance of changing the subject.

Turning to me, her voice very melodious, she embarked again, "My dear, I wanted to talk to you this evening. I just have to know everything about you and Christina.'

"This crazy old woman is impossible!" I thought furiously. "Her only motive was to sell her daughter."

Meanwhile, the man, more curious than surprised, moved closer to her, ready for a long, intimate conversation. On the surface he seemed to be paying attention to her, but his eyes invited me to join the entertainment of mocking her antics. This three-way game was beyond my interest tonight, so I left them to their own game and joined the two older men I first noticed in the other room. Approaching them, I heard them discussing art.

"You are wrong, sir," said one of them. "Real, profound art is based on tragedy. There, strong emotion moves the hand of the artist. The birth of a painting you can compare with a birth of a child. It created through the artist's love and suffering. The painting actually becomes the artist's child. Every new brush stroke transfers energy, part of one's life, the warmth of one's blood, the deepest thoughts and truest feelings — all to the painting, to the child."

The man continued, "The Russian artist Tropinin, who executed the famous portrait of poet Alexander Pushkin, wrote that art is the expression of your feelings, it is in your heart, not in your hand. These are very true and very powerful words. Unfortunately, we now have too many craftsmen — not real artists."

This conversation captivated my attention! I interjected, "Pardon me, but can I join your discussion? Your point of view is extremely interesting, and I agree with you that real art is based on the tragic experiences of the artist. Remember, Shelley said, 'they learn in sufferings what they teach in songs.'"

"But allow me to disagree with you about craftsmanship. Craftsmen have always existed. Techniques have been learned from family members who were also artists. The ability to paint was inherited by sons from their fathers, from one brother to another, to uncles, nephews, and so on."

"Were they all geniuses? No, not all of them; only one, or a selected few, had the gifts of talent and vision beyond craft. The others learned techniques of how to work with brushes and pencils, how to mix colors and interpret shadows, light and dimensions in their paintings and sketches."

"Consider art history — Italian painters for example — Annibale Carracci was the most famous and perhaps the most talented of the Carracci family. Another fine example would be the Bernini family. Remember Raphael's

202

father was also an artist, although Raphael's real teacher was Perudgino — Or the Spaniard, Bartolommeo Carducci, whose youngest brother Vincenzo, was more brilliant than him — Consider the Flemish Bruegels, de Mompers and other families."

"If you examine this theory you could soon cite many other examples of craftsmanship existing at a time when art was not only for the satisfaction of the artist's internal needs, but was also a tool for earning money. Just look at the life of those painters who worked, let's say, for the court — Van Dyck, for example. Could he work completely for his pleasure or did he have to earn a living? Could he put his soul into his work? No, he could not — he was a court painter, and naturally was restricted by the work he was commissioned to do. He was always in a hurry to finish one portrait in order to start another to satisfy his numerous, capricious clients."

One of the men interrupted me, "But at the beginning of his career, I assume he was not like that. His early paintings of landscapes, religious compositions, and some Italian portraits were done with inspiration, not executed so theatrically and decoratively as his later work when he was in England. He was a man of great talent who, under the circumstances, became a craftsman. His English period was productive, but the quality of his work deteriorated. He did not have enough time to absorb himself, and that's why there were repeated backgrounds, dresses and jewelry were repeated on different portraits."

"Are you an art historian?" I asked, assuming by his knowledge I was correct.

"No, I am a frustrated artist, and this friend of mine is a frustrated poet. We have spent our lives trying to achieve something, to compete with others, to climb the steps of success, always looking at our fellow artists and the heights they reached, forgetting the main purpose of our lives — art itself. And now we realize that we have gone nowhere; we pushed our ability in a different direction."

"Art requires your fullest attention, your heart, your intellect, your soul — everything, and if you do not focus on these, you will fail as an artist. Ambition is useful, but in art it does not override attention to your inner vision. You may disagree with my point of view, but I talk from my own experience."

Now the poet turned to me, looking very melancholy, "I am afraid our vision of art is dying. Poetry of this type is also dying. Artists are still searching with determination for new forms to express themselves — to intent on impressing others that they often forget about the content and depth of their work."

"In my opinion, writing poetry focuses on the word and its meaning — managing to imply a lot by writing minimally. Many crucial elements of poetry are now forgotten or ignored. A poem has to have a musical pattern as its background. Poetic expression, profound thought and deeply spiritual emotions are other elements of real poetry. Levels of meaning can be mysteriously indirect — combining these elements is the poet's difficult task."

"I don't think modern poets follow such a pattern. Byron and Shelley, Shakespeare and Keats, Pushkin and Block died and with them, their spirit of poetic expression. True sincerity and wit are replaced by artificial emotions of our 'civilized' society."

"I remember the words of T.S.Eliot," added the artist. "He said that poetry is not a turning loose of emotion or an expression of personality, but an escape from personality. My fear is that poetry is very personal. And, of course, only those who have personality and emotions know what it means to want to escape from these things. Well, it is not that easy to be an artist; it is much easier to be a critic nowadays. They know exactly how it has to be done, but do not have the ability to do it themselves. They can make us famous or they can ruin our art... we all depend on them."

I disagreed and was just beginning to discuss modern art and modern critics when we noticed all the guests had already left. Christina looked at me from across the room, and as I read a questioning message in her eyes I ensured her silently that I would stay. I exchanged phone numbers with my new friends, hoping to meet them again soon.

When everyone left the party, what remained was a mess throughout the house. Christina's mother lingered on, busying herself with cleaning, but unfortunately, the old lady made much more of a mess until Christina asked her to just go home. As the old crow reached for her coat, she slipped me a charming smile and an all-understanding look before slamming the door theatrically behind her.

Finally, we were left alone. Christina led the way to the bedroom, the only place in the house that showed no signs of the party. I followed her in silence. In the intimacy of her bedroom we both felt uncomfortable, as if we were strangers who had just met.

Christina burst into tears that she had feebly tried to hold back. I did not move to comfort her and sat stoically by her, waiting for her crying to end. She could not control her sobs, and sitting there, she looked like a distorted clown with mascara smearing down her cheeks. Feeling pity for her grow in me, I moved closer and took her cold hands in mine. Her body was tense and shaking from the violence of her crying. Covering her shaking knees with my hands, I looked in her eyes, and with this she stopped crying and straightened up as if by a pulled string.

My rational brain seemed unaware of my surging emotions as I reached for her hair, my hand drifting down to her breasts, desire for her body reawakening in me. I undid her dress zipper and pulled it from her shoulders. She did not resist and turned her face to me, and as our lips met, I dimmed the light near her bed. Caught in this moment, we made love passionately, wrapped in the pity and tenderness we felt for each other, knowing that this would be the last time we would be together.

Unaware of how much time had passed, I carefully reached for my clothing heaped on the floor. I did not want to disturb Christina, asleep and exhausted in my arms. Immediately she responded to my movement and opened her eyes.

The room was dark and through the window I saw the moon coming through fog, fighting for its freedom. And to the night I recited:

> On the balcony
> Winds
> Play the reeds
> And the strings
> Of my silence.
>
> As in darkness
> I stand
> Holding night
> In the palm of my hand
> ...and remembrance.
>
> And the sun, coming on
> And the dawn
> Will soon leave
> But pink ash
> Of the moment
>
> And the wind
> (No, not I)
> Will then brush
> From the palm
> Of my hand
> ...all remembrance.

"It is beautiful..." said Christina dreamily. "It must be a woman who wrote it — only a woman can make a poem sound like music. Who is she?"

"Anastasia," I replied, almost whispering her name.

206

"Tell me about her," she asked in the silence of the night.

With some hesitation, I began recounting my memories of Anastasia. I described her as a Russian Princess who once lived in the mysterious Castle of Seeon; how I met her and fell in love; how she disappeared from my life and all I was left with was just... remembrance.

I felt a new urgency to talk about Anastasia, and Christina closely clasped her naked body to mine, resting her head on my shoulder, an attentive listener. I felt after our love-making my words were cruel for Christina to hear, but nothing stopped my flow of emotions and words. I finished my story, wondering what Christina's reaction would be. The darkness of the room was lit by a streak of pale moonlight, and in this I could see her wide-eyed gaze fixed on my face and my story.

"You met her in Berlin, Jerry? You love her — I know you do. You have changed since you came back from Berlin."

After a pause she spoke, "You did not call me for almost a month. I felt abandoned and lonely when I met Tom. We spent a wonderful evening together and I stayed overnight, and since the following day was Saturday, we spent another two days together. You know, Jerry, I did not even feel I had betrayed you. I forgot about everything in the world being with Tom. He knows so much, and he was patient with me, taking me to museums and theatres. You never were, you never really respected me, all you saw was my body. Am I right, Jerry? Tell me, if I am right?"

She got up and turned on the light. In its brightness I saw the beauty of her body, felt the warmth of our love-making still around me — and I knew she was right. Something had shifted between us... Anastasia stood between us... and Tom.

Startled by this thought I exclaimed, "Tom! What about Tom? Why does not he answer the phone? Why is he absent from your birthday party?"

Christina became slightly embarrassed. "He is in Munich attending an art historians congress. I pleaded with him to postpone his trip but he could not. Or, may be, he felt that I still belong to you."

Now it was my turn to be surprised. "Are you in love with Tom?" I felt how banal my question was.

"Am I?" asked Christina. "All I know is that you love the shadow character, and there is no place in your heart for the poor myself. Tom just phoned me from Munich, Jerry. I am flying to join him."

"So, this was our last night stand," I told myself almost regretfully.

I recalled two lines of Pearl Buck's poem: "Yet comes bad day/ I go you stay," but did not repeat them aloud.

Christina's intuition was right. I could not get Anastasia out of my mind. Kissing Christina's cheek, I covered her cold shoulders with her gown and promised to call her as soon as I could.

In the solitude of my car, I was overwhelmed by the events of the evening and laughter was my only response. It was inappropriate but uncontrollable. What an interwoven mess! Drama, a love triangle, disappearances and I, Inspector of Scotland Yard, was part of it all — it was my personal life! How unrealistic life is — surrealism — just as I felt at the party last night. I never liked Dali, but yet he was right on target. I had a new definition of realism.

Chapter 11

Tom Intervenes

Without goodness man
is a busy, mischievous, wretched thing,
no better than a kind of vermin.
— Sir Francis Bacon

When Tom called me, a week later, I was not in any mood to talk to him. I knew he'd want to recount his trip to Munich and would probably, albeit inadvertently, mention the lovely time he'd had with Christina. I could just imagine them visiting the Seeon Castle and walking through the cemetery arm-in-arm, kissing in the dappled sunlight under the large trees surrounding the Leuchtenberg's graves... a scenario I'd rather imagine for Anastasia and myself. Tom, of course, didn't even hear the hesitation in my voice and insisted on coming over immediately.

"Jerry, it is imperative that I see you now," he said. "I have to explain my news in person and it can not wait!"

I thought his behavior somewhat rude, but he was my best friend. I was impressed, even flattered in a way, that he wanted to see me two hours after his plane had landed. If I had been him, I know I would have wanted to spend the time with Christina.

"All right, Tom. All right," I sighed heavily. "If it can't wait, then please come over."

In what seemed like moments later, Tom appeared breathless at my doorstep.

"Jerry!" Tom shouted as his smiled broadened, "Jerry, I must tell you the extraordinary news!" and he embraced me as if I had died and come alive again.

This exuberance could only mean the extreme... "OK," I thought, "so you're trading in the life of a bachelor to tie the knot, huh?"

I really was feeling like a lost failure.

I abridged my thoughts and only asked, "Does it have to do with Christina?"

At this, Tom let out a merry laugh. "Christina?" he exclaimed. "Why? No, not directly... it's you, my friend, I came to talk to."

Tom's vagueness bothered me. I predicted it would take a long story first to reach the "news" that drove him here. Nonetheless, curiosity did have me and I invited him into my flat.

"Jerry, let's have a drink first. I have a long story to tell and I know it will make you thirsty," said Tom, still excited.

Handing my friend a drink, I settled back and gave him my attention.

Tom started, "I arrived in Munich for the symposium on Neo-classical art..." I watched his hands, already twitching in anticipation of the story he would tell.

"The day was dreary and gray, and there was the chill of frost in the air. There was also a north wind, driving pedestrians from the streets. Decaying leaves left a dank odor in the gardens where I had smelled such aromatic flowers in my previous trip. There were few people out that day as I walked alone — just several elderly people tottering along beside their dogs. I was already in low spirits. Christina could not join me immediately. Walking alone in the foul weather, I became depressed and decided

210

that since I had a few more hours to spare before the first meeting, I would cheer myself up by browsing through an art gallery or two."

"Since I was near Kunsthalle, I decided to go there and see their collection of twentieth-century art. The first painting my eyes fell upon was *Seven Tired Men* by Holder. I don't know if you are familiar with this painting — but, in it, seven figures are painted in such way that their posture speaks of their hopeless outlook on life, and without the viewer even seeing their faces. Even if you are not depressed, you become so when looking at this painting. Rarely have I seen a painting that expresses, so pointedly, the hopelessness of the human race."

"I quickly turned my back on this painting and what do you think I saw on the other wall?"

He paused to sip his drink.

"Couldn't he skip the details and get to the point!" I thought. Politely I smiled, stifling the urge to bark out my true thoughts.

Tom relaxed into the chair and continued, "A triptych by Beckman, hardly more cheerful than Holder's work, was my other viewing pleasure. It had been recently purchased by the museum from America, where Beckman died in 1950. Sometimes misery can completely surround you, you know? Anyway, I was hardly in the mood to deal with the power of either work. I left Kunsthalle in a hurry, and quickly walked to the *Franziskaner Stube* at the Opera Platz to have a large glass of schnapps — a sure-fire remedy for the blues."

At this point in Tom's discourse, I felt compelled to clear my throat, rather loudly. "Ahem. Tom?" I said. Tom waved his hands in the air as if to stop my rude interruption.

"Now Jerry, just listen. I'm working toward the point." He continued, "After my meeting I joined several Bavarian colleagues for a traditional dinner — pig knuckles, cabbage, potatoes and sausage, washed down with numerous glasses of Paulaner, the beer my host apparently favored. We talked business during the dinner, but when we had our Unterberg with cigars after dinner I decided to bring up the Leuchtenbergs. I thought my companions perhaps would know something about their art collections. Two had never heard of the family or of their Bavarian connection, but the third surprised me."

"Leuchtenberg... Leuchtenberg... I think I read something in the *Suddeutche Zeitung* in connection with this name. In fact, I'm almost positive. Something about a swindle," he mused.

"My ears perked and I asked, 'Can you remember anything else, or do you still have the newspaper that mentioned the case?'

My colleague promised to contact me once back at his office if news concerning the Leuchtenbergs resurfaced. His phone call the next morning woke me up.

"I found the article, but I have better news. There was a television story this morning.' he said quite excitedly. A man by the name of Fritz Leuchtenberg was arrested for forging his stepfather's checks. He had cashed several before anyone noticed his signature did not match his stepfather's."

"Did the news say anything else?" I asked and by this time, wide awake.

"Well, the reporter mentioned their association with the Royal House of Russia and the Seeon Castle in Chiemsee," my colleague said." Tom paused, "Now Jerry, I remembered you had been followed at Seeon Castle and had later received a menacing letter — most likely by the same person."

Tom continued his story, "The television reporter had stated that this man was being held at the Central Police Station. I dressed hastily and took a taxi to the police station. I asked to see the chief, explaining I had important information concerning the prisoner, Fritz Leuchtenberg. The man who received me was small and fat, with a jolly round face and beady eyes. He was sloppily dressed and a chainsmoker.

'What can I do for you?' he asked in a heavy German accent.

Avoiding his line of exhaled cigarette smoke, I said, I can give you some information about one of your prisoners — Fritz von Leuchtenberg.'

Hearing this news, the chief gave my his attention and ordered some coffee for both of us. I proceeded by retelling him your story — the abandoned Bermuda yacht, Van Dyck portrait, Anastasia, and her father's mysterious disappearance when she was a child. I also told him about the threatening letters you received, Jerry.

'Do you mean to tell me,' the police chief said, 'that your friend from Scotland Yard encountered difficulties pursuing his investigation and has failed to solve his case?'

I did not correct the police chief because he was obviously enjoying his connection in this case. He pompously leaned back in his chair, gloating over his chance for one-upmanship with Scotland Yard.

'I am going to interrogate the young man more extensively,' he said, lighting still another cigarette. 'Your friend's investigations may prove very useful. Thank you for telling me what you know about the Leuchtenbergs.'

How long will it take to interrogate Leuchtenberg?' I asked the chief.

'I will have some information for you within three days.'

'I'll expect your call.' I said, and on that note we shook hands and I departed."

Tom's story was taking me completely by surprise. To learn that he may have located that scoundrel who had threatened me in Munich was clearly fortuitous. I wondered what else this story would unravel to tell. I did not want to interrupt my friend's train of thoughts, however. He was obviously on a roll, his hands waving in the air, the ice of his drink long since melted.

"As you know," Tom continued, "the symposium was to last three days. I dreaded the reserved attitude I would need to have through these meetings, my excitement well beyond control. I tried to reach you, Jerry, and when that failed I called Christina, begging her to join me earlier than we had originally planned. Someone had to be involved with me there!"

'You want me to drop everything I'm doing and take the first plane to Munich?' Christina asked incredulously.

'Absolutely, I need you here. I think I may have a terrific lead on Jerry's case.'

There was a long silence on the other line. And then, laughing, Christina agreed.

'Alright, I will come. Meet me on the next flight from London at the Munich airport. What odd situations you and Jerry get entangled in — together and apart.'

I was overjoyed. "What a wonderful woman!" Tom said, still laughing.

I couldn't help but laugh with Tom, at his relived excitement. I jumped up to pour ourselves more drinks and sat back down as quickly as possible. Tom barely even missed a beat.

"The next flight from London," Tom went on, "arrived in five hours. With time to spare, I walked past Kunsthalle again to see an exhibition I had missed of Nolde's 'unpainted paintings'. I needed a small distraction that day..."

"Nolde's paintings were considered by Hitler a degenerate art. But since Nolde was an Aryan, Hitler did not imprison or kill him — he just prohibited Nolde from painting and forced the local police to keep him under close scrutiny in his native town of Seebul."

"Nolde was too great an artist to have his creativity thwarted by an 'ukaz', but he also realized that if he painted in oil, the smell would help his tormentors denounce him. He therefore switched to watercolors, and not only changed his metier, but also his subject. He had rarely, if ever, painted figures in his previous oil paintings. But in his

214

watercolors, which he called 'unpainted paintings,' he did paint many human figures."

"Jerry, I was so engrossed in the exhibition I almost missed Christina's flight! I urged the taxi driver to move quickly and arrived at the airport just as her plane was landing. My anticipation of seeing Christina burst when she emerged from the passport control booth. I hugged her and kissed her, sharing the same excitement seeing each other again."

Christina and I rented a car at the airport on the suggestion I made to spend the day in the countryside, taking advantage of the crisp autumn sunshine. Christina gladly agreed and we drove to — where do you think — Chiemsee and the Seeon Castle. On our way there I told Christina what I knew about the Leuchtenbergs from your stories, Jerry."

"When we finally reached Seeon Castle, the same old custodian who you met was still there. He remembered you well, and considered you a 'true aristocrat, who was not too hurried to listen.' I laughed at that, remembering your annoyed description of him."

"But he turned out to be quite helpful; when I told him that you had been followed in the cemetery, he told me that after your visit, the same derelict who had come the day before turned up again, claiming to be a Leuchtenberg. The man pestered him about some documents concerning his family he believed were hidden in the Castle. The custodian was convinced that this young hoodlum was deranged and finally told him not to come to the Castle anymore or he would call the police. Needless to say, this was the same man who was recently arrested in Munich."

At this point, I couldn't stay quiet any longer.

"I knew it!" I said, jumping up and grabbing Tom's arm. "The man who followed me was a Leuchtenberg!"

Tom laughed and motioned for me to sit back down.

"Wait, my friend," Tom grinned. "There's more."

215

I did as he asked, wondering if this tale would somehow lead me to Anastasia.

"When Christina and I returned to the hotel," Tom continued, "the concierge told us Orff's *Carmina Burana* would be performed that night at the Munich Opera. We decided to go even though the spectacle is hard to classify as an opera and pleasantly, we were not disappointed. It was a splendid performance. Christina was impressed by the set which consisted of an enormous doll, the singers and dancers entering the stage by emerging from its insides on all different levels. I thought that the voices were excellent, particularly the falsetto singer who performed the defrocked bishop."

"Christina was delighted, having never heard Orff before, and I told her what I knew about the composer — that he was a Bavarian who was as interested in the musical education of children as in composition. Orff taught choral classes to children and he was one of the few contemporary composers who had superb knowledge of human voices as soloists and choral ensembles."

"I also told Christina about Orff's opera, *Antigone,* which faithfully follows Sophocles' tragedy. Instead of ending the opera with an orchestral clash, Orff chose to finish the tragedy by having the same bass note played slowly and repetitively, in unison on eight pianos."

"We walked out of the opera in a happy mood and had our dinner at the *Franziskaner Stube* next to the opera. In order to digest the heavy Bavarian food we had a few Unterbergs after dinner and retired to bed exhausted by the long day. In the morning, we were interrupted by the shrill sound of the telephone. Although I was unable to answer this call, a second call came minutes later. This time when I lifted the receiver I heard the police chief's voice, not the dial tone.

'Could you arrange to be here in an hour?' he said excitedly. 'I have some news for you.'

216

I jumped with alacrity from the bed. I suggested to Christina that she join me at the police station, but she refused. Not only did she want to stay in bed, but she also told me how intensely she dislikes policemen, regardless of whether they are English or German — excepting you of course, Jerry. Anyway, she wanted to see the fashionable shops in the city, so I gave her directions on how to reach Teatiner Strasse."

"I arrived at the police station and was immediately directed to the chief's office. He looked much more dignified that day, well-groomed and well-dressed. Perhaps after realizing that I had connections with Scotland Yard, he decided to cut a more impressive figure."

'We have repeatedly interrogated the prisoner,' said the chief, now classifying the Leuchtenberg as such, 'but he denied having anything to do with the Bermuda affair. We are, however, quite thorough, as I told you, and we carefully examined his Canadian passport for every entry or exit stamp. We discovered that he was in Bermuda not long before your Scotland Yard boss was called to investigate the yacht affair.'

'So he did have something to do with the Bermuda affair?' I exclaimed.

'It would appear that way,' the police chief replied. 'We had several of our investigators quiz him simultaneously every day for exceedingly long hours, and last night from his cell, he asked the guard to bring him before us as he wanted to confess. I was called from my home early this morning. When the Leuchtenberg was brought in, looking pale and haggard, he told me his story.'

At this point, Tom, who was thoroughly enjoying his story, started enacting the different voices. Fritz von Leuchtenberg, the delinquent youth, had a toughened but whining voice. The police chief's voice was stern and unforgiving. I sat back in my seat and watched Tom as if he were an entire cast of characters, performing in my living room purely for my benefit.

217

Fritz von Leuchtenberg," Tom continued in the police chief's voice, "was six years old when his mother married Herzog von Leuchtenberg. Fritz was adopted by his step-father, but they never got along very well, especially after Fritz's mother died. He had an uneventful childhood and had no desire to learn anything at school. At a fairly early age, when he was merely twelve or so, the truant officers soon recognized the boy as one of a gang who spent their time causing mischief on the streets instead of studying.

Herzog von Leuchtenberg tried all sorts of persuasions to change his stepson's lifestyle: bribery, punishment, ca-joling. Nothing worked. When Fritz turned twenty, he was living in his stepfather's apartment, spending his al-lowance freely and performing menial jobs only when he needed more money. Herzog von Leuchtenberg decided to have a serious talk with his stepson.

'Fritz,' he said, 'I have decided to sell our home. The allowance I have given you is enough to attend school and it is enough to start a business. I hope you will use it wisely and build a future for yourself.'

'The money you've given me is worth nothing!' the youth cried. Herzog von Leuchtenberg was visibly upset by his stepson's outburst.

He decided to continue, ignoring Fritz's reply, 'I have also decided to pursue a dream I have had since childhood. I am going to sail around the world. I will give you the itinerary I've worked out, however it will probably be sub-ject to change.'

'And do you expect me to be happy for you? After abandoning me for a trip around the world?' Fritz lashed out.

'Fritz, I never treated your mother with disrespect! She was my love and I treasured her. Her early death hurt me as much as it did you. And I am trying to care for you. But my efforts are to no avail!' Herzog von Leuchtenberg answered, nervously playing with his cane.

218

'You fraud!' Fritz shouted, and his eyes flamed as if he might do his stepfather physical harm. The look was not lost on Herzog von Leuchtenberg.

'I also want to tell you something which will surprise you,' the older man said in a whisper, 'you have a half-sister named Anastasia. I have made out my will and I am leaving everything to her. She is a valuable member of society — you are not.'

At this, the stepson howled. 'What!' he cried out. But he knew his stepfather's words were not a ruse. Fritz knew that the man was speaking the truth.

'Where is the will?' the boy cried out. 'Where is it? I demand to know!'

Herzog von Leuchtenberg merely shook his head, saying nothing. The boy stormed out of the house, rage burning in his eyes. Herzog von Leuchtenberg left that evening for Bermuda to begin his journey around the world."

"Tom," I asked, finally. "Is this true, what you're telling me?"

"Absolutely, Jerry," my friend replied.

"Word for word?" I asked, incredulously.

"Well, perhaps the dialogue isn't exact, but the events are true enough. Now just listen, Jerry. We're coming to the most exciting part."

"As I said," Tom went on, "that night Herzog von Leuchtenberg departed, leaving Fritz only enough allowance to help him through the next year or two. Fritz's reaction to his stepfather's decision was one of rebellion and anger. Why should an unknown and illegitimate sister inherit all the money. He was the legally adopted heir! He should receive all of his stepfather's fortune!

During the next two months, Fritz nurtured his anger — and when he had no more money left, he decided to locate his stepfather and get his revenge. He borrowed money from his friends and flew to Bermuda where he found the yacht anchored. And, once no one was in sight, he had no hesitancy to break into the yacht.

219

Fritz immediately noticed the beautiful painting, but what he was interested in was the will. He started to pull out different drawers, one after the other, until his stepfather entered the cabin.

'What are you doing here?' asked his stepfather.

'I am looking for your will. I want you to change it. It is not just to disinherit me in favor of Anastasia. I am your legitimate son. I should be heir.'

'You must be out of your mind! Get off this boat immediately before I make you leave.'

'I have no intention of leaving until you change the will!' the youth cried.

After hearing this, Herzog von Leuchtenberg started to push Fritz out the door. Fritz pushed back and they struggled for a while until the boy hit his stepfather with a powerful blow to the chest. The old Leuchtenberg lost his balance and fell backwards, hitting his head on the sharp edge of a table. He moaned for a few seconds and then lay still. When the stepson turned him around, he realized that his stepfather was dead.

For a moment Fritz panicked but then he collected his wits. He sat and waited until darkness, and then he hauled his stepfather, a heavy poker tied to his body, onto the yacht's dinghy. He rowed a few minutes into the open ocean and then heaved the body over the edge of the boat and into the sea.

He returned to the yacht and spent the entire night searching for papers and documents. He did not find the will but found a checkbook and account statement issued by the Bayerische Bankgeselschaft in Munich. He then removed every bit of paper, including the checkbook from the yacht — stripping it of identification. He wanted to take the painting but realized that by doing so, he would run a greater chance of exposure.

Under the cloak of darkness, Fritz Leuchtenberg released the yacht from the anchor and sailed it a few miles into the sea. He then abandoned the yacht and rowed ashore in the dinghy with all of the papers safely with him.

Once in Munich, Fritz started to forge his stepfather's signature on the German checks — and you know the rest of the story from there."

Tom looked very content after having told me the entire story. My friend had indeed done an excellent job of detection, but there were still some loose ends that he had yet to explain.

"And the will," I asked. "Has it been found?"

"I asked the police officer the exact same question," Tom answered, smiling like the Cheshire cat. "He told me about a safe deposit box at the bank in Herzog von Leuchtenberg's name. 'The bank will have to open the safe for us when they know about the murder,' he said. And then he invited me to accompany him as a witness while he examined the contents of the box."

"Well, Tom," I exclaimed, "what was in the box!"

"We proceeded to the bank," Tom continued, his hands waving all about him, "and within half an hour the deposit box was ours for inspection. It contained only one document: the last will of Herzog von Leuchtenberg. It listed various real estate possessions, a yacht, one more bank account and the painting of Charles I. It also contained a letter by Dr. Leo van Puyvelde, verifying the portrait's authenticity. All of this was to be inherited upon his death by his daughter, Anastasia, whose address in Athens, Jerry, I am giving to you now."

I could hardly refrain from shouting for joy. Not only were all the pieces fitting together perfectly, but I had also finally located my beloved Anastasia. I was still curious, however, as to the sentence young Fritz Leuchtenberg would receive.

"The chief told me," Tom answered, "that Fritz could be brought before the Court in Munich for falsifying checks, but that he could not be charged for the murder committed in Bermuda. 'That problem is for your friend in Scotland Yard to solve,' he said, with a slightly mischievous smile."

The chief's smile couldn't have been half as mischievous as Tom's — or my own.

Epilogue

Even before Tom could ask for another whiskey I was on the phone to Scotland Yard, asking for Sir Alexander, "I must speak with him. It's urgent!" I told the receptionist.

"You sound so excited, Jerry," she said. "You're practically yelling in my ear. But unfortunately, Sir Alexander is at his country home today."

"But this news cannot wait!"

"Well then! I'll find him for you immediately!"

Within minutes I received a call from my chief. Before he could utter a sound, I told him everything Tom had told me and that the mystery of the abandoned yacht was solved. Sir Alex was quite happy, but he couldn't understand why I had insisted on calling him at his country place.

"I know you're excited, Jerry," he said, "but couldn't the news have waited until tomorrow? What is so urgent?"

"But Sir Alexander," I answered, "I have also located Anastasia! She's living in Athens. And the old Leuchtenberg named her as his heiress. I must see her!"

"That story is something else, dear Jerry. You were right to call. And if I were you, I would fly to Greece on the next plane." I took the chief's advice and left him to find another detective to finish the case of Fritz Leuchtenberg's murder.

During the plane ride, I was so excited I paced the aisle impatiently, back and forth, until the hostess, concerned by my behavior, finally grew so suspicious that she asked the captain to talk to me. I identified myself as a Scotland Yard detective, not on official duty but on a personal mission to reclaim love. The captain was very sympathetic but insisted I keep to my seat. The flight seemed endless.

Athens airport was a disaster; conditions hadn't improved any since my last visit. Our socialist government still had not listened to the perennial requests of the Greek government to return the Elgin marbles to the Acropolis. After pushing my way through the crowds of tourists and Greeks, I finally hailed a taxi and gave Anastasia's address on Heraklitos Street.

The street's name evoked only one memory in my mind: Because of Heraklitos, my marks in Moral Science at Oxford were not as praiseworthy as in my other courses. But I was so excited upon arriving at my destination that I did not haggle with the taxi driver who asked for one hundred drachmas when the meter read twenty.

The house on Heraklitos Street had six floors and twelve tenants but, unfortunately, there were no names next to the different doorbells. I decided to push every bell and bedlam broke loose. A dozen excited tenants converged on various landings shouting at me in Greek. This language is completely alien to my ears but I remembered from my course in Esthetics dogma of the ancient Greeks.

"Kalon Anastasia," I yelled back.

One of them seemed to understand what I wanted. Arriving below to meet me, he showed me to the sixth floor, rang a doorbell and discreetly disappeared. As the door was opened, I gasped for joy at the sight of Anastasia, beautiful as ever. The look of surprise on her face quickly melted and we fell into each other's arms, unable to say a word. Regaining sensibility from the shock, Anastasia invited me in, where we sat down on a couch, holding hands and smiling endearingly.

"How did you find me, Jerry?" she asked.

"It is a long story, my love."

As I told her the complete story, I added cautiously, "I should tell you this, so that you won't have to read about it, or hear it through rumor. Your father, I'm afraid, was murdered by his adopted son."

Anastasia was visibly shocked and started to cry. I took her hand and gently changed the subject, asking, "Why are you in Greece, Anastasia?"

In spite of her distressing news she responded at length, "You remember, Jerry, I was studying certain female companions of famous men. My latest venture into this field was the most daring one. I decided to investigate Aspasia, the beloved and admired companion of Pericles and Alkibiades."

"She was a stranger to Athens, coming from Millet, and Pericles could not marry her since, like a fool, he had previously promulgated a law that forbid Athenians from marrying foreigners. But Aspasia was in love with Pericles and she bore him a son — even though Pericles could only recognize the child and offer him legal status after his so-called legitimate children had died."

"The only thing I can remember about Aspasia is that she cut off the tail of Alkibiades dog," I interrupted, so excited to be discussing things again with her.

"You should be ashamed of your ignorance, Jerry. You obviously failed to read Plutarch. It wasn't Aspasia who cut the dog's tail, but Alkibiades himself, in order to divert the Athenian's attention from his graver faults. But I forgive you, and love you as much as Aspasia loved Pericles."

I was overwhelmed with joy and kissed her lightly, with love.

"Why did you leave me in Berlin, Anastasia?"

She thought for a while, trying to choose the right words, "I was afraid I was falling in love with you. I wanted to avoid the fate of my mother, who had fallen in love with a Russian, my father... and you know the tragic outcome of that affair. Yet, here I am, almost following in her footsteps. In time, Jerry, I realized that you were my fate.

225

And, being a detective, you would discover this mystery and solve it."

Taking her into my arms, I told her how much I had been waiting for this moment to express my love for her. Neither one of us would have envisioned the possibility of true love in our lives before meeting each other.

I thought it seemed ironic Anastasia counted on my detective skills to find her... Scotland Yard and the Bermuda police expected me to solve the mysterious portrait/yacht case...and it had all been successfully brought together by Tom, my friend, the art historian. Maybe my father had been right judging me a better art historian than detective!

After this startling reverie I broke the silence and approached a different subject by saying, "Anastasia, you could claim as part of your inheritance the Van Dyck painting of Charles I and possibly your father's yacht... but I have to warn you that the litigation required to make your claim valid may prove to be a protracted venture."

Anastasia made a quick decision, retorting, "I don't want the painting, I don't want the yacht, I want you, Jerry!" and giggling, tumbled me into bed.

And so, dear readers, this is the last view you have of us before we close the bedroom door. Wish us well. Perhaps we will live happily ever after, until death do us part?

Postscript

It took one year of legal wrangling before Anastasia's inheritance was settled. Dear Anastasia decided not to keep the painting or the yacht, reminders of her father's brutal murder.

Our lives have changed somewhat since then. I am teaching Russian art history at Oxford, and Anastasia is publishing her third volume on *Reclaiming Women in History*. We are living together in a comfortable flat, not far from Christina and Tom, who are happily married. Christina is the proud, overbearing mother of four children, and Tom, quite successfully, works as a detective for the art-theft department of the Scotland Yard. As for Perdoul, we all saw him recently in London, where he came to buy a painting at a Christie's auction. He is director of a small museum in one of the Russian provinces. Thanks to the portrait of Charles I, and Van Dyck's genius, our lives were painted with different strokes.

I have recently learned, however, that some American fool bought this portrait of Charles I and is meticulously searching for the painting's provenance. Auguri!

Appendix

Attribution of two portraits, that of *Isabella Brant* and of *Suzanne Fourment and her Daughter,* to Van Dyck was only recently confirmed.

In 1621, after his first stay in England, Van Dyck returned to Antwerp where he was eagerly met by Rubens. Supposedly, during this time, Van Dyck presented to Rubens three portraits:

1. *Self-portrait with Rubens*
2. *Isabella Brant*
3. *Susanna Fourment with her Daughter*

Isabella Brant, the first wife of Rubens, who died young from tuberculosis leaving him with three children, was painted sitting in an armchair as a queen in front of her palace. Originally Van Dyck was supposed to have painted this portrait to please his teacher. The painting was in the Crozat collection and was then attributed to Van Dyck. After its arrival in the Hermitage, the portrait was considered to be painted by Rubens.

Susanna Fourment was a sister of Rubens' second wife, Helena, whom he married when she was only fifteen and he was fifty-three. The portrait was in the collection of Count Choiseul. Although it was sold to Catherine the Great as a work of Rubens for 7,800 francs, in the catalogue of the Choiseul Gallery *(Recueil d'estampes gravees d'apres les tableaux du cabinet de Monseigneur le duc de Choseul.* Par les soins du Sr. Basau. 1771, p. 83) it was listed about the portrait of Susanna Fourment that "Van Dyck pinx". Both portraits were listed in the Hermitage Catalog (Somof A. *Catalogue de la galarie des tableaux.* St. Petersburg. Companie d'imprimerie artistique, 1899–1901, vol. 2, p. 365, plates #575, #635) as the work of Rubens.

In 1893, the famous German art historian, Wilhelm Bode, while on a visit to St. Petersburg and examining the Hermitage collection, pointed out two paintings insisting they were not by Rubens but by the young Van Dyck, who at his early stage imitated his teacher brilliantly. In his book, *Great Masters of Dutch and Flemish Paintings,* 1909, London-New York, p. 311–314, Wilhelm Bode writes: "The Young Lady with Her Little Daughter" (#635, now ascribed to Rubens), supposed to be Susanna Fourment and her daughter, Katherina, both full-length, is as masterly as it is charming; it was acquired from the Choiseul collection. But also the famous portrait of Isabella Brant, with the triumphal arch of Rubens' palace in the distance, seems to me a masterpiece of the pupil's, not of the teacher's. I imagine that it is the picture which Van Dyck painted of Rubens' wife when he left his home to go to England. The rich coloring, the brilliant warm tones, the delicate gray shadows, the drawing of the slender hands, are all characteristics of his work, and opposed to the manner of Rubens".

Bode suggested that the portrait was executed before Van Dyck's stay in England, but does not refer to any particular sojourn. Bode also gives his opinion about the similarity of both artists:

"Van Dyck's individuality comes out so strongly in all these pictures that we are rarely in doubt as to whether we are to attribute them to him or to his teacher, even though — as a consequence of the master's great influence upon the pupil — the two artists are so much alike one another at this time that at first glance they may be confused."

In the meantime, the well-known Belgian art historian, Max Roozes, who wrote about Western art collections in

Russia, differed in his opinion about these two paintings from Wilhelm Bode. Max Roozes was sure that Rubens would never keep at home a painting of his wife executed by somebody else but him. Roozes and Somoff suggested that the portraits could have be started by Van Dyck but definitely finished by Rubens. These two paintings were listed in the catalog of Rubens' work compiled by Roozes *"Louvre de P.P. Rubens: histoire et description de ses tableaux et dessins.* Antwerp, 1892, pp. 131, 181, 182).

Both Roozes and Bode had strong supporters among the Russian art experts. The Russian magazine *Starye Gody* published letters by their readers who supported either Roozes or Bode's expertise. Someone called James A. Schmidt claimed that Rubens' signature was on both frames on the reverse of the paintings.

After the Russian revolution, the Soviet government sold the portraits of *Isabella Brant* and *Susanna Fourment with Her Daughter.* The paintings were sold in Berlin and bought in 1930 by the American art collector, Andrew Mellon. In 1937 he gave both of these paintings to the National Gallery of Art in Washington. They are listed as painted by Van Dyck.

List of References Compiled by Jerry Gramtrub

Books

1. Aldanov, M. Yunost Pavla Stroganova I Drugii Haracteristiki. Belgrade, 1937 (in Russian)

2. Alexander, J.T. Catherine the Great: Life and Legend. New York, Oxford: Oxford University Press, 1989.

3. Anastasia. I Am Anastasia. The Autobiography of the Grand Duchess of Russia. Translated by Oliver Coburn. New York: Horcourt, Brace,1958.

4. Andrews, P. The Rulers of Russia. Chicago: Stonehenge, 1983.

5. Art and Autoradiography: Insights into the genesis of paintings by Rembrandt, Van Dyck, and Vermeer. New York, Metropolitan Museum of Art, 1982

6. Bernardy, F. De. Eugène De Beauharnais, 1781-1824. Paris, Librairie Academique Perrin, 1973 (In French)

7. Bode, W. von. Great Masters of Dutch and Flemish Paintings. London: Duckworth and Co., 1909, pp. 311-314.

233

8. Botkin, G. The Real Romanovs, As Revealed by the Late Czar's Physician. New York: Fleming H. Revell Co, 1931

9. Botkin, G. The Woman Who Rose Again. New York: Fleming H. Revell Co, 1938

10. Brown C. Van Dyck. Ithaca, N.Y.: Cornell University Press, 1983

11. Carmichael, J. A Cultural History of Russia. London: Weidenfeld and Nicolson, 1968

12. Carpenter, W.H. Pictorial Notices of Sir Anthony Van Dyck. London: 1844

13. Catalog des Tableaux du Cabinet de M. Crozat, Baron de Thiers. Paris: de Bure, 1755 (in French)

14. Conway, M. Art Treasures in Soviet Russia. London, 1925

15. Coughlan, R. Elizabeth and Catherine. Empresses of all the Russians. New York: G.P. Putnam's Sons, 1974

16. Cust, L. Anthony Van Dyck, Historical Study of his Life and Works. London: 1900

17. Custine, Astolphe, Marquis de. Empire of the Czar: a Journey Through Eternal Russia. New York: Doubleday, 1989

18. Grandjean, S. Inventaire Apres Deces De L'Imperatrice Josephine a Malmaison. Pairs: 1964 (in French)

19. Gul, R. Ia Unes Rossiiu: Apologiia Emigratsii. Niiu-Iork: Most, 1981 (in Russian)

20. Higham, FMG. Charles I. Westport, Connecticut: Greenwood Press, 1979

21. Howarth D. Lord Arundel and his Circle. New Haven, London: Yale University Press, 1985

22. Hugh Trevor-Roper. The Plunder of the Arts in the Seventeenth Century. London: Thames and Hudson, 1970 (Walter Neurath Memorial Lecture, 1970)

23. Jackman, S.W., ed. Romanov Relations. The private correspondence of tsars Alexander I, Nicholas I and the Grand

Duke Constantine and Michael with their sister Queen Anna Pavlovna (1817-1855). London: MacMillan, 1969

24. Kempt, B. Sir Robert Walpole. London: Weidenfeld and Nicolson, 1976

25. Knackfuss H. Van Dyck. Translated by Dodgson C. Bielefeld and Leipzig: Velhagen and Klasing, 1899

26. Knapton E.J. Empress Josephine. Cambridge, Mass: Harvard University Press, 1963

27. Koehne B, von. Die Sammlung Gotzkowski in der Ermitage. St. Petersburg, 1882

28. Krupenski P.N. Taina Imperatora. Parizh: Medny Vsadnick, 1927 (in Russian)

29. Larsen, E. The Paintings of Anthony Van Dyck. Luca, 1987

30. Leikhtenbergski G.N. Die Bibliothek Des Herzog Georgii Nicholaevich von Leuchtenberg und Beitrage Aus Auderem Bezitz. Berlin, P. Granpe, 1929 (in German)

31. Levinson-Lessing V.F. Istoria Kartinnoi Galerei Ermitazha, 1764-1917. Leningrad: Iskusstvo, 1985 (in Russian)

32. Levinson-Lessing V.F. The Hermitage Leningrad: Dutch and Flemish Masters. London and Prague: Paul Hamlyn, 1964

33. Maria, Grand Duchess of Russia. Education of Princess. A Memoir. New York: Viking Press Inc, 1930

34. Maria, Grand Duchess of Russia. A Princess in Exile. New York: Viking Press Inc., 1932

35. Millar, O. The Age of Charles I: Painting in England, 1620-1649 (Catalogue of the exhibition held in the Tate Gallery, 15 Nov. 1972 - 14 Jan. 1973). London: Tate Gallery, 1972.

36. Millar, O. Van Dyck in England. London: National Portrait Gallery, 1982

37. Nieuwenhuys, C.J. Description De La Galerie Des Tableaux de S.M. Le Roi Des Pays-Bas, Vec Quelques Remar-

ques Sur L'Histoire Des Peintures Et Sur Le Progres De L'Art. 1843 (Bruxelles: Imprimerie De Delevingne et Callewaert) (in French)

38. Noel W.H. Madame Du Barry. New York: Charles Scriner's Sons, 1904

39. O'Connor, H. Mellon's Millions: the Biography of Fortune. New York: John Day, 1933.

40. Passavat, J.D. The Leuchtenberg Gallery. Munich: 1852

41. Piper D. The English Faces. London: National Portrait Gallery, 1978

42. Pulitzer, A. The Romance of Prince Eugene, vol. 1,2. New York: Dodd Mead and Co, 1985

43. Puyvelde, L. van. Flemish Paintings. The age of Rubens and Van Dyck. New York, Toronto: McGraw-Hill, 1977

44. Puyvelde L. van. Van Dyck. Bruxelles: Elsevier, 1959

45. Puyvelde L. Van Dyck's Style During his English Period. 1946

46. Robinson J.M. The Dukes of Norfolk. A Quincentennial History. New York: Oxford University Press, l982

47. Roozes, M. Art in Flanders. London: l9l4

48. Roozes, M. L'oeuvre de P.P. Rubens: Histoire et description de ses tableaux et dessins. Antwerp: 1892 (pp. 131, 181, 182) (in French)

49. Russki Biobiblographicheski Slovar Pod Redakziei Polovzeva, R.A., tom 19. St. Petersburg, 1909 (in Russian)

50. Schaefer, E. The Work of Anthony Van Dyck. New York: Brentano, 1913.

51. Semenov-Tian-Shanski, P. Etudes Sur Les Peintres Des Ecoles Hollandaise Flamande Et Neer Landaise Guon... St. Petersburg: Imprimerie, "Herold", 1906 (in French)

52. Somof, A. Ermitage Imperial: Catalogue de la Galerie des Tableaux. St. Petersburg, 1899, 1901 (2 vols) (in French)

53. Starkey, D. The English Court: From the Wars of Roses to the Civil War. London, New York: Longman, 1987

54. Strong, R.C. Van Dyck: Charles I on Horseback. New York: Viking Press, 1972

55. Tiutcheva, A.F. Pri Dvore Dvuch Imperatorov. Vospominaniya. Dnevnik. 1853-1882. Moscow: 1928-1929 (in Russian)

56. Tschernavin T. Escape From the Soviets. Translated by N. Alexander. New York: Dutton, 1934

57. Turner, P.M. Van Dyck. London: T.C. and E.C. Jack.

58. Turnerelli, E.T. What I Know of the Last Emperor Nicholas and his Family. London: Edward Churton, 1855

59. Tourneux, M. Diderot et Catherine II. Paris: 1899

60. Ukazatel Sobranii Kartin Iz Redkich Proizvedenii Khudozhestva, Prinadlezhavshich Chlenam Imperatorskogo Doma I Chastnym Litsam Peterburga. Vystavka 1861 Goda. St. Petersburg: Tip. Gogenfeldena, 1861 (in Russian)

61. Vasilchikov, A.A. O Portretakh Petra Velikogo. St. Petersburg: 1872 (in Russian)

62. Verzeichniss Der Bildergallerie Seiner Koniglichen Hobeit des Prinzen Eugene, Herzog von Leuchtenberg in Munchen. Munchen: 1846 (Gerdruckt bei j. Georg Weiss) (in German)

63. Vigel, F.F. Zapiski. Moscwa, Artel Pisatelei, 1928 (in Russian)

64. Vorres, I. Last Grand Duchess. The Memoirs of Grand Duchess Olga Alexandrovna. New York: Charles Scribner's Son, 1965

65. Vrangel N. Les Chefs-d'oevvres de la Galerie de Tableaux de L'Ermitage Imperial a St. Petersburg. Munich, London, New York: 1909 (in French)

66. Walpole, H. Aedes Walpolianae; Or Description of the

Collection of Pictures at Houghton-Hall in Norfolk. London: J. Hughs, Printer, 1752 (2nd ed)

67. Walpole, H. Anecdotes of Painting in England With Some Account of the Principal Artists. London: Chatto and Windus, 1876

68. Walpole, H. A Catalog of Classic Contents of Strawberry Hill Collection. London: Smith and Robbins, 1842

69. Waliszewski K. The Romance of an Empress Catherine II of Russia. New York: Archon Books, 1968 (reprint 1898 ed.)

70. Williams R.C. Russian Art and American Money. 1900-1940. Cambridge: Harvard University Press, 1980

Journal Articles

71. Bilbasov V.A. Ekaterina II i Didro. Russkaya Starina, tom 42, mai-june, 1884 (in Russian)

72. Blunt, A. Royal collection of paintings. Apollo, vol. 77, Aug., 1962, pp. 444-447

73. Borenius T. Addenda to the work of Van Dyck. Burlington Magazine, vol. 79, l941, pp. l99-203

74. Brown D. Van Dyck in London. Art International, vol. XXVI, #3 (July, August), pp. 29-33, l983

75. Felkerzam A. Yantar i ego primenenie v iskusstve. Starye Gody, str. 3-15, Nov., 1912 (in Russian)

76. Gluck, G. Reflection of Van Dyck's early death. Burlington Magazine, vol. 79, pp. l93-l99, 1941

77. Leikhtenbergski N. Vospominania. Russkaya Starina, #5 1890 (microfilm) (in Russian)

78. Lightbrown R.W. Van Dyck and the purchase of paintings for the English court. Burlington Magazine, vol. 111, pp. 418-421, 1969

79. Liphart E. Kartiny v sobranii Kniazei L.M. i E.L. Kochubei. Starye Gody, 1890 (in Russian)

80. Makarenko N. Sobranie Kniazei L.M. i E.L. Kochubei. Starye Gody, Noyabr-Dekabr, str. 3-14, 1890 (in Russian)

81. Malinovsky K.B. Opisanie imperatorskich zhivopisnych kollekzii. Muzei, #1, str. 173-186, 1980 (in Russian)

82. Millar O. Charles I, Honthorst and Van Dyck. Burlington Magazine, vol. XCVI, pp. 36-42, 1954

83. Millar O. Some painters and Charles I. Burlington Magazine, vol. 104, Aug. pp. 326-330, 1962

84. Puyvelde L, van. Van Dyck. Review. Gaz. Beaux. Arts, s.6, v. 58, pp. 247-248, O' 1961 (in French)

85. Puyvelde, L. van. The young Van Dyck. Burlington Magazine, vol. 79, pp. 177-185, 1941

86. Robinson F.M. The romance of art. Van Dyck at the court of Charles I. Magazine of Art, vol. 10, pp. 65-67, 1887

87. Sir Anthony Van Dyck. Editorial. Burlington Magazine, vol. 79, pp. 173-174, 1941

88. Sitwell, S. Van Dyck: An appreciation. Burlington Magazine, vol. 79, pp. 174-177, 1941

89. Trubnikov, A.A. Nasledie Velikoi Kniagini Marii Nickolaevny. Starye Gody, Mai, str. 46-50, 1913 (in Russian)

90. Trubnikov, A.A. Materialy dlia istorii zarskich sobranii. Lozhi Rafaelia. Starye Gody, July-Sept, str. 34-38, 1913 (in Russian)

91. Vrangel N.N. Kartinnaya Galereia gerzogov Leihktenbergskich. Niva, vol. 15, #574, str. 1044–1073, 1884 (in Russian)

92. Vrangel N.N. Iskusstvo i gosudar Nickolai Pavlovich. Starye Gody, July-Sept., str. 53-163, 1913 (in Russian)